# Mercy Row Clann

## Book 2 in the Mercy Row Series

## Harry Hallman

Octane Interactive, LLC
Publishing

Mercy Row Clann
By Harry Hallman
www.mercyrow.com

As with all my writing, I dedicate this book to my family.
A special dedication goes to all the men and women who served and continue to
serve in the United States military.

A special thanks to my brother William Hallman for his invaluable input, especially
about vintage era autos.

Published by
Octane Interactive, LLC - Publishing

ISBN-13: 9780692203897
ISBN-10: 0692203893

# 1

CORPORAL JAMES BYRNE wiped the sweat, blood and bits of brain from his eyes and face. Using his government issued trenching tool he started to dig. The soil was dry, sandy and full of rocks, making it difficult to dig a foxhole of a size that would protect him. Cannon fire from German Panzers and field artillery was incessant. He dug as fast as he could and when the foxhole was large enough for him to fit halfway, he rolled in. Lying in the hole, on his stomach, he started to dig again. Eventually he was able to completely fit in the hole and, at least, get some cover from the rain of shrapnel.

It was a miracle that he and his three other squad members were alive. They had lost seven men, almost two thirds of his squad, including Sergeant Mitchell, the squad leader. The Sergeant had taken a direct hit from a Panzer shell. Byrne had been nearby when the Sergeant just exploded into pieces. *I should be dead,* Byrne thought. He couldn't understand why he wasn't hit by the shrapnel that obliterated Mitchell, but that's the way it is in war. You just never knew when it was your time.

As the ranking man, Corporal Byrne was now the squad leader. "Everybody in your holes?" Byrne yelled, so he could be heard over the bomb blasts.

"Yep."

"Yeah."

"I'm in, but it's not the hole I wanna be in." Private Ken Mallory said. Mallory was Byrne's best friend, and also from Philadelphia.

Byrne and Mallory hadn't known each other before they met at Fort Dix, New Jersey for induction and training. Byrne refused to go to officer's training school and instead asked to be in the infantry and ended up with Mallory, in Sergeant Mitchell's squad.

After training and a year at two different bases in the states, the squad was herded onto a troop transport and crossed the Atlantic Ocean, landing In French Morocco. Ground transportation and some good old-fashioned marching eventually got them to the Kasserine Pass in Tunisia where all hell broke loose. The German's, under Field Marshall Erwin Rommel's command, had stopped the undertrained U.S. troops and were now pushing them back.

"Yeah, Mallory, you'd want to be up Rommel's asshole," Private First Class Pauli Fazoli yelled over the bomb blasts. Fazoli was born in the Bronx and enlisted as soon as he turned eighteen.

"Fuck you Fazoli. Learn ta talk, will ya? I can't hardly understand your Bronx ass." Mallory quipped back. "And the hole I was talking about was your sister's."

"Can you two shut up? I'm trying to listen to the bombs go off," Private William "Nevada" Gentry said. Gentry was born in Southern New Jersey, but his family moved to Nevada when he was ten years old.

"Fuck you, Nevada!" Mallory and Fazoli said together.

"Okay guys, settle down. Dig in as deep as you can. We'll stay here for a while and when the shelling slows down, we'll make a break for it. Keep your heads down," Byrne said.

As if to punctuate Byrne's warning, three blasts hit just behind the small ridge to their right.

"Holly shit Pop, we gotta get out of here. Now!" Nevada yelled.

"No, stay put." Byrne yelled back. The other squad members started calling Byrne "Pop" when they found out he was twenty-nine years old. Most of the men in the squad were under twenty and even Sergeant Mitchell had been only twenty-four. So, the nickname Pop stuck.

"I mean it Pop. We need to go," Nevada said.

"I said no. Shut up and stay down. Two more blasts hit the ridge and showered all four men with sand and rocks.

"I changed my mind. Let's go. Up and at 'em," Byrne Yelled.

All four men got up at the same time and started running west. Just as they had cleared the area, two more blasts ripped into their hurriedly dug foxholes. They ran, in a zigzag pattern, as fast they could. Blasts were hitting all around them. They were also taking small arms fire from German troops who were advancing. There was a large sand and rock ridge approximately one hundred yards in front of them and they headed for cover there. Fazoli was in the lead, Mallory followed him with Byrne close behind. Nevada was in the rear.

Fazoli was the first to make it to the ridge. He leaped over it, got his footing, turned and started shooting back at the German troops. Mallory did the same, and then Byrne jumped over the ridge. "Where's Nevada?" Byrne asked.

"Looks like he's hit. About fifty yards back," Fazoli said.

"Cover me," Byrne said and jumped back over the ridge and started running back for Nevada.

"What the fuck are you doing? He's dead. Get back here," Mallory yelled.

Corporal Byrne kept running as Fazoli and Mallory fired their carbines to give him cover. Like a baseball player stealing a base, Byrne slid to a stop on his rear end, grabbed Nevada, slung him over his shoulder and started to run back to the ridge.

The German soldiers were getting closer and bullets were hitting the sand around Byrne's feet as he ran toward the ridge. He had no time to think. He just ran as fast as he could. When he reached the ridge, he pushed Nevada up and over and started to climb over himself. That's when he felt a sting in the left lower part of his back. At first, it was like a bee sting, but a split second later, the pain turned into a hot poker. The momentum pushed Byrne up the ridge. Both Mallory and Fazoli grabbed him and pulled him over to safety.

It was a weird feeling. Byrne could hear everything, but couldn't move or see anything. It was kind of like a radio show. Mallory was yelling, Fazio answering him. *Strange very strange*, he thought.

"How's Pop, Faz ?" Mallory asked.

"Got it in the back. There are two holes so I think it's a through and through.

"How about Nevada?"

"Upper back. He's alive. Don't know for how long."

"Get back up here. I need your help."

When Fazoli pointed his rifle over the ridge, he said. "Oh fuck."

What he saw was thirty or forty German infantrymen running toward them. He started shooting.

"Faz, we either leave now, or we stay with Pop and Nevada." Mallory said.

"What the fuck? I haven't had a good fight in a long time. You know how us guys from the Bronx are?" Fazoli answered. "Bayonets?"

"Yeah, sure. Why not." Mallory said as he fixed his bayonet on his rifle.

Both men showed no fear, as they were taught by the tough streets of Kensington and the Bronx, but inside they were shaking.

Byrne could hear everything. He wanted to yell, "*Get out of here. Leave us. Save your own lives,*" but he couldn't talk. Then Byrne heard a rumbling noise and the ground started to shake. "*Maybe I died and the ground is opening up to take me,*" Byrne thought irrationally.

"Holy mother of Christ Fazoli yelled, as two US M3 Lee tanks pulled up on either side of them.

"Get behind the tanks," The tank commander yelled from the turret as he opened up his machine gun on the German troops.

Fazoli grabbed Nevada, Mallory grabbed Byrne and they dragged them back behind the tank on the left. Fazoli looked at Mallory and he made the sign of the cross. Mallory did the same.

"I didn't know you were Catholic," Fazoli said to Mallory.

"Every other day of the year I'm nothing. Today I'm Catholic." Mallory said and smiled. Then he made the sign of the cross again but this time forgetting to touch his head.

Fazoli smiled.

The tanks continued to fire at the Germans as a Jeep rolled up. A medic jumped out and helped Mallory and Fazoli load Byrne and Nevada in the Jeep. Then they jumped in and pointed their rifles to protect their rear as the Jeep turned and headed away from the tanks. The medic examined his patients, administered some morphine and did a fast dressing of their wounds.

"How are they doc?" Mallory asked.

He's," pointing at Byrne, "lost a lot of blood. Looks like the bullet went through, but I can't tell if it hit any vitals. The other one here," pointing to Nevada, "was hit in the back. We just have to get them back and let the field docs work on them.

Even though the noise from the Jeep was loud, Byrne could hear everything the medic had said, and prayed he would get to see his family again. Slowly, the Jeep noise started to fad and he could hear Mallory saying, "Stay with us Pop," but it sounded as if Mallory was far away. Finally, all noise stopped and he couldn't hear, see, feel or smell.

# 2

MIKE KELLY PICKED up a baseball bat and patted it on the palm of his hand, checking to see if the weight was right. He swung it a couple of times to practice his swing, and tapped it on the floor. When he was satisfied, he stepped closer to the chair, pulled the bat back and placed it on his shoulder.

"Did I ever tell you I played ball in high school? I was pretty good. My coach said I had the makings of a professional. Yeah I know, coulda, woulda, shoulda. I had to leave school and get a job to take care of my Ma. So I'll never know. Barry, before I take a couple practice swings on your leg, tell me why you've been stealing from people in North Philly?" Mike asked.

"I swear Mike. I never—"

Mike interrupted Barry, "Do you think we're stupid, Barry? We know you've been doing it. I just want to know why and who else is working with you. Whata ya say Barry?" Mike asked in a deliberate calm manner.

"Mike please. I didn't...," Barry started to plead but was interrupted when Mike's bat slammed hard on his knee. Barry screamed in pain.

"You were saying Barry?" Mike asked and paused to allow Barry to regain his composure.

"Mike, come on. You know me." Barry pleaded. Mike placed the bat on his shoulder again. "Okay, okay," Barry shouted. "I did, but only once. I swear."

"Barry, Barry, Barry. Don't lie to me," Mike said as he smashed the bat on Barry's other knee. "Now tell me the truth. Everything!"

"Okay, okay," Barry whimpered. "I've been, for nine months now."

"How much?"

"I don't know. Fifteen grand maybe," Barry confessed still whimpering.

"Who's in on it with you?"

"Just me. I'm sorry Mike. I'll pay you back I swear," Barry pleaded.

"You will? Every penny?" Mike asked acting interested.

"Every penny, Mike, I swear on my kids. I'll take it back to the people we... I stole it from."

"You know Barry we don't have a lot of rules. Just a few. The first rule is you never steal from the gang or anyone in it. The second rule is you never steal anything, not even a candy bar, in Kensington or the wop gang's territory," Mike said.

"I know Mike. I Know. I fucked up. That's all. It'll never happen again," Barry pleaded.

"Okay Barry, but I have to punish you. Wouldn't look right to the other guys if I didn't. You understand. Right? Put your hand on the table," Mike said is a low voice.

Barry tentatively placed his hand on the table and stiffened in anticipation of Mike hitting his hand with the bat. A crushed hand was better than dying, he decided. Mike turned away from Barry and faced Brian who was standing, not far away, in the back of the room. He motioned to Brian to move a few feet to Brian's right. Then Mike turned and swung the bat with all his force, smashing it into Barry's left temple. The blow knocked Barry from the chair to the floor, his head split and bleeding. Mike hit him three more times to be sure he was dead.

"For a minute, I thought you were going to let him go," Brian said.

"Oh no. Couldn't do that. Take his ass over to K&A, and drop him on the sidewalk tonight. I want everyone to see want happens when you break our rules," Mike said.

"Do you think he was telling the truth?"

"No. He lied. He has no children," Mike answered. He was working with the other guys in his crew. When they see what happened to Barry, they'll stop." Mike paused and said, "After they find him and tell his mom, take over five grand and tell her we're very sorry for her loss. Tell her he was a good man and he'll be missed."

# 3

"MARCH 15TH, 1943-TUNISIA

*Dear Mom:*

*I'm sorry I haven't written in a while, but we have been on the move and this is the first opportunity I've had to write.*

*Mom, please don't worry, but I'm writing from a hospital in Tunisia. I was wounded during a battle at the Kasserine Pass, but I'm healing well. I can't give details in this letter, but I'll tell you everything when I'm home. That's the good news. I'll be coming home. The Army is discharging me. I'll let you know more when I get a firm date. My friend Nevada was also wounded. I've written about him before. The docs say he may never walk again. I guess in that way I'm lucky.*

*I can't tell you how much I'm looking forward to one of your home-cooked meals. As you can imagine the food here is not so good. Boy, do I miss soft pretzels and Pat's steak sandwiches.*

*Your letters finally caught up with me and it's a joy to read them. I'm so happy that Rose and Mercy have opened Mercy Row to the families of fallen soldiers. I've lost so many friends this last year. It's the least we can do to try to help soldiers' families. I want to help Mercy when I get home. I'm sure they can use some legal assistance and whatever else I can do. Please tell her and Grandma Rose I send my love.*

*If you see Tony Junior, tell him I said hello. He's a great guy and I'm happy for Mercy and him. Have they set a date for the wedding yet? Oh, and tell Tony I forgive him for joining the Navy. They have it so soft. I'm joking, but don't tell him that.*

*I can't believe Charlie's seventeen. I can only hope this war will be over before he's old enough to be drafted. It seems that most of the new replacements we get are his age. It doesn't seem right to have kids that young see the horrible things I've seen.*

*Charlie seems like he is doing very well in school. I hope he can get into Penn when he graduates. I'm sure Dad can arrange that and Charlie's smart and probably doesn't need help.*

*Jakey's up to his old tricks, I see. He's a good kid, just a bit rambunctious. Don't be too hard on him. He wrote me a letter and told me how he wants to join the Army and kick Hitler's ass (sorry for the curse but that's what he said). Thank God, he's only sixteen, because I think he would join up if he could. I'm not sure Uncle Sam would recover from that.*

*Is it possible Georgie's going to be ten in May? Fifth grade. Wow! I got the picture you sent. He's getting big fast. Seems like just yesterday when he was born. Every time I think about that year, I miss Grandpop and Uncle George. What a waste that they died the way they did.*

*Please tell Dad I send my love and that I'm looking forward to getting back and working at Byrne Construction. I miss that. He looks good in the picture you sent, maybe a bit grayer but I guess that comes with age. Speaking of age, it seems Uncle Frank never gets older. He looks the same as ever. Is he ever getting married? I guess not. I love that guy. Tell him when you see him.*

*How is Don Amato? You mentioned in the letter that he had some heart trouble. I hope it's not serious. He needs to retire and let Uncle Tony take over. He deserves to enjoy his old age.*

*Well, I have to go. The nurse is here to poke and prod me for some tests. Tell everyone I send my love and I miss them all. See you soon, I hope. I love you Mom, Dad. Take care.*

*Love,*
*Jimmy*
    *PS*

*Tell Uncle Mike, Grady and Brian I said hello. I miss getting together with them on Friday nights drinking beer and discussing how we'll fix all the world's problems. You mentioned Uncle Mike had another boy, James Joseph Kelly. Tell him I said congratulations and thanks for naming him after me. He'll get a laugh out of that.*

# 4

JACOB BYRNE WAS sitting in his Father's old office, now his for almost ten years, contemplating how fast time had passed. *Had it been ten years since his father committed suicide and the Johnson moonshine gang out of Oxford, hired by the Chicago mob, murdered George Graham?* He placed the letter from Jimmy that he had just finished reading on the desk. It had been twenty years since he first met Jimmy and his mother Molly.

The night they met had been the start of the war between his gang and Sal Sansone's Italian Mob out of South Philly. Everything had turned out good for him. He met Molly married her, adopted Jimmy and now had four children of his own. He had taken his revenge and killed Sansone and his successor Capci. He then brokered a deal with Don Amato that allowed both gangs to earn, in peace, for ten years.

In the '30s, the Chicago Mob attempted to take over his and Franklin's operation, but he was able to kill the assassins they sent and eventually Don Amato convinced the commission to reign in Chicago. There was only one loose end from those days and, if all went well, that would resolve soon.

"Yo, Jacob. Wake up, "Franklin Garrett said for the second time.

"Sorry Frank. I was just thinking back about when we first met Jimmy and Molly. You know it's been twenty years."

"Yeah, I know. Twenty years, prohibition, your marriage, the depression, two gang wars, four kids and war in Europe and Asia. A busy twenty years I would say."

"It has been. Well, everything except the marriage and kid thing for you. Do you ever wish you had kids Frank?"

"Knock on wood," Franklin said and tapped the wooden desk. "No. Don't want them and hope I don't have any I don't know about. I told you a long time ago, I have your kids and I can send them home at night."

"You never change Frank," Jacob said.

"Change is overrated. Molly told me that Jimmy was wounded. How's he doing?"

"He says he's healing and by his letter, I think he's as well as can be expected. He's happy he's coming home."

"Christ! That is good news. She didn't mention that. When?" Franklin asked in excitement.

"Not sure. He said he'd let us know," Jacob replied.

"Fucking Heinies. I wish they had let me back in the Army."

Jacob laughed and said, "You're a bit long in the tooth to go back in the Army Frank."

"Fuck the Army! I tried them all, Army, Navy, Marines but they wouldn't take me. Too old they said. Their loss. Shitheads. What else did Jimmy say?" Franklin asked.

"Let's see," Jacob said as he picked the letter up. "He did mention you. He says tell Frank he's a womanizing son of a bitch that couldn't shoot straight when he was a young man in the Army let alone now that he's an old fart."

"Give me that," Frank said as he grabbed the letter from Jacob's hand. "You prick, he didn't say that. He says he loves me and that I look much younger than you." Both men broke out laughing.

Jacob and Franklin had first met in jail when Jacob was just seventeen. Jacob had been arrested for stealing from an Italian who had come to North Philly to sell hot watches. Franklin was arrested for nearly killing a contractor who was installing sewer pipe the wrong way on one of Jacob's father's construction sites. Franklin was construction manager of the site at the time.

Franklin saved Jacob from an inmate who tried to rob and rape him. From that time on, they became the best of friends, actually more brothers than friends. Franklin taught the younger Jacob the construction business and a year later, they both formed the beginning of their North Philly criminal enterprise. Jacob became the leader of his mob named the K & A Gang after they killed Mickey Mahoney, head of the Girard Avenue Gang, and consolidated both groups.

In the '30s, Jacob took over Byrne Construction, when his father killed himself rather than suffer with cancer. As the depression ended and the construction business picked up, he left day-to-day gang operations to Franklin. Franklin, with the help of Mike Kelly and Grady Hanlon, built a thriving gambling and robbery ring and controlled all of North Philly. Don Gerardo Amato, the leader of the South Philly Mob, had become a close friend of Jacob and Franklin's and they worked together for their mutual profit.

Franklin reached in his pocket and pulled out a watch. "I still have that watch you acquired from that grease ball. If it hadn't been for him, we might not have met," Franklin said.

"Yeah, brings back memories," Jacob said pensively. "Speaking of history, did Tony and Grady get back yet?"

"They did. I have a present for you," Franklin said, as he placed a newspaper in front of Jacob.

Jacob looked at the paper and then back to Franklin. The headline read "Frank Nitti, Chicago Mob Boss Commits Suicide."

"Finally! This deserves a toast," Jacob said as he got up to get a bottle of Irish whiskey and two glasses. He poured the whiskey, picked up his glass and said, "To my Father and George," and poured some of the whiskey on the floor. Franklin also poured some whiskey on the floor and they tapped glasses.

Jacob poured two more drinks. Franklin picked his up and said, "May you be in heaven a full half hour before the devil knows your dead." Both men touched glasses and drank the whiskey."

"Do you think my Dad and Graham are in heaven, Frank?"

"In heaven or the infernal regions, I have no idea, but wherever they are, I'm sure they're raising hell." Both men laughed.

"Papa, do you have a minute?" Mercy Byrne said as she walked through the open office door.

"Sure. What is it sweetheart?"

"I'm not interrupting something important am I? You two were having a good laugh when I came in," Mercy said.

"No, No. We were just talking religion," Franklin said. "Here, have a seat."

"I have a surprise for you," Mercy said slyly as she pulled Tony Amato Jr. into the room.

"TJ! How are you kid?" Jacob said as he got up and shook hands with Tony.

"Franklin also got up and shook Tony's hand and said, "You're looking really fit. Built like a brick shithouse. That boot camp did you some good."

"Yeah, well you know, up early, working out and all that," Tony replied.

Jacob sat down and offered Mercy and Tony a chair. "TJ, we were just having a little touch. Can I pour you one?"

"I'll take one Dad," Mercy said.

"You?" Jacob said surprised.

"Yeah, I think I'll need it," Mercy replied.

Jacob poured four shoots, stood up, held his glass up and said, "To Tony Junior. May you come home safe."

They all tapped glasses and Tony said, "Alla tua salute!"

"Dad," Mercy said, her tears welling up in her eyes. "Tony and I are married."

"What?" Jacob said flopping back in his chair. "Where? When?" His eyes opened wide. "You're not preg—"

Mercy interrupted him. "No! How can you say that? No. I know we talked about getting married next year, but Tony's shipping out in a couple of weeks. We just wanted to be married with the war and all. We went to Connecticut yesterday and got married. Who knows when Tony will get back."

Franklin offered Mercy a handkerchief.

"Oh boy! Does your mother know?" Jacob asked.

"Yes. We talked this morning. I told her we wanted to tell you ourselves."

"Uncle Jacob, I'm sorry. I meant no disrespect to you," Tony Jr. said.

"How did your mother take it?" Jacob asked tentatively.

"She wasn't happy, but eventually she understood. She made me promise that we will have a big party when the war's over and Tony's home," Mercy said.

Jacob got up and kissed Mercy on the cheek, and then he hugged Tony Jr. and said, "TJ, I guess you're going to have to start calling me Pop or Dad or something."

Franklin also got up, kissed Mercy's cheek, and hugged Tony Jr. and said, "You can call me Uncle Frank."

"That's what I always call you."

"Oh! Well then, you won't have to learn anything new."

"Where are you stationed TJ?" Jacob asked.

"I got a ship, destroyer out of Norfolk, the USS Maddox," Tony Jr. said.

"That's not so far away. You can get home often," Jacob said.

"The scuttlebutt is we'll be doing convoy duty, so I'm not sure when we'll dock. You can bet I'll be home as much as I can," Tony Jr. promised as he took Mercy's hand, looking her in the eyes.

"So you have two weeks home now?" Jacob asked.

"That's right Unc... Dad," Tony Jr. answered.

"How about you two take a week and stay at the Pocono house? After that, you come home and we'll get together. Your Dad and Mom, Don Amato and us. We'll have a little going away party," Jacob said.

# 5

USS Maddox
 "*Mercy, L'amore della mia vita:*

 *I can't tell you enough how much I miss you. Every day away from you seems to be an eternity. If only I had the skills of a poet, I'd write you a love sonnet that would go down in history as the most beautiful poem every written. But, since I'm no poet, I give you a ballad by a famous Italian poet from the 13th century—Guido Cavalcanti. I know you're learning Italian, but I translated this for you until you get better.*

> *I FOUND a shepherdess in forest glade*
> *Lovelier, me thought, than any star to see;*
> *Her rippled tresses wore a golden hue,*
> *Her eyes were bright with love, her cheeks flushed deep*
> *As roses are; the while she tended sheep,*
> *Her feet were bare and sprinkled o'er with dew;*
> *She sang as maids in love are wont to do,*
> *Adorned with every grace she seemed to be.*
> *I greeted her forthwith in Love's own name*
> *And asked her if she chanced in company;*
> *She answered gently that alone she came*
> *Awandering through the wood, and thus spake she:*
> *"Know thou that when the birds sing merrily*

*'Tis then this heart of mine doth crave a lover!"*
*Threon, since she had told me of her plight*
*And I could hear the birds sing merrily,*
*Unto myself I said: "Now is the season*
*With this sweet shepherdess of joy to reason!"*
*Then did I crave her favour, if to kiss*
*And to embrace she reckoned not amiss.*
*She took me by the hand in tender way*
*And said that she had given her heart to me;*
*She led me underneath a verdant spray,*
*Where flowers of every colour I could see;*
*So fond, so blithe was everything anigh*
*I thought the god of love himself stood by.*

Okay, I know, I'm a fathead, but I can't help it. You know I love you more than life. I'm hoping this war gets over soon, so you, our baby and me can be together. I'm going back to school so I can get a real job and give you everything you deserve. I'm not going to work with my grandfather and father anymore.

Speaking of the baby, how are you feeling? You mentioned in your last letter, which by the way I got pretty fast, that you were feeling ill in the mornings. I think that's normal. I asked a couple of the guys here that have children and they said their wives were sick in the morning, but it goes away after a while.

In your letter, you asked me to tell you about my work. I can't tell you where I'm at. They would just black that out anyway. Most of the time, I'm mopping the floors, cleaning my guns, and kissing the chief's ass so I don't get kitchen duty. Once in a while, we practice shooting. My job is to shoot down airplanes. A few times, we were able to shoot at kraut planes. Got my first kill last week. Pretty keen! Huh?

I have become good friends with a guy named Billy Thompson. He cracks me up. A funny guy. I told him, when the war's over to move to Philly and we could start some kind of business together. I don't think *he will. He's from Texas and you know people from Texas never want to leave. The way he talks you'd think Texas was a separate country. Anyway, he's a great guy and I want you to meet him someday.*

*I gotta get going. I am on duty in a few minutes. I'll write again soon.*

*All my love,*
*Tony"*

# 6

AFTER HE CHECKED his airplane, Karl Ackerman reached up and patted the under-wing of his Junkers 88 dive bomber. "How are you old girl? Did you have a good night's sleep? We have a job for you today and all we ask is that you get us back safe." Ackerman was a squadron leader assigned to the Luftwaffe's KG-54 bomber group.

Ackerman pulled himself up and into the plane and took the pilot's seat, checked his instruments, and asked, "Ready Ernst?

"Yes sir," lieutenant and navigator Ernst Nagel answered. "Where we going?"

"Hunting along the coast. Maybe we'll get lucky," Ackerman, answered. "Franz, you back there?"

"Yes sir, ready when you are," radioman Franz Engle answered.

"Bergman?"

"Yes sir," gunner Gerhard Bergman answered.

"Okay then. We go," Ackerman reached over, patted the Saint Christopher statue and then made the sign of the cross and said, "Im Namen des Vaters, des Sohnes und des Heiligen Geistes."

Tony Amato Jr., TJ to his shipmates, had shipped out on the USS Maddox, designation DD-622, on April 14 1943. He had hoped for duty on a carrier, but he soon learned to love the destroyer. He thought of his ship as a Jaguar, sleek, fast and deadly. The Maddox, being a new ship, was first assigned convoy duty and TJ had made one uneventful trip across the Atlantic to Africa and then returned to Norfolk.

When he returned from his first assignment, he was able to get a four-day leave to see Mercy who surprised him by announcing he was to be a father. Two weeks later, the Maddox was deployed to Oran, Algeria, where she became a unit of Task Force 81 and the invasion of Sicily. As the assault troops opened the amphibious battle of Gela, the Maddox was on antisubmarine patrol off the coast.

"Hey TJ, your wife got any sisters?" gunners mate Billy Thompson asked as he looked at the picture of Mercy on TJ's bunk wall.

"If she did, none of them would want a hayseed like you," TJ said jokingly.

"Awe shit TJ. I told you I am cowboy not a hayseed."

"What's the difference? You both smell like cow shit." TJ joked.

"Oh yeah! My cow shit smells a whole lot better that that fucking cheese you're always eating. What's it called tag u lotti?" Billy joked back.

"It's Taleggio. Say it! Taleggio."

"Tal-e-go."

"Shut the fuck up. You're too uncivilized to eat it anyway.

TJ had become very good friends with Billy Thompson. Each operated one of the Maddox' Bofors Mark 1 anti-aircraft guns and had bunks close to each other.

"How's Mercy doing?" Billy asked being serious for a minute.

"Billy, she gets prettier and prettier every picture I get. She says she's fine and that the doc says the baby's good," TJ answered.

"When'd you say that baby's coming?"

"Doc says middle of December.

"Well, let's hope it doesn't look like you."

"Screw you. You wish you had my looks," TJ said as he wet one finger with his tongue and rubbed it across his eyebrow.

"We have rattlesnakes back in Texas that look—" Thompson was interrupt by the ships alarm. "Let's go."

TJ and Thompson grabbed their helmets and lifejackets and hightailed it to the aft gun position. TJ took the left gun and Thompson the right gun. The gun crews were already in position and loading the Bofors.

"You see 'em?" TJ asked the spotter.

"Not yet."

Karl Ackerman's Junkers was in the lead position cruising at 400 kilometers per hour. He had been leading his group in a twenty-five-kilometer circular pattern for about an hour when he spotted two US ships, a cruiser and a destroyer. He ordered half the squadron to attack the cruiser and he and the other half of the squadron set their sights on the destroyer.

"There they are. Ten o'clock." one of the Maddox' gun crew yelled. "Bombers."

TJ steadied his aim and waited for them to come in range. "You see them Billy?" he asked.

"I see the bastards," Billy yelled.

"Wait for them. Wait," TJ said. A few seconds later he yelled, "Shoot."

Both guns started the familiar rhythmic noise, created by the forty mm shells being forced through the Befors' barrels.

Ackermann pushed the plane into a forty-five-degree dive and aimed it at the destroyer. The ack-ack began immediately. Several shells burst in front of the plane, but none hit. On his right side, he saw Werner Fritz' plane take a direct hit and explode. He said a short prayer for the crew.

"Okay Ernst. Here we go," Ackerman yelled.

As the plane came into machine gun range, he opened fire. Ackerman liked to strafe a target first so he could get his bearings and then he would come around and drop all nine hundred kilograms of bombs from the main bomb bay. If he missed, he would come around a third time and drop the bombs from the secondary bay.

"Got the son of a bitch," Billy yelled as he kept shooting at the second plan that was driving toward them.

The bullets from the airplane peppered the deck and bounced off the Bofors' protective shields. One of the gun crewmembers was torn in half as the impact of several of the 7.92 mm rounds hit him.

"Fuckers," TJ yelled as he took aim at Ackerman's plane and fired.

Ackerman saw several more blasts to the right and left of him as he pulled back on the column and started his accent.

"That was close," Ackerman said as the airplane turned sharply to the left in order to come abound on the Maddox again. "What do you say, Ernst? Shall we try that again but with bombs?

Ernst didn't answer. Ackerman turned a saw Ernst had been hit with shrapnel. The right window was shattered and half of Ernst's face was missing. Blood was spattered on the controls and on Ackerman. He had not noticed the gore, being so intent on inflicting as much damage as he could to the Maddox.

As he straightened out the plane he yelled, "Wichser" in frustration. Then he touched the blood-soaked Saint Christopher statue and said a short prayer for Ernst.

"They're coming around again," TJ yelled. "Wait for them."

Ackerman turned sharp left again and took a course directly at the Maddox. The telltale puffs of smoke from the Maddox's guns were visible a split second before explosions ripped Heinrich Wilhelm's plane apart. Explosions continued to burst around Ackerman as he pushed his plane's nose down. Miraculously, none hit his airplane.

All of Ackerman's years of experience and training were engaged as he drove directly at the rear of the destroyer where the aft magazine was located. When he thought he was in the right spot, he let the main load of bombs go.

TJ saw the bombs release from the bomb bay and knew in an instant that they would hit the boat near him. He yelled, "Merc—" and was interrupted by the explosion of the bombs' direct hit. His last and fleeting thought was for Mercy and his unborn baby.

Ackerman turned his plane to the right, hoping he could come around and place his secondary load on the front of the ship. As he turned again and straightened his plane for his third attack, he saw that the Maddox was on its side. The bombs had found the ammo magazine. He flew over the ship, turned around and strafed the survivors in the water. He then set a course for home. He reached out and gently touched the Saint Christopher again and cried for Ernst.

# 7

ROSE REILLY GRAHAM stepped on the Route 60 trolley at the Front Street and Allegheny Avenue stop. The trolley would take her to Broad Street and then she would transfer and go south to Jacob and Molly's house. Still spry at the age of sixty-three, Rose preferred to walk or take the trolley car on her excursions. Ever since the war began, Rose had refused to have anyone drive her, believing the boys overseas needed the fuel more than she needed to ride in a car. She handed the driver two dimes and said, "Two please, with transfers." The driver looked at her and then Mercy and handed Rose the two transfers.

Mercy Byrne Amato often stayed overnight at the Mercy Row homes, where she worked. As a young child, assassins attempting to kill her father Jacob had shot Mercy in the arm. While in the hospital recovering, Mercy suggested that her father use the then abandoned homes on the one hundred block of West Wishart Street as temporary residence for homeless. Jacob agreed and had the homes refitted. He asked Rose, then recently widowed, to head up the Mercy Row Foundation, which he named for Mercy. Mercy worked with Rose on weekends and after school until she graduated, two years before, and then started working fulltime. Mercy and Rose, with the help of Nate Washington, helped many families, over the ten years since the Mercy Row foundation had been created. As the depression ended, World War II started. They changed the Mercy Row Foundation's focus to helping families of fallen or severely injured service men and women.

As Mercy walked behind Rose down the aisle of the trolley, a man suddenly put his arm out blocking her way and said, "I like blondes. You're a good looking broad. You know that?" From the way the man slurred his words and the smell of liquor on his breath, Mercy knew he was drunk.

"Thank you. Could you please move your arm so I can find a seat?" Mercy said.

"I like you. What say we go get a drink?" the drunken man said.

"Sir, move your arm!" Mercy said.

"Take it easy sister. I'm just trying to be nice," the drunken man said as he put his hand on Mercy's stomach. "Oh, look, you're having a baby." As he said this, his hand moved up toward Mercy's breasts.

Mercy made a fist and punched the man square on his nose. "You fucking bitch. You broke my nose," the man screamed as he got up from his seat.

Mercy backed up a couple of feet and as the man came at her, she brought her knee up into his groin. The man doubled over in pain. Several nearby male passengers realized what was happening and grabbed the man, threw him to the floor and kicked him several times, then dragged him to the door and threw him out of the still moving trolley. The man tumbled and landed in the gutter. A green car pulled up and two men picked up the still unconscious man, put him in the backseat and sped past the trolley.

"You okay, Miss?" one of the men who had helped her asked.

"Yes, I'm fine. Thank you."

"Young lady, you got quite a wallop," the man said.

"Four brothers. You learn a lot. Thank you again," Mercy said as she took a seat next to Rose.

"Are you all right?" Rose said as she rubbed Mercy's stomach.

"I'm fine Rose."

"I don't know what this world's coming to. A lady can't even take a ride without some low life accosting her. In my day—" Mercy interrupted Rose's angry tirade.

"It's okay Rose. I'm okay. Please calm down. Your blood pressure. You know."

"That young man should be in the Army not getting drunk and bothering decent women." Rose said.

By the time they arrived at the Byrne house, Rose had calmed down. As they walked to the door, Mercy stopped and said, "Rose, let's keep this to ourselves. My Mom's worried enough about Jimmy. She doesn't need to be worrying about me." Mercy put her arm around Rose and they entered the house.

A half hour later, Rose, Mercy, Molly, Jacob and Franklin were all sitting at the dining room table discussing the Mercy Row foundation.

"We have all of the homes filled with families," Mercy reported.

"How are you doing with cash?" Jacob asked.

"We're fine, Jacob," Rose said. "The interest on the money you have in trust, plus the money you, Molly and Franklin get from your fundraisers does us just fine."

"Mom's old store helps a little too," Mercy said. "Since we reopened it, we get the ladies of the houses to volunteer to work there. It generates enough cash that we can give our families a little extra spending money. Most of the mothers are working at the Frankford Arsenal, so we have an area in Uncle Frank's old house that we use for the children to play until their moms get home. Some of the non-working Moms watch over the kids."

"Ummm, my old house is a play center for children! Now that's interesting."

"Oh, come off it Frank. You know you love children," Molly said.

"As long as they're not mine," Franklin said laughing.

"And we set up a couple of pretzel stands on Front Street and get the children of our families to sell the pretzels when they're not in school. It doesn't bring in much, but it does teach the kids how to work," Rose added.

"How's Nate doing? I thought he'd be here," Jacob asked.

"Uncle Nate's working on some repairs and said he would come over when he's finished," Mercy said.

"Nate's doing okay. After Helena died, he just wasn't himself, but he's doing better now. They had been married a long time you know," Rose said.

Nate Washington was the first employee of the Mercy Row Foundation. In 1933, Nate was standing on a corner in West Philly when a car pulled up and the driver asked where the nearest hospital was. The driver was Jacob Byrne and he was trying to get Mercy medical care after Chicago Mob assassins shot her. Nate ended up driving Jacob's car to the hospital while Jacob held Mercy. Jacob gave Nate his business card and asked Nate to contact him in a couple weeks when things calmed down. It took Nate a month to get an appointment with Jacob, but when he did, Jacob asked if he would like to be the Foundation's custodian. Nate accepted.

During the ten years that Nate had been working for Rose and Mercy, he had learned to do everything necessary to keep the Foundation operating smoothly. Not only did he make all the repairs, he often helped with the office work, as well as driving their guests to medical appointments. When his wife died, he moved into a Foundation apartment in Jacob's old home. His only son was now serving in the Army Air Corp.

The doorbell rang. "I'll get it," Mercy said.

When Mercy left to answer the door, Molly asked, "Rose, how's Mercy doing? She always tells me she's fine, but I know she just doesn't want me to worry."

"Mercy's a very strong young woman, but every once in a while, when she stays over, I hear her crying in her room. She misses Tony. You know how emotional we get when we're pregnant. Other than that, she seems fine."

"Yeah I remember," Jacob, said looking at Molly. Molly looked back at Jacob with a look that meant that he should shut up now. Jacob shrugged his shoulders.

"Well, does anyone want more coffee or maybe something stronger?" Franklin said picking up the pot.

"Yeah. Break out the Irish," Jacob said. "We'll have a toast to the continued success of Mercy Ro—" Jacob was interrupted by a blood-curdling scream.

Franklin pulled his pistol from his shoulder holster and he and Jacob ran to the front door, followed by Molly and Rose. Mercy was standing in the doorway, her hands to her face. On the ground just outside the door, there was a cigar box with a twenty-inch garter snake crawling next to it. As the snake slithered away and dropped into a small patch of grass, Jacob and Franklin began to laugh. Molly put her arm around Mercy and asked, "Are you all right?"

"I'm okay. It just startled me," Mercy said and started laughing.

"Who would do such a thing?" Rose asked.

They all turned as they heard muffled chuckling coming from the stairway. Jakey, Molly and Jacob's sixteen-year-old, son was standing on the third step from the bottom with his hands over his mouth to stifle his laughter.

"Jakey, you come with me," Rose said as she walked over and grabbed Jakey by his ear and walked him into the dining room. The others followed her.

"Do you not know your sister is having a baby? If you frighten a woman with child, the child can come out deformed," Rose said.

Mercy held her hand to her mouth to stop from laughing.

"I'm sorry Grandma. I won't do it no more," Jakey said and laughed.

"Oh you're incorrigible," Rose said as she released her hold on Jakey's ear.

Jakey rubbed his ear and said, "Hey that hurt."

Everyone laughed.

"All of you sit down. I'll go make some sandwiches," Rose said and walked into the kitchen.

"Jakey, go help your Grandma," Molly said.

"I'm no woman. That's women's work."

"Get your ass in there, now!" Jacob said sternly, or you'll be more women than you want to be."

"Aww all right!"

When Jakey left the room, they all laughed again. The doorbell interrupted them.

"Sit down Mercy. I'll get it. It's probable Nate," Franklin said as he left to answer the door.

Mercy sat and they all started discussing plans for the next Mercy Row fundraiser. A couple of minutes later, Franklin came into the room. His face was pale and somber and he held a telegram in his hands. He said, "Mercy, it's for you."

# 8

MERCY WAS SITTING, her arm hanging over the sofa. In her hand, she held tightly to a telegram from the Navy Department. She had read it countless times since she first received it two days before, and still couldn't believe the words printed on it.

*"The Navy Department deeply regrets to inform you that your husband, Gunners Mate First Class Anthony Amato, was killed in action in the performance of his duty and in service to his country. The department extends its sincerest sympathy for your great loss. On account of conditions his body cannot be returned.*

*If further details are received, you will be informed. To prevent possible aid to our enemies, please do not divulge the name of his ship or station.*

*Rear Admiral Thomas the Chief of Naval Personnel."*

Mercy dropped the telegram, put her hands to her face and cried. She had cried so much during the last two days she didn't think she had any tears left, but she did. *"Why God? Why him?"* she thought.

"Mercy, come eat some lunch," Molly said as she entered the sitting room.

"No. I can't eat."

Molly sat down beside Mercy, took her hand and kissed it and said, "You know, when my first husband James was killed I felt as if my world had ended. It was as if a light had gone out and I was all alone in the dark. I was scared, grief stricken. I was angry with the Army. I hated the Germans. Worst of all, I was furious with God. How could God let this happen?"

Molly put her arm around Mercy's shoulder and continued. "Then, one day I realized I had to be strong for Jimmy. He deserved a mother who could take care of him. And Mercy, you too have a child who deserves your love, your strength, and your guidance," Molly patted Mercy's tummy. "Now come to lunch. You have a baby," Molly patted Mercy's tummy again, "that needs nourishment."

Mercy leaned over, kissed Molly on the cheek and whispered, "Thanks Mom."

Mercy and Molly walked to the dining room, where Jacob, George, Charlie and Jakey were waiting. All, even Jakey, were in a somber mood. They ate in silence, until Jacob said, "Mercy, there's a memorial mass Thursday at St. Nicholas in South Philly. The Amato's are taking care of everything. After the mass, we'll have family and close friends at our house."

"Papa, I don't know. I can't… I can't be around people. I just can't," Mercy said tears in her eyes.

Jacob rose from his seat, put his hands on Mercy's shoulders and said, "Mercy, we know it's hard. I wish I could make it all better like I did when you were a kid and hurt yourself. I can't. I can't and it kills me." Tears welled up in Jacob's eyes as he continued, "We owe Tony a proper send off. We owe his mom, dad and Grand Pop Amato. You're a Byrne. You're tough and you do what is right for your family. You can do this."

Mercy reached up and squeezed Jacob's hand, but said nothing.

# 9

ON THE DAY of Tony Amato's memorial, the family had two 1939 Chrysler Imperial limousines take them to Saint Nicolas church in South Philadelphia. Mercy held up well at the church, where she was comforting Tony's mother. When she stepped back into the limousine, for the return trip to her home, her strong demeanor dissolved and she began to weep again.

Molly took Mercy's hand and held it in her lap. Rose held Mercy's other hand, lightly patting it. The trip back to Jacob and Molly's home was about three miles. As they drove North on South Broad Street, they passed city hall, by law the tallest building in Philadelphia, and continued North on Broad Street. Mercy aimlessly stared out of the car window barely noticing the various red brick homes and modern office buildings.

"Look, the Inquirer building," Rose said trying to lighten the mood. "That's my favorite newspaper." Moss Annenberg purchased the newspaper and not long after was convicted of tax evasion and sent to prison. His son Walter Annenberg took over management and the Inquirer was now giving the Evening Bulletin a run for the money.

Mercy said nothing and continued to stare out the window seeing nothing.

As Mercy's limousine stopped for a red light, at the corner of 401 North Broad Street, a beat up green 1939 Chevy sedan pulled up beside them. As she became aware of the car, Mercy noticed that a man in the passenger seat was staring at her. He was about thirty and had a ruddy complexion. His nose had a bandage on it and his right eye was black and blue. With a start, Mercy realized she had seen this man before. He was the drunk who accosted her on the trolley. A chill went up Mercy's spine. When the light changed, the sedan sped past the limousine and was soon out of sight.

Noticing Mercy's discomfort, Rose asked, "Are you okay Mercy?"

"I'm okay Rose. Thank you." Mercy replied thinking it better not to bring up that unpleasant experience with her mother in the car.

"We're almost home. You should have some time to freshen up before everyone arrives." Molly said.

"Okay Mama."

Once past Fairmount Avenue, the limousine made a U-turn and pulled up in front of the Byrne home. The second limousine, where Jacob, Franklin, Mike, George, Jakey and Charlie were passengers, pulled up behind them. Jacob got out of the backseat of his limo and opened the door for Mercy, Rose and Molly. As Franklin and Mike exited the vehicle, a beat up green sedan with four male passengers passed by the house going south on Broad Street. Nobody noticed.

Jacob had arranged to have a photo of Tony Amato printed and placed on a stand near the entrance to his home. There was a book on a small table where guests could sign in and a place to put the envelopes. After an hour or so, the table was stacked with envelopes containing Mass cards and cash.

Mike waved to one of his men to come to him and motioning to the envelopes said, "Pat, get a bag and put these in it and put it in Jacob's office. If you take anything, I'll cut your fucking balls off."

As Pat left to get the bag, he said under his breath," Póg mo thóin!"

Jakey, who had been standing near Pat asked, "Hey Uncle Mike, what's Póg mo thóin mean?"

"Where did you hear that?" Mike asked.

"That guy you were talking to."

"Oh yeah," Mike said looking after Pat.

"What's it mean," Jakey persisted.

"Look Jakey, I'll tell you but don't ever say it to an Irishman. It is a very bad thing to say. It means 'kiss my ass'."

"What's so bad about that? I tell people to kiss my ass all the time," Jakey said.

"It just is, so don't say it," Mike said and walked off to find Pat. Jakey left to find Charlie so he could share this new curse word with him.

Mercy, Molly and Rose were sitting with Tony's mother and sisters in the living room. Guests were in a line taking their turn to offer them their condolences. Mercy thought to herself, *if I have to hear that Tony's a hero one more time I'm going to scream. I don't want him to be a hero! I want him alive! I want him here when the baby's born! I want him to see his baby get married. I want him to see his baby have babies!* Mercy abruptly got up and rushed out of the room.

Molly started to get up to go after her, but Rose held her back saying, "She needs a few minutes alone."

Mercy opened the door to the bathroom and stepped inside. She turned on the cold water and soaked a washcloth, placed the cloth over her face, and held it there for a minute. When she took it away, she looked in the mirror and said aloud, "Hold it together girl."

"As Mercy left the bathroom, Don Gerardo Amato walked up to her. Mercy hugged him and said, "Pop Pop, what am I going to do? I miss him so much."

"I know; I know. We all do, but he is with God now," Amato said as he made the sign of the cross. "He is safe now. Mercy, we have to honor Tony by living, by bringing up his baby in the best possible way. You know this. Don't you?"

"Yes Pop Pop. I know."

"The Roman's had a saying, Virtus et honos, which means honor and virtue. Sometimes, the soldiers would add the word strength as a prayer to their God before a war. I tell you this because you also should pray to God to give you strength, honor and virtue, for our little one," Amato said as he placed his hand on Mercy's stomach.

"I will, Pop Pop. I will."

"Good. Then my bella bambina, come with me now. The commissioner of parks and recreation wants to present you with a letter from the city council. They are naming a park in South Philadelphia after Tony."

# 10

**THE GUESTS LEFT** several hours after Mercy received the official letter from the commissioner of parks. Molly, Mercy and Rose retired to the kitchen for coffee and Jacob and Don Amato were in the living room. Franklin had gone to meet Brian and Nate to check on their operations centered on Columbia Avenue in North Philly. A few years after Nate started working for Mercy Row, Jacob and Franklin recruited him to help build K&A Gang's business in the North Philly Negro neighborhoods. Since the beginning of the war, the Columbia Avenue corridor had seen marked increase in middle class Negro residents and had become one of the gang's busiest operations.

"Another drink Don Amato?" Jacob asked.

"Jacob, after all these years? I have told you to use my first name," Don Amato said.

"Force of habit I guess. It seems comfortable to me," Jacob said holding the bottle up and nodding to it.

"Yes, yes please. I am becoming accustomed to this Irish whiskey of yours."

Jacob poured two whiskies and said, "Well, the Italian's have great wine, and we Irish have this." They both drank.

"Where are the boys? I wanted to give them some money to buy some candy," Don Amato said.

"I sent Charlie and Georgie to the movies to see that new film Bataan. Jakey's upstairs. He wanted to stay around in case Mercy needed anything."

"Jacob, you know Mercy will be okay. She is a strong woman. You remember how she was when she got shot. Santa Madre! She was one tough kid."

"Yeah. I know she'll be all right. I just hate seeing her hurt like this. Tony was the love of her life," Jacob said.

Don Amato made the sign of the cross, his eyes welled up with tears and he said, "Tony loved her too, but he is with G—" A crashing sound coming from the front door interrupted Don Amato. Then there was another crash and the sound of the door falling to the floor.

Four men entered the house; two went directly to the living room, which was adjacent to the home's entrance. The leader motioned to the other two men to check the other rooms.

"You two sit down," the man told Jacob and Don Amato pointing a pistol at them. They complied.

The man walked up to Don Amato and smashed his pistol against Amato's head, knocking him out, and said, "We're not here for you old man." He then pointed the pistol at Jacob's head, and said, "Do you know who I am Byrne?"

Mercy and Molly, having heard the noise, moved out of sight to the sides of the entrance to the kitchen. Mercy picked up a butcher knife and Molly grabbed an iron skillet. Rose stayed seated at the kitchen table, not sure what to do. As they heard the men coming closer, Molly and Mercy squeezed themselves tightly against the wall so they couldn't be seen. The first man walked into the kitchen pointing his gun at Rose and she screamed.

"Shut the fuck up you old—" The man was interrupted when Molly's skillet hit him in the face breaking his nose and knocking him to the ground.

The second man rushed in and started to point his pistol at Molly. Mercy drove the twelve-inch knife through the back of the man's neck. It came out through the front spurting blood on Molly. He dropped to the ground gurgling. Mercy pulled out the knife and handed it to Molly and said, "Here, take this in case the other one wakes up." Then she started tentatively toward the living room.

Rose, who had come around the table to see if she could help, grabbed the skillet from Molly and hit the man on the head again. "He won't be waking up too soon," Rose said. "He called me old."

At the same time Mercy was dealing with her assailants, Don Amato was unconscious in his chair and two assailants had guns trained on Jacob.

"You fucking Mick. Do you remember me?" the leader who had a bandage on his nose and a black eye said.

"No. Should I?

"My name's Johnson."

Jacob eyes showed a flicker of recognition.

"That's right. My brother was Caleb Johnson. I say was because the he's dead now! The family of the man you killed murdered him because you made him help you. My Pa drank himself to death because of you. Now I'm going to kill you. Then I'm going to find your daughter and fuck her until she bleeds."

Jacob's eyes betrayed his surprise that he knew he had a daughter.

"Oh yeah, me and her go way back. I met her on a trolley. I like fucking pregnant women," The man said licking his lips.

The surprise in Jacob's eyes turned to rage and he jumped up from his chair and grabbed Johnson's gun. Johnson smashed his fist into Jacob's face and both of them fell to the floor. Johnson's gun and arm were under Jacob's body and he was on top of Jacob. Jacob, still holding on to the gun, twisted it so the barrel was pointing at his own side, found the trigger and pulled. The bullet passed through Jacob's side and into Johnson's heart. He went limp, still lying on top of Jacob.

Johnson's man seeing this, started toward Jacob, his gun pointed at Jacob's head.

"Hey what're you doing?"

"The man, startled, turned around and pointed his gun at the doorway. Standing in the door was Jakey with his hands behind his back.

"I'm not here to kill a kid, so fuck off or I will," the man said and started to turn again to finish Jacob off.

"Póg mo thóin," Jakey said as he took the revolver, his grandfather had given him, from behind his back and pointed it at the man.

"What the fuck did you—" The man started to ask, turning back toward Jakey, when a bullet ripping through his chest interrupted him. He fell backward landing on coffee table. Blood was oozing from his mouth, but he was still alive.

Jakey slowly walked up to him and said, "I said Póg mo thóin!" Then he shot the man in the head.

# 11

AS MERCY ARRIVED at the living room, she saw Jakey shoot Johnson's man. Seeing Jacob had been shot, she rushed to his side. He was unconscious but alive. "Jakey, take that," pointing at the gun, "to the kitchen and guard the man with mama and grandma. Tell mama to call an ambulance for Dad. Don't kill that man, hear me?"

Jakey nodded yes and ran off to the kitchen while Mercy picked up a cloth napkin and applied the cloth to Jacob's wound. She tied it in place with a sash from the drapes. She then checked on Don Amato who was coming around and trying to get up.

Mercy, seeing the blood dripping down Don Amato's face, said, "Just sit there Pop Pop. Your head's bleeding."

Mercy took a handkerchief from Jacob's pocket and handed it Don Amato. "Here, hold this to your head. It'll help stop the bleeding."

Molly called for an ambulance and then rushed to the living room after asking Rose to stay with Jakey and the still alive intruder.

Seeing Jacob bloodied and laying on the floor, Molly yelled, "Oh my God! No! Is he..."

"No, he's alive Mom. He's alive," Mercy said.

Molly rushed to Jacob's side and started to turn him over. "No, don't move him. It could make it worse," Mercy said. "Can you try to get hold of Uncle Frank or Mike, or anyone? Ask them to come here? I'll take care of Dad."

Twenty minutes later, the ambulance arrived and took Jacob and Don Amato to the Episcopal Hospital at Front Street and Lehigh

Avenue. Mercy told Molly and Rose to go with them, promising to follow as soon as Franklin or Mike arrived. Meanwhile, she and Jakey tied the unconscious intruder to a chair and waited.

Shortly after they secured the man, Mike arrived with Grady and six of his men. Mike stationed two men at the front and another two at the rear entrance to the house.

"Mercy, Pat and Sean will drive you to the hospital." Pointing to the bound man Mike said, "Grady and I will see to him." What hospital did they take Jacob to?

"Episcopal," Mercy replied.

"Where are Charlie and Georgie?

"They went to the movies."

"Jakey, give me that, "Mike said, holding his hand out for the gun that was still in Jakey's hand."

"No. I might need it."

"You go with Mercy. Your Mom needs you. I'll take care of the gun," Mike said.

Jakey reluctantly gave Mike his gun.

"Jakey saved Dad's life Mike. He shot the man that was going to finish Dad," Mercy explained.

"Go ahead, get to the hospital," Mike said.

As Mercy, the guards and Jakey started toward the now open front door, Mike said, "Hey Jake. Good Job."

Jake didn't turn around, but just put one hand in the air and waved it. On his face, was a wide grin.

# 12

THE RIDE TO the hospital was short, only three miles north on Broad Street, left on Lehigh and on to Front Street and the hospital. Like Allegheny Avenue, Lehigh Avenue dissected North Philadelphia east to west. Lehigh Avenue was also a main route for the PTC trolleys that connected Strawberry Mansion to Port Richmond. It was a wide street by Philadelphia standards but not as wide a Broad Street. On both sides of the street, there was a mixture of two- and three-story red brick row homes, small stores and some factories. Northeast High School, the school that Jacob flunked out of, was located at Eighth and Lehigh.

Both Charlie and Jake were currently attending Northeast High, Charlie in his senior year and Jake in his sophomore year. Both had gone to Catholic school for a short time, but when Jake was asked to leave, Molly and Jacob decided to have both boys go to public school. Mercy continued in Catholic school and in 1939 transferred to the then new Little Flower Catholic High School. She was part of the first class to graduate. Georgie Byrne was still attending a Catholic grade school.

Trying to console his sister, Jake smiled and said, "Dad's gonna be okay. He's tough. Even tougher than me."

"I hope so Jake," Mercy said and patted Jake's hand.

Approximately the same time that Mercy arrived at the hospital, Mike, still at Jacob's home, pulled a leather blackjack from his coat pocket and rested it on the only surviving assassin's shoulder. He tapped it several times and said. "Who sent you?"

"Fuck you!" the man yelled.

Mike hit the man on his shoulder twice and said. "Wrong answer. Let's try again. Who sent you?"

"I said Fuck y—" the man attempted to say, but Mike' blackjack across his mouth stopped him. The force knocked him and the chair on which he was bound to the floor. Grady picked him up and the man spit blood and two teeth on the floor.

"So?" Mike said.

"The Johnsons."

"The who?" Mike asked.

"The Johnsons from Oxford."

"The fucking moonshine hillbillies? You gotta to be kidding me."

"You won't be laughing long," The man said.

Mike hit the man's shoulder again. "Why's that?"

"Son of a bitch, you broke my shoulder."

"Why's that? I'm not going to ask again."

"Because old lady Johnson's on the warpath and she's a witch of a woman," The man yelled.

I'm tired of this. Wrap that towel around his head. We got enough blood on the floor.

As Grady began to wrap the towel, the man yelled in a frighten voice, "What the fuck are you doing?"

Mike said nothing and put two bullets into the man's head. They untied him and laid him on the floor.

"Go call the cops Grady. Tell them there was a break in. They can do the cleanup. Take the towel. No need to give them too much to think about."

# 13

"**HOW MANY TIMES** do I have to tell you that we're part of the Byrne Construction security team?" Mike said in frustration. "Go ask your captain; he knows who we are."

"Mr. Kelly, we have four dead bodies and two in the hospital. It's my job to investigate," Detective Joe Madden said.

"I've told you this five times already. The story isn't going to change, because it's true," Mike said in frustration.

"One more time, and we can call it quits," Madden said.

"Okay. Four mugs broke into the house—" Mike was interrupted.

"Why would they do that?"

"How the fuck should I know? A robbery? Maybe they didn't like a house we built. I don't know. They broke in and me and Grady were in a back room. They attacked Mr. Byrne and he was able to shoot one of them. We heard the gunfire, rushed in, and saw two men entering the kitchen where Mrs. Byrne was. Grady took out one man in the kitchen with his pistol and it jammed. He scuffled with the other man and was able to grab a knife and stabbed him. One of the men was holding a gun and pointing it at Mr. Byrne. I shot the man before he could finish shooting. We called an ambulance and then you guys," Mike said pointing at Madden.

"And these are the weapons you used," Madden asked pointing at two pistols and a butcher knife.

"Yes."

"This one looks pretty old."

"Yeah it's my lucky gun. My grandfather passed it down. He was in the Civil War. I want it back when you're done with it," Mike said.

"Well, Mr. Hanlon's story is pretty much the same as yours—" Madden was saying when Mike interrupted him.

"Because it's true."

"Yes, maybe it is. Cool your heels here for a while. I need to report to Captain Murphy. I'll be back." Madden picked up the weapons and left the room.

Fifteen minutes later, Madden returned with Captain Murphy. Murphy sent Madden for some coffee and then sat down in front of Mike.

"Mike, how the hell are you?"

"Good Murph. How about you? Your family good?" Mike asked.

"Good Mike. Yours?"

"Yep. Got a new kid," Mike said.

"That's right. Congratulations." Murphy shook Mike's hand and continued, "Hey, listen, I'm going to get you out of here in a few minutes. I got people doing the paperwork now."

"Good. I gotta see how Jacob's doing. Hey Murph, you have any idea who these guys were?" Mike asked.

"None of them had any ID on them, but we found a car we think they were driving. It's registered from Oxford Pennsylvania," Murphy said.

"Oxford?"

"Yeah. You know anybody there?"

"No. Never met anybody from Oxford," Mike lied. "If you learn anything let me know."

"Will do."

Detective Madden returned with three coffees and set them on the table.

"Madden, cut Kelly and Hanlon loose. It's a clear case of self-defense. No use wasting any more time on this."

"Captain Murphy, when do you think I can get my gun back?" Mike asked.

"Madden, give him the guns. We don't need them."

# 14

WHEN MIKE AND Grady arrived at the hospital, Mercy, Molly, Rose, Franklin and Brian were sitting in the waiting room. It was evident to Mike that Mercy and Molly were very distraught. Mike said his greetings and sat down beside Mercy.

"It's all taken care of. Have you told anyone what happened?" Mike asked Mercy.

"Just Uncle Frank and Brian. What do you mean it's taken care of?"

Mike explained to all of them what had transpired with the police.

"Where are the kids?" Mike asked.

"I sent them with a couple of men to Mercy Row. I didn't want them here in case..." Molly said and started to cry.

"How's Jacob?"

"We don't know," Mercy said. "The doctor came out and told us Papa had lost a lot of blood and that they were trying to stabilize him. Oh God! If anything happens..."

"It won't," Franklin said, "Your dad's a tough character. He'll be just fine." He paused for a second, looked at Mike and said, "If you don't mind, I need to talk to Mike. We'll be back soon. Can I get anything from the cafeteria for you?"

They all declined and Frank motioned to Grady and Brian to follow him. They walked through the sterile white halls to the steps and then down two flights to the cafeteria. Franklin hated the smell of hospitals. It always seemed to him that hospitals had a chemical smell mixed with the byproducts of human suffering. He was anxious to leave and take care of the business that he knew had to be done.

Mike, Brian and Franklin took a seat at a table and Grady bought coffee and placed a cup in front of each of them. What's the plan, Frank?" Grady said.

"First, we need to find out who did this. Did you get any info from the police?" Frank said.

"Nah, all they know is the car's from Oxford. One of them was alive when we got to the house, so we convinced him to tell us. It was the Johnsons."

"What Johnsons?" Frank asked.

"You know, the hillbillies. You remember?" Brian said.

"What? Those fucking hicks?"

"Yeah," Mike said.

"How the hell did they get the clout to do this?" Frank said.

"Don't know, but we should find out," Mike answered.

"We will, just as soon as we see how Jacob is. Brian, go pick up a few guys and bring them here to go with us. Have some men watch Jacob here and the family at Mercy Row. Nate can get a few of his guys to help. I want the kids and the ladies there where it easier to protect them," Franklin said and paused. "Tony's gonna want in on this. Grady, can you call and tell him to bring a few men and meet us here?"

"How's Don Amato? Mike asked.

"Tony took him home. Doc wants him to rest," Grady said as he left to call Tony.

"Let's get back. Maybe there's some word about Jacob," Franklin said.

When Frank and Mike returned to the waiting room, Jacob's doctor was talking to Molly, Mercy and Rose. Franklin could tell by the shocked look on Rose's face and tears from Mercy and Molly's eyes, the news wasn't good. Frank suddenly felt deflated. It was as if someone just took all the air and blood from his body and left him as an empty shell. For the first time in his life, Franklin felt true despair. *Jacob couldn't be dead. It was impossible*, he thought. Frank stumbled, as his legs began to buckle.

Mike caught him by his arm and asked, "You okay Frank?"

"Yeah. Yeah I'm fine." Franklin said, snapping out of his daze. Then he walked up to the doctor. "How's Jacob?"

Molly and Mercy began to cry and Rose put her arms around both of them as tears ran for her eyes as well.

"Mr. Garrett, are you okay? You look pale," the doctor asked.

"I'm fine doc. How Jacob's doing?"

"Mr. Byrne has a gunshot that went into the right side," the doctor explained pointing to a spot on his own torso approximately ten inches below his rib cage. "It went through his torso and exited on the right side of his back." Again, he pointed to a spot on his own back. "Luckily, no vital organs were hit."

"So he's good," Frank said with excitement.

"Well, unfortunately he lost a lot of blood. We patched him up but Mr. Byrne is currently in a coma."

"Coma! When will he wake up?" Franklin asked.

"We just don't know. He could come out of it anytime or never. When and if he does wakeup he could have some damage to his brain functions," the doctor said, "or he could be perfectly normal. We won't know until he's awake."

Franklin just looked at the doctor for a long time saying nothing and then said, "No, he'll be fine. Jacob's going to be fine."

"Lady's," the doctor said, "I can take you in to see him, but no other visitors until he's awake."

Mercy rose from the waiting room chair, hugged Franklin and said in his ear, "I know you have to do what you have to do. Please be careful. And please, please keep my family safe."

"Of that you can be sure," Franklin said and kissed Mercy on the forehead. He hugged Molly, assuring her that Jacob would be fine, and then he hugged Rose. The women walked off with the doctor.

"Okay, boys, let's go to Oxford," Franklin said. Franklin, Mike and Grady, who had returned from calling Tony, left the hospital and waited in Franklin's car until Brian returned with his men. Shortly after, Tony Amato Senior arrived with three of his men from the South Philly Mob. Altogether, there were twelve men. Enough Franklin thought *to take care of some fucking hicks.*

They took the same road they had taken ten years before and the last time any of them had visited Oxford. It was an hour and a half drive south on route US 1. Franklin, Mike, Grady and Brian were in Franklin's car and the others followed in three additional vehicles.

Approximately an hour after they started driving, Franklin saw a restaurant, pulled into the driveway, and parked under a large sign that said *Kennett Square Pennsylvania Mushroom Capital of the World*.

"Brian, tell the others were getting some food. Before we go any further I want to brief everyone on how we're going to do this," Franklin said.

"Sure Boss," Brian said as he walked off.

"How's Brian's kid doing?" Mike asked Grady.

"He's okay. His left arm is paralyzed and he has a limp, but he's healthy again," Grady replied. "Every summer we worry about the kids getting polio. My wife's a wreck until the cold weather comes," Grady continued.

The men had just started walking to the restaurant, when Mike yelled, "Fuck!" And started spitting on the asphalt.

"What the hell's wrong with you?" Franklin asked as he hit Mikes' back, thinking he was choking.

"Shit! I got a fucking fly in my mouth. It tastes horrible," Mike said and spit again.

"What, these little things?" Franklin asked swatting flies from his face.

"They're everywhere. Let's get inside," Mike said and started trotting toward the restaurant's entrance.

Once they were all seated, Franklin started to outline his plans for their retaliation on the Johnson gang. His main point was they had to hit them hard and fast so they ceased to be a threat, but they didn't need a lot of bodies around getting the authorities riled up.

"One thing! I don't want the old lady killed. I want her scared enough that she stops fucking with us. We already killed four of them and—" Franklin was interrupted by the waitress.

"What can I get you fellas?"

"Beers all around and Italian hoagies," Tony Amato said. "That okay with you guys?"

Everyone agreed and as the waitress started to walk off, Mike asked, "Hey sister, why so many flies outside? You got some dead bodies buried out there?"

The waitress laughed and answered. "No bodies Hon, just mushrooms. We call those little bastards mushroom flies. Every year this time, they swarm and get into everything. The nasty little things hatch in chicken dung the farmers use to grow the mushrooms. One thing," she paused for a couple of seconds for effect, "don't get any in your mouth!"

Mike looked up at her, his eyes opened wide and asked, "Why, they poison or something?"

"No, they just taste God awful," she said and walked off to get the beers.

Franklin continued briefing them and when they were finished, he paid the bill and left a sizable tip.

"Thanks Hon," the waitress said and when they left the restaurant, she walked over and picked up the phone and dialed.

Franklin had prearranged that Mike would ride with Tony Amato's men, so he could keep them reigned in if this got too hot. Tony and his crew were well known for their violence and Franklin wanted to keep the killing to a minimum.

"Tony. Ride with me, will you?" Franklin said. "Mike, can you ride with your guys?"

Frank opened the back door of the sedan, let Tony in first and then followed. Brian and Grady got in the front.

"Tony, I didn't get a chance to talk to you at the memorial. I want you to know how sorry I am about Tony Jr. He was a great kid," Franklin said.

"Whata you gonna do Frank? It's war," Tony said, his eyes glistening. He turned his head away so Franklin couldn't see.

After twenty minutes, they turned off US 1 and started south on Limestone Road. They immediately saw the flashing lights of several police cars. They were about one hundred yards up the road.

"What going on up there?" Grady asked.

"Stop here Grady," Franklin said. "Looks like an accident. I'll go see what's happening. Brian, you're with me. Keep the other cars back here."

Brian and Franklin walked the hundred yards to where the police were. As they approached the police vehicles, men carrying rifles came toward them from both sides. They had been hiding in the brush beside the road. Franklin guessed there must be forty or fifty men all pointing their rifles at Brian and him.

"Yo! What's going on?" Franklin asked.

A man wearing a badge walked up to Franklin and motioned for him and Brian to raise their arms. They compiled and the man first took Franklin's pistol and then Brian's. He handed the guns to another man and turned back to Franklin. Saying nothing, he punched Franklin in the stomach. Franklin bent over and the man hit him again with an uppercut. Franklin fell to the ground. Brian grabbed the man to stop him from hitting Franklin again. Two other men grabbed Brian, knocked him to the ground and kicked him.

The man then pulled Franklin up to his feet and said, "I'm Sheriff Dan Maxwell. Now, Mr. Garrett, I have orders to keep you alive. Nobody said I can't beat you and I will if you don't do as I say."

Franklin looked at the sheriff somewhat surprised that he knew who he was. "Oh yeah, Mr. Garrett, I know who you are, but this guy over here I don't know." The sheriff said pointing to Brian. "Nobody told me to keep him alive." He pointed to a man and bent his finger motioning him to come forward. "This is Tim Johnson. Your people killed his brother yesterday. You know what the Bible says Mr. Garrett?"

"I haven't read it lately," Franklin answered.

"Well, let me give you a Bible lesson then. Deuteronomy 19:21 says, And thine eye shall not pity; but life shall go for life, eye for eye, tooth for tooth, hand for hand, foot for foot," the sheriff said as he pulled his revolver and handed it to Tim Johnson.

Tim Johnson pointed the revolver at Brian's head and pulled the trigger.

"You fucking bastard!" Franklin yelled as he lunged for the sheriff. The sheriff kicked Franklin back to the ground, grabbed his revolver from Tim Johnson and hit Franklin on the head with it. Franklin fell back unconscious.

Grady was watching from the car when Tim Johnson killed his brother Brian. He jump from the driver's seat, pulled his Colt .45 and started shooting at Johnson and the sheriff.

"Grady, get back in the car. You can't hit anything that far away. We have to get out of here!" Tony Amato yelled. Grady ignored Amato and emptied his clip. Then he ran to the rear of the car, popped the trunk and pulled out a Springfield rifle. Seconds later, using the car's bumper as support, he aimed the Springfield at Sheriff Maxwell's chest and squeezed the trigger. Maxwell fell backward with a bullet in his heart. Grady loaded another cartridge and aimed at Tim Johnson. In the seconds it took Grady to empty his .45, get his rifle from the trunk, aim and kill Sheriff Maxwell, Johnson's men recovered from the surprise and started shooting back. Some of them, also had long-range rifles and bullets, hit the car's windshield and the dirt around Grady.

"We gotta go. Too many of them." Tony Amato yelled again as he grabbed Grady's shoulder and pulled him to the rear door of the car. Amato pushed Grady in and then jumped in the driver's seat, started the engine and turned the car around speeding back to the others in Franklin's and his crew. Seeing Tony speeding toward them, the men quickly got in their cars and also turned and sped up the road and back on to US 1 travelling north.

In the backseat of the car Tony Amato was now driving, Grady was saying "Motherfuckers," repeatedly.

# 15

MIKE DROVE TO the Episcopal hospital as soon as he arrived home from Oxford. He asked Tony Amato to meet him there and told his men to go home, but to be available when he called. He sent Grady home to tell Brian's wife and other family members what had happened to Brian.

Tony Amato, who was in fact if not name, the boss of the South Philly Italian gang, was waiting for Mike by the front door of the hospital. Upon seeing Mike starting to walk up the pathway, he singled to the four men he had stationed in a car in front of the hospital that it was okay.

"Mike, how you doing?" Tony asked as he hugged Mike and kissed his cheek.

Mike always felt uneasy when the Italians greeted people with hugs and kisses. He understood it was their custom, but with the Philadelphia Irish, you only kissed or hugged women. It was very rare if you even hugged your father or brothers.

"Not so good Tony. Worried about Frank and pissed off about Brian. If I had those shit eating hicks here I'd kill them all," Mike said.

"I'm sending one of our best lawyers to Oxford to make inquiries. He'll find out if Frank's..." Tony hesitated and then continued, "He'll find out what's going on."

"I hope so. Let's go talk to the ladies," Mike said opening the door and waiving Tony in first.

When Tony Amato and Mike Kelly entered the hospital waiting room, they saw Mercy sitting on one of the benches. Seeing them, she stood up and hugged Mike, then Tony."

"How's your Dad doing?" Mike asked.

"No change, Uncle Mike."

"Where's your Mom and Rose?"

"Rose went back to Mercy Row to take care of the boys. Mom's in with Papa. I think she dosed off. I couldn't sleep so I came out here."

"Better go wake her up. We have some bad news," Mike said.

Mercy's eyes reacted before she could speak. She hesitated and the said, "No, let my Mom sleep. She needs it. Tell me."

Mike and Tony explained what had happened that evening, leaving out nothing.

"What are we doing about Uncle Frank?" Mercy asked, feeling very queasy. She didn't know if it was the bad news or her pregnancy.

"I have a lawyer going to Oxford to find out what's going on," Tony said.

"What about Brian's family. Is someone with them?" Mercy asked.

"Yeah. Grady's there and some of the guys' wives will bring food and stay with the family," Mike replied.

"I can't believe Uncle Brian's gone. Do you think they killed Uncle Frank?" Mercy asked suddenly realizing what danger Franklin was in."

Mike said, in a not so convincing voice, "Nah, he'll be okay. He's like your Dad. He'll be fine."

Mercy's eyes filled with tears and she put her head on Mike's shoulder and said, "I pray to God you're right."

Franklin Garrett was in a five by ten foot cell in the Oxford jail. His right eye was swollen and oozing blood. The left side of his mouth was badly bruised and cut. Franklin's chest was aching and every time he took a breath, he felt a sharp pain. He was sure he had a broken rib or two.

*At least I'm alive*, he thought. He had felt sure that the hicks were going to kill him, but to his surprise, old lady Johnson told her son to load him in the car and take him to the jail. Before her son could get him off the ground, the old woman kicked Franklin in the face several times. He blacked out and when he woke, he was in the jail cell.

When Franklin's head cleared, he asked the jailer for some water. The jailer laughed, went away and then came back with a bucket. As Franklin came closer to the cell door to get his water, the jailer lifted the bucket and threw the contents at him.

"You fucking bastard. That's piss," Franklin yelled.

The jailer laughed again, turned and left.

# 16

ALAN SCHECHTER, THE Amato family's top lawyer, arrived at the Oxford City Jail at 9am sharp. His rule was that if you were trying to get something from somebody in power, do it early in the day. People tended to more pliant before they had to deal with too many other people trying to get something. Schechter walked up to the desk officer and said, "There was an incident last night near US 1. Your police officers, for no reason, abducted a man. Is that man here?"

The desk deputy looked up at Schechter, squinted and said, "And who are you?"

"Aaron Schechter. I'm Franklin Garrett's attorney," Schechter said with authority as he handed the officer his card. "Is he here?"

"He's here. Hold on. I'll be back," the deputy said as he walked over to an office door in the corner of the small lobby.

"Sir, there's a guy outside, says he's a lawyer. He's looking for Garrett."

Tommy Thompson had been second in command at the sheriff's office and had taken over this morning for the now departed Sheriff Maxwell. "Tell him he's not here."

"I... I think I told him he was," the deputy said sheepishly.

"God damn idiot! Tell him you made a mistake. Shut the God damn door behind you," Thompson snarled.

"I'm sorry Mr. Schechter I was wrong. He's not here," the deputy said.

"Is that so," Schechter said as he started walking toward Thompson's office door.

"Hey, stop. You can't go in there," the deputy yelled.

Schechter paid no attention and opened the door. The deputy ran after Schechter, caught him by the arm and said, "I told you, you can't go in there.

"Do you really want to assault an officer of the court?" Schechter said looking at Thompson."

"Leave him," Thompson said.

The deputy took his hand from Schechter's arm and, Schechter walked into Thompson's office, took a chair and said, "My name is Alan Schechter, and I'm Franklin Garrett's lawyer. I want to see him," Schechter said handing Thompson his card.

"I am sorry Mr. Schechter, but we have no Franklin Garrett here. Deputy Wallace was wrong. He's a bit of a dunce, but he's my brother-in-law so we keep him around. You know how it is."

"Is that so? Well if I don't see Garrett right now, my next visit will be with a high-ranking State Police Officer out of Harrisburg. I might even invite someone from the FBI office in Philadelphia," Schechter said calmly.

Tommy Thompson starred at Schechter for a full minute, while he pulled together his thoughts. He hated big city people who thought they could push everyone around. He especially hated uppity Jews. If he thought he could get away with it, he would throw him in the cell next to Garrett. Finally, he decided he didn't need any higher authorities meddling in his business. He got up, walked to the door and yelled, "Wallace, get over here. Take Mr. Schechter to see Mr. Garrett." He turned to Schechter and said, "You got fifteen minutes."

"Sherriff, before I see Mr. Garrett, please give me the details of why you're illegally holding him," Schechter said.

# 17

MERCY TOLD HER mother the news Mike brought the night before. Molly was dumbfounded and heartbroken. She had come to love Brian and his family, especially his son who had contracted polio in 1938. *The poor kid*, she thought, *how would Brian's wife be able to care for him without Brian?* She resolved that Brian's family would never want for anything again as long as she was alive.

The news that affected her most was that Franklin was missing and could be dead. When Molly first met Franklin, so many years ago, she thought he was a rather lecherous man who didn't think much of women. He was certainly not the type of man she would choose but as time went by, Molly saw a different side of Franklin. Yes, he was a womanizer, but he was also a good man. He always treated his women well, and he loved Jacob and her children. Molly knew Franklin would do anything to keep Jacob safe. Eventually, Molly began to see Franklin as the brother she never had, and she loved him as a brother.

Franklin Garrett was hunched over sitting on his jail cell bunk that consisted of a hard wood platform with no mattress or pillow. He reeked of the urine the guard had soaked him with the evening before. The galvanized bucket that served as a toilet emanated such a stench that Franklin had taken his shirt off to cover it. It did no good. He had been given no food or water since he arrived at the Oxford jail.

*I've had it worse*, Franklin thought, remembering spending ten days trapped in a trench during the Great War. The Germans had pinned down his company. They couldn't get supplies. They drank rainwater and ate whatever they could find, which twice consisted of the rats that shared the trenches with them. *I survived that and I will survive this*, he thought. *That is, if the old witch doesn't kill me.*

"Garrett. There's a shyster here to see you." Deputy Wallace said as he unlocked the cell door. Franklin slowly lifted his head as Schechter entered the cell.

"Oy vey," Schechter exclaimed as the stink of Franklin and the cell attacked his senses.

Schechter put his briefcase down and holding his nose with one hand, he put his other hand out to shake Franklin's. "Mr. Garrett, my name is Alan Schechter. Tony Amato sent me to see if I could help."

Franklin started to laugh. Schechter's muffled high-pitched words reminded him of the munchkins in the movie The Wizard of Oz. He took Schechter's hand and shook it. "Sorry my accommodations aren't better Mr. Schechter," Franklin said.

"Sorry," Schechter said taking his fingers from his nose, "Alan Schechter. Tony sent me. This stench is unbearable."

"Tell me," Franklin said, "Good to meet you Mr. Schechter. You here to get me out?"

"That may be harder than I first thought. They're charging you with killing their sheriff."

"I didn't. The fucking bastards killed Brian. I don't know who killed the son of a bitch sheriff, but I am happy they did," Franklin said and spit on the floor in disgust.

"You're going to have to sit tight for a while. I have to go back to Philly and try to work my magic. Apparently, some old women and her family run the town and the new sheriff is scared shitless of her," Schechter said.

"Yeah, old lady Johnson. Her son killed Brian," Franklin said in disgust.

"I'll do everything I can to get you out," Schechter said.

"Better hurry. Looks like these bastards are going to starve me to death. I haven't seen a crumb or a drop of water since I've been here," Franklin said.

Schechter opened his briefcase and handed Franklin a paper bag. "I brought this for the trip home. I think you need it more. Do you like pastrami?" Schechter asked.

"Thanks," Franklin said as he opened the bag and wolfed down the sandwich.

"Let me see if I can get you some water," Schechter said as he walked to the cell door and yelled, "Deputy Wallace, Deputy Wallace."

"You ready to come out?" Wallace asked.

"Not quite yet. I need some water for Mr. Garrett," Schechter said.

"No can do."

"How much do you make each month Deputy Wallace?"

"What do you care?

"Just curious."

"Almost two hundred dollars a month," Wallace said proudly.

"Tell you what. I'm going to give you two hundred dollars now," Schechter said, pulling out his wallet, "and if you continue to bring Mr. Garrett food and water until he's released, I'll give you six hundred dollars. That's four months' pay. What do you say?" Schechter held out the two one hundred dollar bills.

Deputy Wallace starred at the money, looked over his shoulder and grabbed it from Schechter's hand.

"Now, be a nice boy and get Mr. Garrett some water," Schechter said and turned back to Franklin. "Let me update you on what's going on back home Mr. Garrett."

When Schechter finished updating Franklin and was sure Deputy Wallace had provided the promised water, he said, "It may take a few days for me to get our FBI contacts in line. Right now, I have to get back to Philly and report to Don Amato. The deputy will bring you food and water and I'll be back tomorrow to check on you." With that, he asked Wallace to open the door and he left Franklin's cell.

As he walked through the door to the offices, two men grabbed Schechter by the arms and manhandled him into a chair. "Mr. Schechter, my name is Mrs. Johnson," Old lady Johnson said in a slow deliberate voice. "We don't like Jews here in Oxford. You're not welcomed here."

"Mrs. Johnson, last I checked we live in a free country and I can travel where I want. As a lawyer, I have the right to see my client whenever I want," Schechter said.

"Not in Oxford, Mr. Schechter. If you come back, Sheriff Thompson may not be able to protect you. As I said, Jews are not welcomed in Oxford. Oh, and here, take this with you." Old Lady Johnson said as he threw a one hundred dollar bill in Schechter's face. "Deputy Wallace decided he didn't want your money after all."

"If Mr. Garrett is hurt or dies under any circumstance, Mrs. Johnson, two things will happen. I will bring the FBI here to have an investigation and you'll be the first to go to federal prison. And, Mr. Garrett's friends in Philly will burn your town, your home and your family to the ground. Clear?"

"I think you have the wrong impression Mr. Schechter. I don't want Garrett dead. I want him to suffer."

# 18

IT HAD BEEN three days since Amato's lawyer Schechter visited Franklin in the Oxford jail. Those days had been hell on Franklin. Each morning and every evening since Schechter's visit, Deputy Wallace turned a fire hose on Franklin. He claimed it was to keep him clean, but Franklin knew it was part of their plan to break him.

Once a day, at noon, they fed him the only meal of the day. It consisted of a milk bottle full of water and three pieces of white bread with butter. Once they included two slices of moldy American cheese. Every evening at midnight and again at 4am, the night guard would bang his nightstick on the jail bars to wake Franklin. The cell was filthy and they wouldn't empty the bucket he used as a toilet, so his waste overflowed on the floor.

"Hey Garrett. Your Jew lawyer was here again. Thompson wouldn't let him in," Deputy Wallace said.

"I have a right to see my lawyer."

"Maybe in Philly, but not here. We say who gets to see who," Wallace said as he turned the water on and pointed the hose at Jacob. The force of the water threw Franklin back against the wall and then to floor. Wallace laughed and said, "I'm getting pretty good at this."

The water pushed Franklin's head against the cell wall, and cut his lip. When Wallace turned off the water, Franklin stood up. It was hard, very hard, but he didn't want to give Wallace the satisfaction of seeing him hurting. His lip bleeding, Franklin slowly walked to the cell door and said, "Hey Wallace, you got any kids?"

"No," Wallace replied.

"You married?"

"No. What the hell do you care?" Wallace answered.

"I can understand that. You're one ugly son of a bitch. That's good Wallace, that's real good," Franklin said.

Bewildered, Wallace asked, "Why's that good?"

"Because it's going to make it much easier for me to cut your throat, "Franklin said and spit a glob of blood in Wallace's face.

"You fucking Harp!" Wallace yelled and turned the hose on Franklin again. Franklin fell backward, rolled himself into a ball and slid as far under the bunk as he could.

# 19

AT THE SAME time Franklin was being tortured in the Oxford jail, the doctor attending Jacob at the Episcopal Hospital in Philadelphia, ran into the waiting room and urgently motioned to Mercy and Molly to follow him. As they made their way to Jacob's room, Mercy's heart filled with dread. *No, no, he can't be dead*, she thought as she ran ahead of her mother. When she entered Jacob's hospital room, the doctor was at Jacob's bedside blocking her view of her father's face. As she came around the bed she yelled, "No, no Papa!" Molly entered the room a few seconds after and hearing Mercy, she started crying.

Then Mercy saw that the doctor was rubbing Jacob's lips with ice and that Jacob's eyes were partially open. His head was slowly moving back and forth, as he tried to come to grips with where he was.

"No Mama. Papa's okay. He's waking up," Mercy said.

"Oh Jacob," Molly said as she grasped his hand. She was still crying, but these were tears of happiness.

"Mercy took Jacob's other hand and said, "Papa wake up. Time to get up."

Jacob's head rolled toward Mercy; his eyes opened a little more and he smiled.

"He was showing signs of consciousness and I thought it would be best to have someone he knows here when he woke up. I'm sorry if I frightened you," the doctor said.

Molly grabbed the doctor, hugged him, and still crying said, "Thank you, thank you."

After ten minutes, the doctor asked Mercy and Molly to stand by in the waiting room while they worked on Jacob. He promised to come get them in an hour or so. Molly told Mercy she would go find a payphone and call Rose and the boys with the good news.

Within thirty minutes, the waiting room was full of men from the K&A Gang, residents of Mercy Row and neighbors. After an hour, Tony Amato and some of his men arrived. The well-wishers came with food, as was customary for those who were ill. The aroma from bowls of Cannelloni, steak sandwiches from Pat's Steaks, hoagies from DePalma's, pastries from the German Bakery at Front and Clearfield, homemade roast beef sandwiches with horseradish and soft pretzels created an atmosphere akin to an old country feast. Patients, doctors and nurses joined in the festivities until the hospital administrator shooed them back to work and asked the well-wishers to keep quiet. "After all, there are sick people here."

As Jacob's visitor's munched on the hoagies and steak sandwiches, the doctor emerged from Jacob's room and told the family they could visit now. They generally only allowed three visitors at a time, but, as if he had a choice, the doctor said it would be okay if all the children, Rose, Tony Amato, Mike, Grady and Nate visited. The others, he said, would not be allowed. The well-wishers were disappointed and finally asked if they could just walk by Jacob's room. The doctor said he would ask Jacob to see if that would be okay. Jacob agreed.

"Charlie, Jakey, help me sit up will you?" Jacob said.

"No! You have to rest," Molly said.

"It's okay Molly. I'll be fine. I don't want people to see me lying down."

"Okay, but you two be careful," Molly said waving her hand at Jake and Charlie.

"Just prop a couple pillows behind me. That should do it," Jacob said and flinched with pain as they lifted him. "It's okay, just hurts a little. Okay doc, I'm ready.

Molly was on Jacob's left side with Rose next to her, then Charlie, Jake and Georgie. Mercy was on his right side, with Mike, then Tony Amato, Grady and Nate Washington as the visitors started by the door. Each looked into the room and either smiled, tilted their heads in greeting or made the sign of the cross blessing Jacob's recovery. A few older Italian men bowed and walked on. At one point, a man with a large speed graphic camera took a flash photo of the family. Later, they discovered that the Philadelphia Inquirer ran a story about Jacob, describing him as a prominent businessman who was beloved by all of North Philadelphia. For the first time in her life, Mercy realized how powerful and loved her father really was.

When the last visitor passed, Mercy shut the door. Charlie and Jake took the pillows from behind Jacob and laid him down.

"Dad, I saved you a Hoagie," Georgie said, holding out the sandwich wrapped in butcher's paper.

"Thank you Georgie. I'm going to save it for later. Okay?"

"Sure Dad."

"Where's Frank and Brian?" Jacob asked looking at Mike.

Molly and Rose gathered the children and took them home to Mercy Row, leaving Mercy to tell her father what had happened. Mercy explained how they had fought off the two men in the kitchen, and how Jake saved his life. Mike, Tony and Grady filled in the rest of the story to date.

"Grady, I 'm sorry," Jacob said. "I can't believe it. I'm sorry."

"You have nothing to be sorry for. The Johnsons killed Brian, not you," Grady said.

"How about his wife and kids? What can I do?"

"Molly's taken care of that, Jacob. You just need to get well. We need you," Grady said.

Jacob put his hands on his head shook it a little, as if to clear his thought, and said. "Okay, how do we get Frank out of Oxford?"

"Pop's got some connections with the FBI. He said he could call in a favor. Maybe get them to help out," Tony said.

Everyone looked at Tony with surprise. Jacob asked, "How the hell did that come about?"

"Something to do with security at the port. We got our guys looking out for krauts trying to blow shit up."

Mike shook his head and said, "The Feds and Mob working together. That's a new one."

"He wants to send a couple FBI guys with our lawyer to see if they can muscle Frank out of jail. They are the Feds, after all," Tony said.

"And what if it doesn't work?" Jacob asked.

"Papa, they're starving Uncle Frank. We have to get him out one way or another," Mercy said.

"We will sweetheart. We will," Jacob said. "How fast can Don Amato set this up, Tony?"

"Tomorrow morning."

"Okay, set it up. If that doesn't work, we'll need a plan B, a more direct approach," Jacob said.

"The problem is, the Johnsons have somehow found a small army. From what our lawyer says, they have the jail well-guarded," Mike said.

"Mercy, I think it's best if you go home and see how Rose and Molly are doing," Jacob said.

Mercy looked at her father with her mother's *you didn't just say that* look and said, "They're fine. I'll stay."

"We can't use Route 1 to get there. They'll be looking for us to come that way," Tony said.

"What if you came from the south? Would they expect that?" Mercy said.

"Maybe not," Tony replied.

"We could go over to Jersey and cross over to Delaware and come north. If they have someone watching us here, they'll just think we're going to the shore," Mike said.

"Mike, Tony, it's important we do this with as little damage as possible. We'll deal with the Johnsons later when things cool down," Jacob said looking at Grady.

Jacob's eyes began to droop and he nodded off, but came back quickly.

"Papa, Mike and Tony will figure this out. You need to rest now," Mercy said.

"We'll need to put Frank on ice somewhere until we work out the charges against him," Jacob continued.

Mercy waved to everyone to leave and said, "Okay, that's enough for tonight."

Mercy kissed Jacob on the forehead and said, "Get some sleep Papa."

"You okay Mercy?" Jacob asked.

"I'm fine Papa. Sleep."

When Jacob fell asleep, Mercy went to the waiting room and asked the floor nurse if they had an empty room she could use. The nurse told her Room 205 was available and Mercy gathered the men and went to the room to continue their meeting.

"Uncle Mike, what's your plan if Uncle Tony's FBI agents fail to get Frank out of jail?" Mercy asked.

"We'll take a lot of our men, go south as you suggested, and come up behind them. We'll take them by surprise and break Frank out," Mike replied.

"Papa said he thought it best to be low key. I think he wants to keep the state police out of this. If you do that, you're going to have to kill people and some of our men may die. And I think the newspapers would want to cover what happened," Mercy said.

"Mercy, we've handled things like this before. It'll be okay," Mike said dismissively.

"If I have a better plan, will you listen?" Mercy asked.

Mike looked around the room at the others. He felt uncomfortable. He loved Mercy like a daughter, but she was a just a kid and he didn't want to hurt her feelings. Tony Amato lifted his shoulders in acquiescence. "Sure," Mike answered.

"Uncle Nate, we'll need your help," Mercy said.

# 20

NATE WASHINGTON LOVED the countryside surrounding Philadelphia. He had spent the first nine years of his childhood living in a small country town in Georgia called Stone Mountain, located near Atlanta. The town received its name from the very large granite mountain nearby. It was more of large hill actually. He had loved exploring the forest that surrounded Stone Mountain and had even climbed the backside of the mountain more than once. From the top, he could see for miles. The pine trees of Pennsylvania reminded him of his childhood home in Georgia and memories of collard greens, corn bread and black-eyed peas with ham hocks was making him hungry.

His thoughts were interrupted when Willy Williams, who was driving the 1936 Ford sedan asked, "Hey Nate. We near Oxford yet?"

"Let me look," Nate replied as he unfolded the map of Pennsylvania he had picked up at the local Texaco station before they had left Philly. "Where we at?"

"Saw a sign that said West Grove a couple miles back," Willy replied.

"Says here Oxford's about ten miles more," Nate said. Nate turned to the three men in the backseat and said. "These hicks don't like our kind very much, so be careful. Willy, look for Limestone Road. When you see it, pull over and we'll wait there."

"Hey Nate. Why we driving this jalopy? Why not the Imperial?" Willy asked.

"What you think it would look like if five darkies come into that cracker town riding in an Imperial?" Nate answered.

"It'd look like we had money, like we do," Willy said.

"This here car may look shabby on the outside," Nate said patting the dashboard," but on the inside it's got one hundred twenty-five horses," Nate said. "The engine in this baby is a Cadillac with milled heads and larger carburetor jets."

"Where'd you get this here car, Nate?"

"Some mechanic friend of Mr. Mike."

"Why do we need all that?" Willy said.

"You'll see," Nate replied.

One of the men sitting in the back of the car said, "Willy, this car's like you, ugly on the outside, but suped-up on the inside. Oh, wait a minute. I was wrong. You're ugly on the outside and inside."

Everyone laughed. "I got your ugly right here,' Willy said and grabbed his crotch.

When Willy arrived at Limestone Road, he pulled over and parked on the side of US 1. A few minutes later, a black 1941 Cadillac drove past Nate and his men and turned onto Limestone Road on their way to the Oxford jail. When they arrived at their destination, Alan Schechter and the two FBI agents who accompanied him opened the door to the sheriff's office.

Deputy Wallace, on seeing Schechter, quickly got up from his desk and opened the door to the sheriff's office and said, "Garrett's Jew's back. Got a couple guys with him."

Sheriff Thompson quickly got up from his desk, grabbed his shotgun from the corner and walked out to confront Schechter. "You were told that you are not welcomed in Oxford Mr. Schechter."

"And good evening to you Sheriff Thompson. Let me introduce my companions. This is Agent Brown and his partner Agent Hightower. They're with the Federal Bureau of Investigation."

Hightower and Brown held their badges up. Hightower said, "We have a court order for you to release Franklin Garrett to us. He's wanted for federal crimes."

Thompson took Hightower's ID, inspected it and then threw it back and said, "Stick that up your ass. He's my prisoner and we're holding him on murder charges. So you can get your G-man asses out of Oxford and take this Jew," Thompson pointed at Schechter, "with you."

Agent Brown said, "Sheriff, you realize we can take him by force if that's what you want." He pulled back his suit jacket revealing his Smith and Wesson."

"And that would be the last mistake you ever made," the sheriff said and whistled. A man came through the front door with his shotgun pointing at the agents. Another man came from the back room, also holding a shotgun. Sherriff Thompson leveled his shotgun at Schechter and said, "Like I said, take this Jew and get the fuck out of Oxford. I suggest you do it quickly."

"We'll be back," Agent Hightower said.

"That I don't suggest," the sheriff replied and he pushed Schechter to the door.

When Schechter and the FBI agents were in the car and heading up Limestone Road, Schechter said, "That went pretty much the way I expected."

"That sheriff's got some big balls ignoring a federal order," Agent Brown said.

"No, he's afraid of old lady Johnson more than the federal government. Anyway, we got what we wanted. You're my witnesses. The sheriff of Oxford refused a federal order and he is illegally holding Franklin Garrett. We have every right to get him by whatever means we have available."

When they reached the intersection of US 1 and Limestone Road, Schechter stopped the car and flashed his lights three times. He looked for a response and saw three flashes from a car parked on the side of US 1, and Schechter turned and headed back to Philadelphia.

Nate Washington said, "Okay, Willy, let's go to Oxford. As Willy turned onto Limestone Road, Nate and the three other men in the car checked their Colt model 1911 .45s and chambered a round.

# 21

WILLY PULLED THE Ford up near a restaurant several blocks from the Oxford jail. The five men exited the vehicle, walked twenty yards to the door and entered Clyde's Clam House. There were only two tables of diners in the otherwise empty restaurant. The floor was dirty, the tables old and the smell of the establishment would make anyone lose their appetite.

"We need a table for five. We heard you have good clams here," Nate said.

The hostess, who was dressed as if he had just come from her shift at a mushroom farm, looked at them with surprise and yelled, "Clyde, you better get over here."

A portly man with a dirty apron standing behind the counter looked up and seeing Nate said, "You boys best turn around and go somewhere else. We don't have any tables available." Then he came from behind the counter with a baseball bat in his hand.

"What's all these tables then?" Nate said waving his arm.

"We don't serve Negros here, so get your asses out the door," Clyde said threateningly and holding the bat high as if ready to hit someone."

"Hey mister, you play ball? You look a little fat to run the bases," Willy said.

"Look boys, I don't want to hurt anyone, but I will. I said get out and I mean it," Clyde said and stepped forward.

"Mr. Clyde, we play ball. We brought our bats too. Maybe we can have a game," Nate said and pulled his gun from under his coat. Willy and other men did the same.

Clyde's eyes grew bigger and the hostess screamed. The diners all dropped to the floor.

"You can go," Nate said pointing the gun at the hostess. She ran out the front door. "You all too," he said to the diners and waived his gun at them. Clyde started to leave, but Nate put his gun under his chin and said, "Not you Mr. Clyde. We have a game to play."

"Here are the rules Mr. Clyde. We bat first," Nate said. Each man began shooting at windows, the cash register, the counter and whatever they could target, until all their guns were empty. "Time to go," Nate said and started out the door. Nate stopped turned back to Clyde and tipped his hat and said, "Good evening Mr. Clyde. Thanks for the game." Then he turned and left the restaurant.

The hostess was the first to arrive at the sheriff's office. She was screaming and incomprehensible. A minute later, several of the diners arrived and explained to Deputy Wallace what had happened. Wallace gathered the extra guards old lady Johnson had provided and told them to go to the restaurant. "I'll stay here and guard Garrett. You go take care of the bastards," he yelled.

The guards, ten in all, jumped into their cars and took after Nate and his men. Wallace told the diners and hostess to go home and then he started to dial Sheriff Thompson. Before he could finish, Mike Kelly burst through the front door and smashed the butt of his shotgun into Wallace's jaw. Wallace fell back into his chair unconscious. Tony Amato and Grady followed Mike and all three went to the back room where the cells were located. Franklin was lying on the hard cot, balled up like a freezing cat.

"Wake up Frank. We gotta go," Mike yelled as he unlocked the cell door.

"Franklin turned over and looked at Mike, then Tony and Grady and said, "What the fuck kept you."

Mike and Tony took Franklin by his shoulders, and with Grady leading, his shotgun pointed straight ahead, went back into the office. Deputy Wallace was still unconscious in his chair.

"You got six large Mike?" Franklin asked.

"What? What's that for?"

"I want to leave old lady Johnson a message. You have it or not?"

Mike pulled out three one hundred dollar bills and said. "That's all I got."

"How about you guys?" Frank asked looking at Tony and Grady.

"Jesus Christ Frank. We gotta go," Mike said.

Tony Amato pulled out a roll of one hundred dollar bills from his pocket, peeled off six of them." Here," he said as he handed Frank the money.

Frank flattened the money out and put Deputy Wallace's right hand on the desk. He placed the money on the deputy's hand and took his left hand and placed it over the money. Franklin picked up the pointed letter opener off the desk and stabbed it into Wallace's hand. It only went in a short distance when Wallace woke up with a start and screamed.

"Help me," Frank yelled.

Mike and Tony placed their hands over Frank's and pushed hard until the letter opener pierced both hands. Mike picked up a metal paperweight and pounded the letter opener into the wood desk. The blood oozed out from the holes and quickly covered the money. Wallace continued to scream.

"Let's go!" Mike yelled.

"Give me your gun," Franklin ordered Mike.

Mike handed Franklin his gun and said, "Make it fast Frank. We gotta go."

Franklin placed the gun on Deputy Wallace's forehead and said, "Thanks for the water."

"No! Do—" Wallace was interrupted when Franklin pulled the trigger.

Mike and Tony grabbed Frank again and ushered him out the door, then to the rear of the jail and down an alleyway where three cars with drivers were parked.

"Jesus Christ Frank, you smell like a cesspool," Mike said." Put him in Grady's car Tony."

They put Franklin in the backseat and Grady followed him and told the driver to go. All three cars headed south out of Oxford on 3rd Street and then Baltimore Pike into Delaware. When they reached Pulaski Highway, Mike and Tony's cars tuned north, and on to Wilmington and Philly. Grady and Franklin's car continued south toward Rehoboth Beach.

"I brought you a sandwich and some coffee. You want?" Grady asked.

"Is that a joke? Shit yeah," Franklin said.

Grady opened the thermos, poured some black coffee into the lid and handed it to Franklin. Then he opened a brown bag and handed Franklin a sandwich. "Roast beef with cheese and mayo. That okay?" Grady asked.

Franklin took the sandwich and wolfed it down. Then he gulped down the coffee. He shut his eyes, smiled and shook his head in delight. Then he held out his cup and his other hand and said, "Please, sir, I want some more," quoting from the book Oliver Twist.

"We got more. Sure, here." Grady said oblivious of the origins of the famous quote.

Franklin sat back in his seat, drank and ate his second helping slowly. "Where we going?" Franklin asked.

"Rehoboth Beach."

"What, we going swimming?" Franklin said sarcastically.

"We got a boat waiting there. It's gonna take us over to Cape May and Don Amato's beach house," Grady said.

"Why Cape May? Why not Philly?" Franklin asked.

"You're too hot Frank. We gotta hide you there until things cool down. We had to get the Feds to issue a warrant for your arrest and—" Grady was interrupted by Franklin.

"Tell me later. How's Jacob?" Franklin said.

"He woke up and is doing good."

"Thank God," Franklin said and sighed. "I was scared you were going to tell me he was gone.

"No! He's good."

"How the hell did you guys get through those guards in Oxford? There must have been ten or twelve of them," Franklin asked.

"We tried to get the FBI to get you out legally, but it didn't work. So, Nate and his men shot up some restaurant and the deputy sent the guards after them. We were waiting in that alleyway behind the jail and when they left, we rushed in grabbed you and that's that."

"How'd you get into town without being seen? Franklin asked.

"We came up on Oxford from the south, where they wouldn't expect us."

"Just the three cars?"

"Yeah. That's it."

"I'm happy to see Jacob is thinking straight. The doc said he might have some problems with his head," Franklin said.

"Nah, he's good, but this wasn't his plan."

"Mike or you then?"

"No. It was Mercy's plan."

Franklin shook his head in disbelief, paused and said, "Grady, I'm sorry about Brian. It's my fault. I should have left him in the car."

"We're all sorry about Brian. I miss him, but I don't blame you. It was the fucking Johnsons that killed him," Grady said.

"We'll take care of that when I get back to Philly," Franklin said and paused. "Hey Grady, find an inn or hotel will you. I need a bath."

"You really do stink, Frank," Grady said and laughed.

# 22

**TWO DAYS AFTER** Franklin escaped from the Oxford jail, he was sitting by the fireplace in Don Amato's home in Cape May. The night he broke out of jail, he took a shower in a hotel room Grady rented for him, then a long bath and a shower when he arrived at the Amato home. Since then he showered four times to try to get the smell of the prison cell from his body. He knew it was only in his mind, but he still could smell the stink of shit, piss and vomit mixed with the dank odor of the jail.

He had eaten a couple of sandwiches in the car, during the ride from Oxford to Rehoboth, but he had to have Grady pull over twice so he could vomit. He vomited again on the boat trip across the Delaware Bay. His stomach had not been ready for so much food. It took another day before he could eat solids and now he was feeling good enough to find a restaurant and get a good meal.

"Grady, look in the phone book and see if there's a restaurant we can go to. I'm going to check and see if I can find a suit to wear," Franklin said.

Grady nodded an affirmative and walked off to find a phone book. Franklin walked up the stairs to check the closets in the bedrooms for a suit that would fit him. Amato's shore home was a large English style, beachfront two-story with porches on the upper and lower floors. It also had a large lookout tower on the roof that faced the ocean. Grady had told him it was built in the 1880s and Amato bought it in 1930 and had it refurbished.

Franklin looked first in the large master bedroom, but the suits there were Don Amato's and didn't fit him. After searching four additional bedrooms, he found a room Tony Amato used and in his closet, there were several suits. He chose a dark gray double-breasted suit and a charcoal gray Fedora. *Tony has good taste*, he thought.

Before he put on his jacket, Franklin strapped on George Graham's old double gun shoulder holster that Grady had brought for him, and filled them with two Colt .45s. He slipped the jacket on and buttoned it, checked himself in a mirror. Seeing the guns didn't show, he put the hat on and went to meet Grady.

Grady had found a restaurant not far from them and that was open all year. As Franklin entered the establishment, it was evident it was a hangout for the locals. At the bar, there was a mix of blue-collar workers in overalls, and banker types in suits. In the restaurant portion, most of the patrons were middle aged to older couples. The décor was the standard sea resort style. A lot of photos on the wall of men holding up large fish, a mounted swordfish and oddly, a mounted hammerhead shark.

Below the shark, seated alone at a table, there was a woman reading a book titled *The History of Whaling in Cape May*. When Franklin saw her, he was first startled by her beauty and then intrigued. While she was very attractive, she was wearing dark framed glasses and her blonde hair was done up in a bun as if she was trying to hide her beauty. She looked, what many men would say, *bookish*.

"Can we have a table near the shark?" Franklin asked the hostess.

"Sure hon. It's not like we're booked up," the hostess replied chuckling.

The hostess sat them at a table near the shark and next to the woman Franklin had seen. The waitress took their orders for steak cooked medium rare, baked potatoes and raw clams as an appetizer. They also ordered two whiskeys and ask for the bottle to be brought to the table.

After they ordered their meal, Franklin leaned over and said, "Excuse me Miss, I couldn't help notice that book you're reading. I didn't know there was whaling in Cape May. I thought that all happened in new England."

The woman looked up from her book, eyed Franklin up and down and said, "Really? Are you telling me you're interested in whaling?"

"Uh, well," Franklin paused taken back by the woman's frankness, "Well, to be honest, I'm not. But, I am interested in you."

The woman looked Franklin up and down again and said, "I'll tell you what. You finish your meal and I'll finish my book. When you're done, I'll let you buy me a drink. Deal?"

"Deal," Franklin said.

When the waitress brought the appetizer, Franklin ate one clam, wiped his mouth, excused himself to Grady and stood up, walked over to the woman's table and sat down.

"How about that drink now?" Franklin said.

"Ummmm. I guess you weren't very hungry. You didn't even finish your appetizer," the woman said.

"I'm on a diet."

The woman cocked her head, ran her eyes over Franklin's body and said, "You don't look like you need to be on a diet."

Franklin held his hand out and said, "Franklin Garrett."

The woman lightly took Franklin's hand in hers and said, "Catherine Avril."

Still holding Catherine's hand, Franklin said, "My friends call me Frank, Catherine."

"I think we will become friends, Frank."

"Yes, I think we will. What're you drinking?"

"Whiskey, neat."

Franklin motioned to the waitress and when she came to the table, he ordered two whiskeys.

"Catherine, don't take this the wrong way, but why are you reading a book on whaling in Capé May. You look more like a women who would read works from Hemingway or Fitzgerald, not a hack history writer," Franklin said.

Catherine smiled and turned the book around so Franklin could see the author's name. It read *Whaling in Cape May by Catherine Avril, PhD*.

Franklin's face flushed. Catherine laughed and said, "It's okay Frank. It happens all the time."

"I'm sorry, I really didn't mean—" Franklin said but was interrupted by Catherine.

"Truly! It's okay," Catherine said and put her hand over Franklin's hand.

"So your PhD is in history?"

"Yes, that would be it," Catherine replied.

"You know, I am very interested in history, especially here in Cape May," Franklin said.

"Oh really!

"It's true. How about we adjourn this meeting to my place and you tell me all about whaling in Cape May?" Franklin suggested.

"This must be a record for you," Catherine said.

"Record? What do you mean?"

"It took you all of five minutes to ask me to get in the sack with you. That must be a record," Catherine said and smiled. She took his hand, stood up and continued, pointing at Grady, "Maybe your friend will let us take that bottle with us."

Franklin walked over to Grady and whispered, "I'm going to be a little busy tonight," and picked up the bottle of whiskey.

"I'll drive back to Philly to see the family, unless you still need me to hang around," Grady said smiling.

"No. You go ahead. I think I'm in good hands," Franklin said as he turned and walked out of the restaurant hand-in-hand with Catherine.

# 23

FOUR DAYS AFTER Jacob came out of his coma, he had regained much of his strength and was bored with the hospital. He asked the doctor if he could leave, but was told that they wanted to keep him a few more days for observation.

"Molly, I don't know if I can stand being in this bed another three days," Jacob said.

Molly was at Jacob's bedside every day and other family members and friends stopped by for the early evening visiting hours. Still, Jacob was use to a full schedule, running the construction firm and meeting with Franklin and Mike about K & A Gang activities. He didn't like being idol, especially when the family was in danger.

"The doctors want to be sure you're okay. It's just three days. They can get along without you for three more days can't they?" Molly said.

"I guess so. At least we get to spend more time together," Jacob said.

Molly rose from her chair, leaned over and kissed Jacob on the lips. He took her head in his hands and drew her closer. His tongue darted in and out of her mouth. After a few minutes, Molly broke off the kiss, put her hand under the covers and said as she stroked him, "Oh my, somebody is really feeling better."

"I wish I could do something about it, but it'll be a while before my wounds are healed enough for that," Jacob said.

"Maybe you can't do anything about it, but I can," Molly said. She walked over to the door and locked it, walked back to Jacob and put her hand under the covers again. As she gently stroked him, he lifted her dress with one hand, slid his fingers down her panties and began a slow rhythmic motion. Molly groaned.

Someone tried to open the locked door and Jacob raised his head. "Don't stop; the door's locked," Molly said and groaned again.

Jacob put his head back on his pillow and closed his eyes. Molly continued stroking, but a little faster now. Jacob arched his back and let out a short yelp as a sharp pain hit his back.

Someone knocked on the door. Molly stroked faster.

"Hello, It's Father Kennedy from Saint Hugh's church. Mrs. Graham mentioned you were in the hospital and I thought I would come by to see if I could help. Hello."

"Give me a few minutes Father. Just in the middle of something now. Won't be long," Jacob said in a strained voice.

Molly increased the tempo of her strokes, as did Jacob with his finger. In less than a minute, both Molly and Jacob's faces contorted in pleasure as both tried not to make any sound. Finally, Jacob laid back spent, and Molly flopped back in her chair.

"Almost done Father," Jacob said and then whispered to Molly, "Hand me a towel please and lock yourself in the bathroom."

Molly did as Jacob asked, quietly unlocked the room door and rushed into the bathroom.

"Okay Father, you can come in now."

The door opened slowly and Father Kennedy walked into Jacob's room.

"Have a seat Father," Jacob said.

"Thank you my boy," Father Kennedy said and sat in the chair next to the bed. "Are you okay my son? You look a bit flushed."

"I'm fine Father, just a little pain when I move around."

"I'm sorry for that. Is there anything I can help you with, Jacob?"

"I'm good Father. Should be out of here in a few days. I'll be back in our Wishart Street house for some months. I'll come by for mass when I am able."

"That would be wonderful. We are always happy to have the Byrne family in attendance. After all, I believe it was your father who built our fine church," Father Kennedy said.

"It was," Jacob said.

"Before I leave, how about a blessing to help speed your recovery?"

"Thank you Father. That would be great," Jacob said, hoping to get the priest out of his room so Molly could come out of the bathroom.

Father Kennedy rose from his chair and made the sign of the cross on Jacob's forehead. He then said, "Lord and Father, almighty and eternal God, by your blessing you give us strength and support in our frailty; turn with kindness toward your servant, Jacob from all illness and restore him to health, so that in the sure knowledge of your goodness he will gratefully bless your holy name. We ask this through Christ our Lord. In the name of the Father, Son, and Holy Ghost. Amen."

"Thank you Father," Jacob said. "I feel better already."

"That's good my son. Now, I'll leave you to contemplate the power of God. Goodbye Jacob," Father Kennedy said as he started toward the door.

"Goodbye Father."

Father Kennedy stopped and pointed at the bathroom door and said, "Jacob, do you mind if I use your facilities?"

"Ahhh, well, ahhh. It's broke Father. I'm waiting for the maintenance people to fix it. There's a restroom by the nurse's area," Jacob said hesitantly.

"No problem, my son; I'll use that one. Goodbye." Father Kennedy said. As he opened the door, he smiled widely.

# 24

THE OLDEST THANKSGIVING Day parade in the nation was about to start. Gimbel's department store created the parade in 1920 to help foster new business. By 1943, Gimbel's was a Philadelphia landmark and its parade was the highlight of the year. Children in puffy snowsuits filled the sidewalks along the parade route. Men with carts yelled, "Chestnuts here. Get your red hot Chestnuts here." And the pickpockets smiled with glee on this, their busiest day of the year.

The women of most families were at home preparing a Thanksgiving Day feast of turkey, stuffing, sweet potatoes and three different kinds of pie for dessert. That was if they could get the sugar needed for the recipes. They would sneak sips of cooking sherry, reminisce about past holiday dinner successes and laugh about their culinary failures. The time the bar of soap unknowingly fell into the mashed potatoes, or the other time when the marshmallows on the sweet potato casserole caught fire.

Mercy couldn't help notice the absence of young men at the parade. The war had changed everything. Once, young fathers placed their children on their shoulders so they could see the floats. Now, their grandfather's, wearing heavy woolen overcoats and fedoras, pushed through the crowd to the front to help their grandchildren get a position to see the parade. Where once young couples snuggled to keep warm on the cold November day and watch the marching bands, there were now just small groups of young women inwardly praying their boyfriends would return safe from the Pacific, Africa or Europe. At home, mothers and wives smiled and joked as they prepared the cranberry sauce and discussed how they could make their ration stamps last longer. But, inside, they were quivering with the fear of not knowing if their husband's and sons were safe, warm and getting enough to eat.

Tears rolled down Mercy's cheeks as she remembered the times when Tony and she would stand arm in arm waiting for Santa to end the parade, and sneaking kisses and sips of anisette from Tony's flask.

Jacob, seeing his daughter's tears, wiped them away with his fingers but said nothing. What could he say? Georgie, Mercy's ten-year-old brother, squeezed Mercy's hand a little tighter and hugged her arm.

"Papa, I'm so happy you're feeling better," Mercy said and kissed Jacob on the cheek.

"Me too, Mercy," Jacob replied as he grabbed George and hoisted him on his shoulders.

"I just wish Uncle Frank were here. You know. Like the old times," Mercy said.

"Me too, but I draw the line at me putting you on my shoulders," Jacob said laughing.

"Okay, I promise I won't ask you to do that," Mercy said. "It's been three months, Papa. Isn't it safe for Uncle Frank to come home?"

"We haven't had any problems with the Johnsons since then, but we're still working on getting the FBI arrest warrant squelched. If we don't do that, they could arrest him," Jacob replied.

"But I thought that was just a made up warrant," Mercy said.

"Yes and no. It was made up, but it had to look real, so our friends in the FBI did a real warrant. You know how the government is. Red tape and slow as molasses. Shouldn't be long now. Maybe by Christmas," Jacob said.

"That would be wonderful. All of us together for Christmas," Mercy said as a wave of sadness engulfed her. It would be her first Christmas without Tony.

Mike Kelly and Grady Hanlon were on the opposite side of Market Street from where Mercy, Georgie and Jacob were standing. Mike had his son on his shoulders and Grady had Brian's son on his shoulders.

Seeing Mercy, Mike waved and Mercy waved back. Mike looked for his men, who should be nearby Jacob and Mercy, and saw Pat O'Malley standing a few people behind Jacob. He had three men, in all, guarding Jacob and once he had seen all of them, he relaxed.

The beginning of the parade that began at the Philadelphia Art Museum was just passing by them. Marching bands from local schools, colorful floats, clowns and local celebrities waving from cars all added to the festive atmosphere. When the parade finished, Santa would climb the fire truck ladder to the Toyland floor at Gimbel's department store. The passing floats blocked Mike's view of Jacob and Mercy.

"Mikey, can you see Mr. Byrne?" Mike asked his son.

"I see him Pop. Mercy and George are there too," Mikey answered.

"You know Mr. O'Malley, Patty's dad?" Mike asked.

"Yeah, I know him," Mikey said.

"Do you see him? He should be a few people back and to the left of Mr. Byrne."

"I don't see him Pop."

"You're sure? Look all around."

"No Pop, he's not there."

"Are you sure?" Mike asked.

"Yeah Pop. He ain't there," Mikey said is frustration.

Mike took his son from his shoulders and said, "Grady, take care of the kids. I'm going to see where O'Malley's got to."

"Want me to go?" Grady asked.

"No. You take care of the kids. I'll be right back.

Mike ducked under the rope and dodging the marchers, made his way across the street to Jacob. A police officer stopped him and asked what he was doing. Mike whispered he was security for Jacob Byrne and the police officer let him go.

"What's up Mike," Jacob asked.

"Not sure Jacob. We didn't see O'Malley. You stay here and I'll look for him."

Before Mike went into the crowd, he found the police officer that had stopped him and asked him stand guard until he got back. He slipped a hundred dollar bill from his pocket and placed in the officer's hand. The officer ducked under the barrier and stood behind Jacob.

Meanwhile, Pat O'Malley was making his way back toward Jacob, after killing the other two guards. He was crouching so as not to be seen. As he got closer, he pulled an eleven-inch stiletto switchblade and held it in the palm of his hand. He saw the police officer turn around and look into the crowd. Making a decision on the fly, O'Malley opened the knife and bumped into the officer. He shoved the knife through the officer's chest and into his heart. The officer slumped back against Jacob.

Jacob turned just as O'Malley pushed the officer aside and came at him. Jacob grabbed O'Malley's knife hand and pushed upward. With his free hand, he punched O'Malley in the nose. O'Malley fell back against the crowd.

"Mercy, take George and get out of here. Get to the Eighth and Market station and wait for me," Jacob yelled.

Mercy started her way through the crowd, George in hand. As she did, O'Malley found his footing and lunged at Jacob again. The crowd started screaming and dispersing. O'Malley pushed Jacob and Jacob tripped over the dead police officer's body and fell to the ground. O'Malley started to push his knife toward Jacob's eye, while Jacob held him back with both hands. Jacob pushed O'Malley's hands to his left and rolled over as O'Malley's knife hit the pavement and fell out of his hand.

Seeing the police officer's gun, O'Malley grabbed for it. Jacob did the same. They rolled to the right, pulling the police officer along with them. Jacob saw the strap holding the revolver in the police officer's holster and unstrapped it. The gun fell out and onto the ground. Both O'Malley and Jacob grabbed for the revolver. Jacob was faster and was able to get the revolver by the handle. As he tried to get his finger in the trigger guard, O'Malley smashed Jacob in the face with his right hand, knocking Jacob back. Now free of O'Malley, Jacob righted the revolver and fired two shots into O'Malley's chest. O'Malley, already on the ground, just rolled over on his back and groaned. Blood oozed from his chest. Jacob stood up, placed the revolver on O'Malley's forehead and fired.

Seeing what had happened, Grady had taken the children to the Eighth and Market Street subway station, meaning to get them home and out of harm's way. He saw Mercy there, asked her to take care of Brian's and Mike's sons, and ran back toward where he last saw Jacob. He met Jacob halfway.

"You okay boss?" Grady asked.

"Okay," Jacob answered out of breath.

"Mercy's at the station with the kids," Grady said." I'll go see if I can find Mike."

"No, stay with them. Get them home. I'll find Mike." Jacob gasped.

As Jacob was about to turn, he heard several gunshots coming from behind him. He reeled around and saw Mike running down Market Street with four men chasing him. They fired several shots but missed Mike. Jacob dropped to one knee and said, "Go Grady. Get the fuck out of here. Grady ran back toward the station and Mercy and the kids.

Jacob took aim and fired the revolver, hitting one of the men, chasing Mike, in the leg. The other men stopped and dropped to the ground as Mike ran on. Jacob fired his remaining two shots at the men, but missed. As Mike reached him, Jacob dropped the revolver and started to run **toward** the station. The three men hesitated and then started running after them, leaving the wounded man.

Mike and Jacob reached the subway just as a train traveling north arrived. Jacob saw Grady and Mercy, kids in tow, get on the first car. He and Mike made it to a middle car as the doors were about to shut. They jumped on. Two of the three men chasing them were able to get on the last car before the doors closed.

Jacob and Mike were catching their breath when the back door of the car they were on opened. Two men with pistols in their hand started through the door. Mike yelled, "Fire. Fire." The passengers got out of their seats in a panic, giving Mike and Jacob a chance to get through the front door and into the next car. The men saw them, but were having trouble getting through the passengers standing in the aisle.

People in the car panicked and someone pulled the emergency brake cord. The subway train came to a stop just as it was pulling out of the underground and up on the elevated platform. The two assailants fell forward to the floor and one of their guns discharged harmlessly into an empty seatback. This caused pandemonium in the car, as passengers forced open the door and started to exit.

Meanwhile, Mike and Jacob had made it to the first car where the children, Mercy and Grady were located. Seeing their car was halfway up the elevated platform, leaving them no safe exit, Jacob bang on the train operator's door. When the operator opened the door, Jacob told him to start the train moving again. The operator was hesitant and Mike pulled his revolver and held it up, not pointing at him, but so he could see it. The operator started the train moving again.

"Mercy, you and the kids get down behind the first seats. Keep low. All of you on the floor behind your seats," Jacob ordered the other passengers.

Mercy did as Jacob ordered laying herself over the children to protect them.

"Get the fuck on the ground," Mike yelled to get some of the hesitant passengers to do as Jacob had ordered.

"Grady, get behind a seat mid-car and be ready. Mike let's get to the back of the car and wait for them."

Grady pulled his revolver and squatted behind the seat several rows from Mercy and the children. Mike and Jacob ran to the back of the train and took position on both sides of the door. Mike pulled his weapon and Jacob looked around for something he could use. He saw a fire extinguisher on the wall behind him and grabbed it. Seconds later, they heard the air-activated door of the car behind them open. Jacob put his hand up indicating Mike should wait.

The door to their car swished open and one of the assailants started through. Jacob hoisted the fire extinguisher up and into the man's face. There was a loud crack and a scream as the man fell backward onto the other man. Both men fell back against the car door. Blood was squirting from the man's nose and he rolled to his left leaving the second man the opportunity to raise his weapon and point it at Jacob. At the same time, Mike pushed Jacob to the side, lifted his weapon and fired twice. The assailant's head reeled backward with two bullet holes just above his eyes.

Mike entered the area between the two doors and held his pistol to the head of the man with the broken nose.

"I know this guy. He's one of ours. Worked with the same crew Barry Brennan was with," Mike said. "Who else is in on this?" Mike asked the man.

The man was couching and spitting out blood, and Mike pressed the gun deeper into the back of the man's head. The noise of the air rushing by and the train made it difficult to hear the man's reply.

"Speak up," Mike yelled.

"Fuck you," the man yelled.

"Look, I know you're working with the Johnsons. One of the men chasing me was one I saw in Oxford. Who else are you working with?" Mike said and hit the man on the back of the head with his pistol.

"The Johnson's? Are your sure Mike?" Jacob asked.

"I'm sure."

Seeing things were under control, Grady motioned Mercy to stay put and walked to the back of the car to see if Mike and Jacob needed help. Seeing the assailant, he said, "You got to be fucking kidding me." Grady shook his head and continued, "This is Pete Hanigan, Jerry's brother. They were part of Brian's crew."

"Yeah," Mike said, "and before that they worked with Barry Brennan."

"Get him up Mike, "Jacob said.

Mike grabbed Pete by the collar and lifted him to his feet. Pete wiped the blood from his nose and sniffed.

"Is your brother in on this Pete?" Jacob asked.

"Doesn't matter; you'll all be fucking dead soon," Pete said.

"Oh yeah, why's that?" Mike asked.

"The Johnsons got men. We got men. You're dead," Pete answered and spit blood on Mike's shirt.

Mike smashed the butt of his gun into Pete's head. "We got men too, Pete. You can't win this," Mike said.

"Not as many as you think!" Pete spate.

Mike looked at Jacob. Jacob nodded.

"You know Pete, a friend of mine recently reminded me of an old Irish saying," Mike said in a low voice.

"Fuck your Irish saying," Pete yelled back.

"No Pete, you're gonna like this one. I'll use the English translation since you're only half a Mick. Kiss my ass," Mike yelled as he pushed Pete, with all his strength, out of the moving train.

Pete's face contorted with fear as he fell backward. A split second later, he hit the guardrail, and continued over the rail to the pavement near the corner of Front and Diamond streets.

Jacob, Mike and Grady walked back to Mercy and the kids. The other passengers were getting up. Mercy was standing in the aisle looking down. All three men seeing her, turned white.

"Papa. My water broke."

# 25

"PAPA, I NEED to get to the hospital. I think we're near the Episcopal Hospital, right?" Mercy said taking control of the situation.

Jacob, Mike and Grady looked at Mercy dumbfounded.

"Papa!" Mercy yelled.

"Uhh, I don't know," Jacob said, coming to his senses. He banged on the driver's door. "What's the next stop?"

"York and Dauphin Station, coming up in a couple of minutes," the driver yelled.

"Don't stop. We need to get to the Huntingdon Station," Jacob yelled through the door.

"I can't do that sir."

"I have a .45 pointed at the door and if you stop before Huntingdon Station I'm going to empty the clip at it." Jacob lied. "Open the fucking door, will you."

The door opened.

"That's better. Don't stop until we get to Huntingdon Station," Jacob said and handed the man a handful of cash.

"Yes sir."

When they arrived at the station, Jacob told Grady to stay behind with the children and when the police arrived to explain what had happened. Jacob and Mike helped Mercy down the station steps, then one block up B Street and over Lehigh Avenue to the hospital entrance.

"My daughter's having a baby. I need help," Jacob yelled.

Two nurses ran over and took Mercy. They placed her in a wheelchair. Jacob learned down and kissed Mercy on the check, and then he whispered, "Let's not mention to your Mother what happened. Let her enjoy this moment. I'll tell her after the baby's born."

The nurses told Jacob and Mike to wait in the main waiting room and took Mercy to the delivery room. As a father of four children, born in hospitals, Jacob was well acquainted with the rules about the birthing process. They did not involve a man, other than the doctor, to be underfoot. Jacob and Mike walked to the waiting room and asked where a payphone was located.

Before Jacob called Molly, he had Mike call the Girard Avenue Club and had several men who Mike trusted drive over to Jacob's house to pick up Molly, Jake, Charlie and Georgie and bring them to the hospital. They had explicit orders not to mention what had happened at the parade. Then Mike called Rose and had Nate bring her to the hospital.

Rose arrived before Molly and insisted that she be with Mercy. The nurse tried to deter her, but Rose firmly told her," Understand this young lady, I will be going to see Mercy so don't waste your breath trying to stop me." The nurse relented. "Oh, and when her Ma gets here, you'll be showing her to Mercy's room as well."

Molly arrived with the boys fifteen minutes after Rose and the nurse immediately took her to see Mercy. The boys joined Jacob in the waiting room. Mercy's doctor arrived thirty minutes after Molly. He examined Mercy and explained that Mercy was certainly in labor and that even though she was three weeks early the baby should be fine. He expected that Molly and Jacob would have a grandchild before the day was out.

Rose and Molly stayed with Mercy while the men in the family were relegated to the waiting room. Jacob called Don Amato and Tony and within the hour, they both arrived at the hospital with Tony's wife, who was ushered off to be with Mercy and the other women.

"Don Amato, I have a favor to ask," Jacob said.

"Of course Jacob, whatever you need; you tell us and we'll do it," Don Amato said placing his hand on Tony's shoulder.

Jacob explained what had happened at the parade and that he no longer knew who to trust in his gang. He asked Don Amato to lend him some of his men to help safeguard Mercy and the rest of the family until he sorted things out.

"Tony, call Mario. Tell him to get some men over to Jacob's house. Have him send a few men here. Tell him we'll give them a bonus for missing their Thanksgiving Day celebration."

"I'll take care of it Pop. I'll be back," Tony replied and left to find a payphone.

"It'll be all right," Don Amato said patting Jacob's shoulder.

"We'll make it all right, Don Amato. I can promise you that, "Jacob said.

"What names has Mercy decided on for the baby?"

"She won't tell us. Says Tony and her worked it out and that she wants it to be a surprise," Jacob said.

Don Amato's men arrived an hour after Tony had called them. Nate returned to Wishart Street and had several of his men placed at the Front Street and Howard Street entrances. No one expected that the Wishart Street location would be attacked, since it was mainly being used for military families, but Jacob's motto had always been "better to be safe than sorry."

"Pop, Jake and I are going to the cafeteria. Can we get you something?" Charlie asked.

"Don Amato, you hungry?" Jacob asked.

"No. No, I am fine. Charlie, maybe you could bring a black coffee for me."

"Sure Pop Pop," Charlie answered.

"Tony, Mike?" Jacob asked.

"Black coffee. Charlie," Tony said.

"I think I'll go with them. I need to stretch my legs," Mike said.

"Bring me a coffee Charlie. You know how I like it," Jacob said. "Mike, fill the boys in will you?"

Charlie and Jake looked at each other and Mike said, "Come on guys."

Don Amato motioned to one of his men to go with Mike.

"You have any idea who's behind this attack on you?" Tony asked.

"The Johnson's. I should have taken care of this sooner," Jacob said.

"You were recovering, Frank is out of commission. I would have waited also," Don Amato said.

"Problem is, they somehow got to some of my men. Now, I have to fight an internal battle as well as the Johnsons."

"It was inevitable, like war was inevitable for America. Men are greedy. They want what others have. We waited, and waited until our enemies attacked us. But, now we will finish it and grind the Germans and Japs into dust. As you will do with your enemies Jacob," Don Amato said. "And we will help."

One of the Amato crew walked up to Tony and whispered something in his ear. Tony turned pale. He looked at Jacob and shook his head.

"What is it Tony," Jacob asked warily.

"They bombed your house. Before my men could get there, they bombed your house," Tony said.

Jacob fell back in his seat and sat there for a moment to collect his thoughts, then said. "Thank God no one was there." Then looking at the messenger he said, "How bad?"

The messenger looked at Tony who nodded.

"When they got there the house was completely engulfed in fire. The fire department was there, but I am afraid the house is, pretty bad.

Jacob's eyes narrowed. "Excuse me Don Amato, Tony. I have to make a call. It's time Frank came home.

# 26

AT 11:52PM ON November 24th, 1943 Mercy's baby was delivered. Molly, Rose, and Tony's wife Carmella, came into the waiting room smiling like the Cheshire cat in the story *Alice in Wonderland*. They took their seats and said nothing. After a long pause, Carmella nodded to Molly and said, "Go ahead Molly, tell them."

"No, I think I'll wait awhile," Molly said jokingly.

Jacob tilted his head, looked up and said, "For Christ sake Molly, what is it?"

"It's a boy, seven pound eleven ounces," Molly blurted out, then leaned over and kissed Jacob.

Carmella hugged Tony.

After the appropriate congratulations, hugs and kisses, Jacob asked, "When can we see him and Mercy?"

"A little while yet. The nurses are cleaning him up. They said we can see Mercy in about thirty minutes or so," Rose said.

"Were you in the delivery room?" Jacob asked.

"No, they wouldn't allow it. We won't be able to hold the baby for a few days. The doctor says they don't want to subject him to our germs."

"But we can see him?" Tony asked.

"Yes dear, we can see him in the nursery. We just can't go in for a while," Carmella said. "The doctor says the baby is healthy and Mercy is doing fine. They should be able to come home in five or six days."

"Well, you can bet your sweet Irish behind I'll be here every one of those day," Rose said.

"Can you believe it? Our baby has a baby. We're grandparents!" Molly said. "I can't wait till they come home."

"What is it Jacob," Molly said seeing a darkness come over Jacob's face.

"Nothing," Jacob lied. "I was just wishing Frank could be here."

"Did Mercy tell you the baby's name?" Charlie asked trying to lighten the mood again.

"She did," Molly said.

"Well, what is it?" Tony said.

"I know, Tony. Right?" Charlie said.

"No."

"Tom, Joe, Jim, Shamus, Francis. Not Ish Kabibble?" Charlie said and laughed.

"No, No," Molly said as she rose from her chair and stood in front of Don Amato. "The baby's name is Gerard Anthony Byrne Amato. Gerard is the English name for Gerardo. It was Tony Junior's wish." Molly bent down and kissed Don Amato's head.

Don Amato put his hand to his mouth as a tear ran down his cheek. Carmella sobbed, and Tony turned so no one could see his tears. Rose hugged Carmella and as she did, she noticed Jake sitting off to the side with a scowl on his face. *Now, what in the devil is wrong with that boy,* she thought?

Fifteen minutes later, the doctor told everyone the baby was ready and they all could see him. After that, they could visit with Mercy. As the family peered through the glass separating them from two rows of newborns, it was easy to pick out baby Gerard. He had his father's swarthy look and Byrne's hereditary thin nose. His eyes were a striking blue color. After everyone claimed Gerard was the cutest baby ever, they all visited Mercy.

One after another, the family kissed Mercy and told her how wonderful she looked for just having a baby and how healthy looking Gerard looked. Jake was last and he leaned down and kissed Mercy on the head and whispered, "I'll get those sons of a bitches sis. I promise you that!"

Mercy whispered back, "You know?"

Jacob shook his head yes and Mercy put her fingers to his lips in a gesture that meant keep quiet.

They all talked for a while and Jacob told Charlie and Jake to go home and get some sleep. "Mike, can you take the boys home?"

"Take Aldo with you. He is in the waiting room," Don Amato added.

Mike nodded and motioned to Charlie and Jake to come along. As they were leaving, Jacob said, "Molly, I have some bad news."

Mike picked up Aldo and the group walked down the stairs to the front door of the hospital. Mike told the men who had brought Molly to stay at the hospital and he took their car. He had two men follow him in a separate car.

"I guess we're going to Wishart Street, "Charlie said.

"Yeah," Mike answered.

"Can we go by our house first, Uncle Mike?" Jake asked.

"Not a good idea, Jake," Mike answered.

"I have to check on something. Something special," Jake pleaded.

"It's not safe Jake," Mike said.

"I don't give a fuck. I need to go there!" Jake yelled.

"Whoa! Take it easy."

"I mean it Uncle Mike. If you don't, I'll just sneak out later and walk there," Jake said.

"Aldo, take us to Broad Street." Mike said realizing Jake would do what he said. At least this way he would be there for protection.

"Thanks," Jake said.

Aldo parked outside of Franklin's home and they walked past a couple of homes to the Byrne residence. When they were close enough to see the damage to the house, Jake said, "Fuck me!"

The windows on the first and second floors were broken and the glass covered the sidewalk. The front door was hanging off a single hinge. Most of the first floor was blackened with fire damage.

A single fire truck was parked in front of the house, and the driver was sitting on the front step. Aldo introduced Mike, Charlie and Jake to Don Amato's men. Then Mike asked the fireman how bad the damage was.

"Pretty bad mister. First floor's totaled. Second floor's pretty bad. Part of the floor caved into the kitchen. Top floors are damaged but not as much. It's out now. I'll stay to be sure it doesn't flare up," the Fireman answered.

"Move, will you. I need to get something," Jake said.

"You can't go in there kid. The ceiling might come down, or a floor cave in."

Jake pushed the fireman off the step and ran into the building and up the steps. "Christ sake kid. Take it easy," the fireman yelled.

Mike ran after Jake, and as he entered the house the fireman yelled, "You people are fucking crazy."

Jake ran up to the third floor and into his bedroom. He pushed open the door partially blocked by a fallen bookshelf and ran to his closet. When he opened the door, it fell off its hinges. Jake threw the door to the side, reached up and grabbed a metal box. As he turned around, he bumped into Mike who had followed him.

"You okay Jake?"

"Yeah. I'm good now. Let's go."

As the pair walked toward the stairs, Jake's foot broke through the flooring and he tripped forward, Mike picked him up and the two ran down the steps and out the door. The fireman was standing with his fists on his hips when they came out. Mike handed him a one hundred dollar bill and said, "Sorry for the trouble."

"Aldo, take us to Mercy Row," Mike said.

"Sure," Aldo replied.

When they were in the car, Mike said, "What's so important about that box that you want to risk getting hurt or worse."

Jake didn't say anything. He just opened the lid of the box. Inside was the revolver his grandfather had given him. Mike nodded his approval and Jake closed the lid.

Aldo had turned right on to Allegheny Avenue and was just passing Twelfth Street, when Jake yelled, "Stop the car."

Aldo screeched to a stop and both he and Mike pulled their guns expecting an attack. "What is it Jake?" Mike asked.

"I want to see what that man over there's doing," Jake pointed to a man who was trying to open a sewer cover on the corner. He had a red haired cocker spaniel on a leash and a burlap bag was lying to the side of the sewer. The bag was moving.

Jake got out of the car, opened the trunk and took out a tire iron. He tucked it in the back of his pants, then walked over to the man, and asked, "What're you doing mister?"

"What's it to you kid?" the man growled.

"Just wondering."

Aldo started to walk over to Jake, but seeing what was happening, Mike stopped him. "He can handle it. He needs to blow off some steam."

"Nice dog you got there, mister. What's his name?" Jake said.

"It's a her. The bitch got herself pregnant and had a litter. I can't take care of a bunch of pups."

"So what are you going to do?" Jake asked.

"I'm gonna dump them and let nature take care of them."

"I'll buy them from you." Jake said.

"How much?"

"I have two bits," Jake said holding out a quarter.

"Get the fuck out of here kid."

"On second thought, you're just going to give me the puppies for free. And your dog too," Jake said.

"And why would I do that?" the man said balling up his fists.

"Because if you don't I am going to break your arm and a leg. That's kind of funny don't you think. It's going to cost you an arm and a leg if you don't give me your dogs," Jake said and laughed.

The man stared at Jake and moved forward to grab him. Jake took the tire iron from his pants and hit the man on his outstretched right arm. The man howled in pain. Then Jake hit him on the leg and the man collapsed. Jake hit the man several more times on the arm and again on the leg. The man was crying when Jake untied the dog leash and picked up the burlap bag. Jake started walking toward the car with the dog and bag. He stopped, turned around and said, "What's the mom's name?"

"The man still sobbing said, "What?"

"What is your dog's name?" Jake yelled.

"Bonnie," the man said.

"If I ever see you with another dog, cat or any animal I'll kill you," Jake said.

When they all got back in the car, Jake opened the burlap bag. Five little red and blond-haired cocker spaniel puppies scurried out. Jake smiled.

Charlie picked up one of the puppies and said, "Ginger."

"What?" Jake asked.

"She looks like gingerbread. So that's her name, Ginger," Charlie said. And I'm keeping her."

# 27

**THE SAME DAY** that Mercy and her baby Gerard came home, Molly received a letter from Jimmy. He said that he was in the states and would be coming home by December fifteenth. Molly laid the letter on the table and sighed with relief. *What a crazy topsy-turvy year it had been.* She thought. *So many twists and ups and downs. More downs it seemed. Jimmy being wounded, Tony's death, the house destroyed, Franklin in jail, the attempts on Jacob's life.* Sometimes, she felt as if her brain would explode. The only thing keeping her sane was Mercy's baby and now her own first baby was coming home and safe. She had worried every day Jimmy was away that he would suffer the same fate as his biological father, who had been killed in World War I.

Molly walked to the living room and paused at the doorway. Mercy was sitting on the sofa, nursing Gerard. Memories of her own nursing of Mercy flooded into her mind giving her a warm feeling. She walked over to Mercy just as Mercy lifted Gerard to her shoulder to burp him. When Mercy was finished, Molly gestured for Mercy to give her Gerard. Molly sat on the other end of the sofa and gently rocked the baby until he fell asleep.

"I heard from Jimmy. He'll be home for Christmas," Molly told Mercy.

"Oh. Thank God." Mercy said as she leaned over and kissed Molly on the cheek. "Did you tell Papa?

"Not yet. He's meeting with Frank and Mike in the dining room. When he's finished, I'll tell him.

Since the firebombing of the house on Broad Street, Jacob and his family had taken over his old house on Mercy Row. He felt good in his old home. It was like a pair of old leather gloves; it fit well and was warm. Back in the '20s, when the homes were first built he and Franklin had each taken four row homes on Wishart Street and converted them into single homes. Both expanded residences were now part of the Mercy Row Foundation. There had been a couple of families living in Jacob's old home, but he moved them to two homes he owned on Lippincott Street. Mercy Row on Wishart Street was a very defensible facility, as it had proven in the 1920s when Franklin and he started the K&A Gang. Franklin offered Jacob the use his Broad Street home until the Byrne residence was rebuilt, but Jacob felt more at ease on Wishart Street.

Twelve hours after Franklin received Jacob's call, he was back in Philadelphia. Amato's lawyer, Schechter was working with the FBI to negate his warrant. Until then he would take his chances.

"Frank, it's time we stopped the Johnsons," Jacob said.

"What do you have in mind?"

"We need to weed out the traitors in our gang first. Nobody's safe until we find them."

"Jerry Hanigan, his brother Danny and Shorty O'Shea are missing. We already know the Hanigan's are involved and O'Shea must be with them. Shorty's brother Denny claims he knows nothing," Mike said.

"Do you believe him?" Jacob asked.

"I don't know. He was part of the Barry Brennan crew. I should've taken the whole crew out after I did Barry," Mike said in disgust.

"No, you did the right thing. We can't kill everyone. It's bad for business," Jacob said. He paused and then continued, "Unless they're trying to kill us."

"So if you wanted to take over the K&A Gang what would you do?" Franklin asked Jacob.

"I'd get some internal support in the gang. Then I'd take out the leadership."

"So, pretty much, you would kill me, yourself, Mike and probably Grady," Franklin said.

"The problem with that is Don Amato's gang. Tony and he wouldn't stand by and let that happen," Mike said.

"Unless they have external support from one of the New York mobs or inside the Amato organization," Jacob said.

"Now you're scaring me Jacob," Franklin said.

"I'm scaring myself. If we're right, the Amato's are targets also." Jacob sat back in his chair and closed his eyes. After a minute or so, he opened his eyes, leaned forward on the table and said, "Back in the summer, there was a story in the newspaper about some of the German generals trying to assassinate Hitler."

"Yeah, they fucked it up. Shame they didn't get that little kraut bastard," Mike said.

"What about it?" Franklin asked.

"They tried to take out Hitler and his closest supporters when they had all gathered for a meeting. Makes sense, right?" Jacob said. "With them out of the way, Germany would be up for grabs."

Franklin leaned forward and said, "You're kidding!"

"No it could work," Jacob said.

"Too risky Jacob," Mike said.

"Not if we're smarter than they are. If we do this right, they'll have to use all their supporters to get to us and instead, we'll get them. Once we get them, then we'll go see the Johnsons."

"I'll call Don Amato and Tony and fill them in," Franklin said.

"No, we need to do this in person. Too risky to use the phone?" Jacob said.

"How do we get to them without anyone knowing?" Mike asked.

"Nate," Franklin said.

"Right!" Jacob said. "They won't expect that."

"Where can we meet? Can't do it here or at the Amotas," Mike said.

"I bought some land, up on the boulevard awhile back. They have a couple of barns on the property. We can use one. The farmers moved out so there's nobody there."

"I'll go talk to Nate," Franklin said.

"I'll write a note to Don Amato telling them where to go," Jacob said, "Mike, how about you go to the property and figure out how we can set a trap."

The next morning, Nate left Wishart Street and drove west to Seventeenth Street then south as if he were going to his Columbia Avenue headquarters. Instead, he passed Girard College, turned on Ridge Avenue and east on Girard Avenue. He then took Broad Street south to the Amato South Philly headquarters. He was sure no one had followed him. Don Amato and Tony agreed to meet Jacob that afternoon.

When Jacob and Franklin arrived at the property on the boulevard, Mike was already there. He guided them to a barn in the middle of the property and suggested they park inside the barn where no one could see it.

"What do you think Mike? Can we work this out?" Jacob asked.

"I think so. If I were going to ambush you, I'd set up in or behind those small buildings to the west and to the east of the barn. You can't see behind them when you drive up the road. And they're far enough away our guards wouldn't probably search those buildings," Mike said.

"We would have to post our men way behind them so they are not seen. That's risky. What if they can't get here fast enough?" Franklin asked.

"What if we put some steel sheeting in the barn and disguise it somehow? That would give use protection long enough for our guys to get to the barn," Jacob said.

"Where're you getting steel sheets?" Mike asked.

"I have some connections within the Budd Company. They're a war effort company and have steel available," Jacob answered. "We'll borrow it."

"I thought we might send a construction crew up here and dig a trench behind those out buildings. We could put some pipe around. People would just think we are laying sewer pipe. Then, when it's done, we can make it look like it is filled in, but it won't be. Our guys can hide in the trenches," Mike said.

"Normally, we would have at least four men guarding any building we and the Don are meeting in. That means they'll need at least seven to nine men to come at us," Jacob said.

"You think they have that many?" Franklin asked.

"With the Johnson's helping, yes. Maybe the Italian's that are backing them will have men there," Mike said.

"No, I don't think so. They wouldn't do anything before we are out of the picture. And if they can get the Irish to kill the Don and Tony, it's better for them," Jacob said.

"Okay, so we have to find at least eight men, plus the four guards, that we trust with our lives," Franklin said.

"Nate can provide a couple of men. Tony and the Don can give us a few men and the rest will be our guys we know are loyal," Jacob said.

When Don Amato and Tony arrived, Mike had them park in the barn. Jacob and Franklin shared their thoughts and explained the plan. The Amato's were not surprised that he might have some disloyal men. He even knew who they might be.

"Jacob, our business is a difficult one. If we owned a restaurant and one of our employees steals from us, we call the police and fire the son of a bitch. But, we can't call the police. We have to be the police, the judge and we have to punish the offender. We don't have jails, so every offense is a capital offense. We had an offender a few months ago and he was punished. Now his cousins are not happy. This is who I believe is helping your traitors," Don Amato said.

"We'll take care of them, after we deal with your threat," Tony said.

"So you agree to our plan?" Jacob said.

"Yes, with one change. Pop won't be there, Tony said.

"No! I will be at the meeting. It would not look right if I was not there," Don Amato said.

"Pop—" Tony tried to say but was interrupted by Don Amato.

"That's it!" Don Amato said swiping his hands together. "I will be there."

"Okay then. Let's set the meeting for December eighteenth at 8pm. That'll give us time to get things ready," Jacob said.

"Mike and me will work on getting the men together. Tony, do you have a few men we can use that you trust?" Franklin said.

"I'll get you some men, Frank," Tony answered.

"We need to start leaking small bits of information about the meeting. Never too much at one time, but enough for our enemy to figure out where the meeting is and when," Jacob said.

"I'll handle that," Mike said.

# 28

JIMMY BYRNE CALLED early the day of December fifteenth and said he would be home mid to late evening. Molly arranged a small impromptu party for family and Jimmy's friends to greet him. They had been at the Wishart Street home since 7pm, and several of Jimmy's friends were tipsy and singing a song popular with the country's military and their families; *I'm Dreaming of a White Christmas*. There was an air of excitement and happiness, even though the war raged in Europe and the Pacific and the Byrne family was once again in jeopardy.

December fifteenth was a cold day and by 9pm the temperature had dropped to eighteen degrees and it began to snow. Mercy thought, *Maybe we'll have a white Christmas*. As she peered from her bedroom window at the Wishart Street house, the white flakes were settling on the cold sidewalks and parked cars. Most of the homes on the street were decorated with colorful lights and candles in their windows. Mrs. Weinstein would be displaying her electric blue menorah when Hanukah began on December twenty-first. For now, she dressed her window with strings of blue lights that highlighted two silver stars.

Many of the homes on Wishart Street also displayed silver stars in their windows. Each star signified that a family member was serving in the military. A single gold star in Mrs. Milkey's window reflected the light from the lamppost outside her home. Her son would not be coming home for Christmas, ever again. Tears streaked down Mercy's cheeks as she thought of how many more gold stars she might see displayed before the war was over. She kissed her fingers and touched the gold star in her own window and said a short pray for Tony.

Mercy's attention was drawn to the guards at the end of the How-ard Street intersection. They were huddled around a fire they had made in a large oilcan. One man started singing an old Irish song:

> Over in Killarney
> Many years ago,
> Me Mither sang a song to me
> In tones so sweet and low.
> Just a simple little ditty,
> In her good ould Irish way,
> And I'd give the world if she could sing
> That song to me this day

She wondered how many of these men would survive the war her family was fighting. Would the family survive?

The men suddenly stopped singing, picked up their weapons and pointed them at a taxi that had stopped at the intersection. Mercy was anxious until she saw a tall familiar figure, in uniform, step out of the cab and start shaking the guards' hands.

She ran down the steps and out the front door, shouting, "Jimmy's here! Jimmy's here!

Before he reached the house, Mercy ran to him and threw herself at Jimmy, who picked her up and twirled her around. He kissed her on the forehead and set her down and kissed her cheek. By then, Molly had reached Jimmy and she hugged him tightly.

"I'm so happy you're home. So, so happy," Molly said.

"Me too Mom. Me too," Jimmy said.

One by one, family members and friends hugged or shook Jimmy's hand. When it was Jake's turn, he stuck his hand out and said," Welcome home Jimmy."

Jimmy grabbed him, gave him a hug and whispered in his ear, "You're not too old for a hug, you little prick."

Jake smiled and punched Jimmy on the arm.

The partygoers circled Jimmy and guided him to the house. On the step and in the entryway, Mike, Grady, Jacob and Franklin blocked the way. Jimmy shook each of their hands and exchanged greetings. As Jacob shook Jimmy's hand, he put his other hand on his shoulder, and said, "Jimmy, we're proud of you. It's good to have you home."

"Get over here you big lummox and gave your old Grandma Rose a big hug," Rose Graham said.

Rose had been standing behind Jacob and Jimmy walked over grabbed her and picked her up squeezing her tightly. He didn't say anything for a minute or so, then he whispered in her ear, "I missed you most of all."

Rose released her hold on Jimmy and blushing said, "You mean you missed my cooking." She grabbed him by the hand and took him to the kitchen. "I made your favorite, potato chip sandwiches," she said pointing to the table and a platter of sandwiches.

"Real Lebanon baloney?" Jimmy asked.

"Of course," Rose replied.

"White American cheese?"

"Is there any other kind?"

"Barrel-brined kosher pickles?"

"Yes," Rose said.

"Gulden's dark mustard?"

"I almost changed to French's mustard because Gulden is a German name, but I didn't. So yes, Gulden's dark mustard."

"And, I hope you bought Wise potato chips," Jimmy said.

"I haven't bought any other chip since you were a boy," Rose said as she tweaked Jimmy's cheek.

"Hey, watch it. I'm a disabled Vet," Jimmy said jokingly.

The expression on Rose's face changed from happy to concern and she asked, "Jimmy, are you okay? Do you still hurt?"

"I'm fine Grandma. I'll tell you all about it tomorrow, but right now I'm eating three of these good boys," Jimmy said and grabbed the platter of sandwiches and ran into the living room.

By eleven o'clock, all of Jimmy's friends left and he promised to get with them before Christmas. Charlie and Jake were sitting on the arms of a chair Jimmy was sitting in.

"Did you kill krauts?" Jake asked.

"What was it like to get shot?" Charlie asked.

"Come on guys. Give me a break. We have plenty of time to talk about the war. Right now, I want to relax and enjoy the family," Jimmy said.

Jake looked disappointed, but said, "Okay general," and saluted.

Georgie was asleep on the floor and Molly, Rose and Mercy were sitting on the sofa. Mercy was rocking baby Gerard trying to get him to fall asleep.

"Mercy, can I hold Gerry?" Jimmy asked.

"Of course," Mercy said and handed Jimmy the baby."

Jimmy sat back in the chair coddling Gerard and said, "I can't believe I'm an uncle."

"I can't believe I am mother either. It's like a miracle. He grew in my tummy. Can you image that?"

"Well, technically it wasn't your stomach he grew in," Charlie said.

"We won't be talking about that around the baby, Charlie," Rose said making a stern face. Everyone looked at Rose and began to laugh.

"You know what I can't believe?" Jake said and paused. Everyone looked at Jake and waited for him to answer his own question. "I can't believe how stinky Gerry smells." Jake held his nose, got up from the arm of the chair and ran over to the other side of the room. Charlie did the same.

Jimmy sat in the chair with an expression of bewilderment on his face. He had no idea what to do.

Mercy laughed and said, "Here, let me take him."

"No, I'll do it," Rose said. "I've been changing all of your nappies for years." She took Gerry from a grateful Jimmy.

"I'll help you Rose," Molly said and the two women left the room with Gerry.

Jake began to laugh and said to Jimmy, "You looked like you were going to crap your pants."

"Funny, Jake. You know when you were a baby I had to change your diaper once. You had the smallest little ding-a-ling," Jim lied.

Jake's cheeks turned red and he threw a pillow at Jimmy. Everyone laughed.

Jacob walked into the living room just as Jake threw the pillow.

"That's no way to treat a war hero, Jake," Jacob said and laughed. "What the hell is that smell. Jake, you been eating beans again?"

"No it w—" Jake was about to say but was interrupted by Jacob.

"Can you all come in the dining room? We need to talk."

Mike, Grady, Franklin and Jacob explained in detail the situation and the plan to resolve it.

"Papa that sounds dangerous. There has to be another way," Mercy said.

"We have to find out who our enemies are. If we don't, the whole family's in danger, including Don Amato and Tony," Jacob answered.

"I'm going with you," Jimmy said.

"Me too," Charlie echoed.

"Yeah, I'm going," Jake said and pulled the gun his grandfather gave him from under his shirt.

"Jesus Christ, Jake, give me that," Jimmy said and grabbed the gun from Jake.

"Give it back," Jake yelled.

"None of you are going," Jacob yelled. "Jake, I told you about that gun. I'm not telling you again."

Jacob rarely yelled at his children and the fact that he did get their attention.

"Look, I need you to be here to protect family in case things don't go the way we planned. Jimmy, this envelop has a key to a safe deposit box at the bank. There's cash and our various bankbooks in the box. Our stock portfolio's there also. You'll find a will. Not that you'll need this, but just in case." Jacob paused then continued "Charlie, Jake, this envelop has the combination to a vault. The vault's in the basement of this house. In the vault, you will find weapons. Don't go there unless it is absolutely necessary. We don't expect they'll come after the family, but you know my motto."

"Better safe than sorry," Jake said.

"Right," Jacob said. "Mercy, the basement in the second section of the house will have food and water and a safe place for you all to stay, if anyone attacks you here. You know where the hidden trapdoor is. If anything does happen, I want you to take Rose, your mother and the kids there until the danger passes." Jacob said.

"I talked to your father about this and he agreed to let my friend Catherine stay with you until this situation is resolved. My place won't be safe. Is that okay with you? Franklin said looking around the table.

"Uncle Frank, are you telling us you have a girlfriend?" Mercy said.

"Well," Franklin paused as though he had to think about it. "Yes, she is. Her name is Catherine Avril," Franklin answered.

Jake looked at Charlie, eyes wide and shrugged his shoulders in disbelief. Franklin had never had, what would be considered, a normal relationship with a woman. He had plenty of women, but usually only for a night or two, and none that had lived with him.

"Of course, Catherine's welcomed," Mercy said.

"I was going to introduce you to her on Christmas, Franklin said embarrassed that he hadn't already done so.

"Okay! That's settled. Jimmy, give Jake his revolver. Jake, put the gun away. We'll give the three of you something better when the time comes. Charlie, Jake. Jimmy's in charge. You do exactly what he tells you to do. I've already talked to Rose and your mother. They know everything you know. Nobody leaves the house until after the eighteenth. Agreed?" Jacob said not expecting an answer.

# 29

JUST AFTER DINNER on December eighteenth, Jacob took Jimmy, Charlie and Jake to the basement, where the vault was located. He dialed in the combination and opened the door. There was a loud whistle as Jake saw the contents of the vault.

Jacob picked out three shoulder holsters and three military grade .45 caliber automatic pistols and handed them to Jimmy.

"Jimmy, Charlie and Jake know how to use these, but you hold onto them. Give them to them after we leave."

"You don't trust us Pop?" Jake said.

"Of course I thrust you, but we don't need to brandish these weapons around the kids any more than we have too," Jacob said.

This placated Jake who was happy not to be considered one of the kids.

Jacob then picked out three M1 carbines and handed one each to Jake, Charlie and Jimmy. Picking up two military ammunitions boxes marked .30 carbines, he handed them to Charlie and said, "Break these out and put clips in different rooms of the house. Be sure everyone knows where you put them. Make it high up where Georgie can't find them. No clips in, unless you need to use them. Keep them hidden until we leave."

Jacob pointed to a shelf and said, "Jimmy, grab six boxes of those .45 cartridges and give Jake and Charlie two each. Keep these on you at all times. See that," Jacob said pointing to a black wood cabinet against the wall. "Behind it, there's a metal door to the safe room. It locks from inside the room. Only use it if you have no other choice.

"Pop, it seems to me that you're expecting a hit on the house," Jimmy said.

"No, I'm not really. I don't think that would gain them anything, but you know what I always say. Charlie, Jake and Jimmy said in unison, "Better safe than sorry," and laughed.

Jacob picked out his favorite two-gun holster and filled it with two .45s, grabbed four boxes of shells and put them in his suit pockets. "Okay boys, let's go upstairs. I don't want to be late for the dance," Jacob said.

Earlier the day of the meeting, Mike had supervised the placement of their men in the ditches he had the construction crew dig. After the ditches were finished, they put plywood over them and covered the wood with a thin layer of dirt. It had started snowing the morning of the meeting and there was now a half-inch covering of snow, making the ditches virtually invisible.

Franklin had placed two men on a rise about half a mile east of the building. One of the men had a high-powered pair of binoculars so he could monitor the movements of the enemy when they showed up. There was a field telephone in the ditch that connected to another phone the lookout had by his side. His job was to keep the men in the ditch informed and to tell them when to attack.

The lookout had seen the attackers take their places behind the two out buildings, just as they had expected. That had been two hours before Jacob arrived. He had informed the men in the ditch and then sent the second lookout to call Jacob.

When Jacob pulled up outside the barn, he turned the engine off, exited the car and then in a loud voice, so the attackers could hear, said, "It's clear."

Franklin, Mike and Grady exited the car and talked about the weather, again so they could be heard. As the four men walked into the barn, the lookout picked up his phone and said, "The bosses are here."

A few seconds later, another car arrived and two men took their place in front of the barn door. After another ten minutes, Don Amato and Tony arrived. Their driver exited, looked around and then opened the door. Don Amato stepped out from the backseat and Tony from the passenger side of the car. They then gave some instructions to their two men is a louder than normal voice.

The lookout picked up the phone again and said, "The Amatos are here." On hearing this, Jacob's men in the ditch picked up their weapons and got ready to move. Nate had insisted that he be allowed to be one of the men in the ditch. He had also brought two men from the Columbia Avenue crew.

Nate rubbed his leg and whispered, "Man I'm getting too old for this."

"You are Nate. You're so old, your dick has done shriveled up," Willy whispered.

"That's not what your wife says," Nate whispered back and gave a quite laugh.

"Shut the fuck up you two," the man Franklin had put in charge whispered.

Inside the barn, Jacob, told the Amatos that the attackers were there and they could expect some action very soon. He showed them to a makeshift conference room his men had made from bales of hay. There were four walls of hay two bails thick, with a small doorway. Between the bales of hay, there was steel sheeting. They would be safe in the conference room.

Jacob took his two .45s out of their holsters and laid them on the table. The other men did the same with their weapons. Don Amato's weapon of choice was the Italian made Berretta M195. He felt that it was more reliable than the American Colt .45. Tony carried a Colt .45 and a Lupara, the sawed off shotgun favored by the Cosa Nostra. He left the small Berretta in his ankle holster.

"Whiskey?" Jacob said holding out a bottle.

Each man turned over the glass in front of him and Jacob poured each a drink. He held his glass high and said, "To my Pop, George, Tony Jr. and Brian." Each man poured four small portions of their glass on the floor and drank the rest.

"I don't think it'll be long now," Franklin said.

The attackers started moving from behind the out buildings and headed toward the rear of the barn. The lookout grabbed the phone and waited. His orders were to wait until the attackers were in place and would be caught between the guards and the men in the ditches. He whispered in the phone, "Eight on the move. Hold."

The attackers took places at the rear and the sides of the building, being careful not alert the guards at the front door. Four of the attackers had Browning automatics and the others had handguns. Suddenly, one of the men opened fire with his Browning, spraying the side of the building at chest height. The four Byrne and Amato guards, as rehearsed, fell back into the building and headed toward the makeshift conference room. All the attackers opened fire.

As the bullets peppered the room easily destroying flimsy wood walls, the guards fell to the floor and crawled to the doorway. One man let out a short scream as several bullets found their mark on the guard's side.

Jacob, the Amatos, Franklin, Mike and Grady grabbed their weapons and lay on the floor. The sound of the gunfire and the noise of the bullets bouncing off the steel were deafening.

Several of the attackers started to the front door of the barn. This is what the lookout was waiting for. He picked up his phone and yelled, "Attack!" Immediately, the men in the ditches threw over the plywood, climbed up the short embankment and started running toward the barn. By the time Jacob's men were half way to the barn, all the attackers were standing on the sides of the barn front doors. Two men with Brownings stepped into the doorway, guns blazing. There was no return fire, so they moved further into the room, followed by several more attackers. When they were halfway into the conference room, Jacob and the other men in the conference room opened fire.

The two men with the Brownings were hit and fell bleeding in front of the conference room door. The other three attackers moved to the sides and returned fire. By this time, the men from the ditches were close enough to open fire. Two more attackers fell wounded. The attackers from outside rushed through the barn doors and dived to the sides to avoid the bullets coming from the conference room. One man was hit in the ankle and screamed as he smashed into the dirt floor.

Jacob's men ran up and, as planned, took prone positions in front of the barn. The attackers were surrounded. Jacob yelled out, "Give it up. If you want to get out of this alive, drop your weapons."

"Fuck you! You Mick motherfucker," a man yelled out. Immediately, there was a loud crack, a scream and another man said, "Shut the fuck up." And another crack. "How do we know you won't just shoot us anyway?" another voice said.

"You don't, but I'm giving you my word," Jacob said. "Shorty, is that you?" Not waiting for an answer, Jacob continued, "You know me. What do you say?"

There was silence for a couple of minutes and then Shorty said, "Okay."

"Drop your guns and put your hands above your head," Franklin said.

When the attackers starting walking to the center of the barn, hands above their heads, Jacob's men rushed in, searched them and pushed them to the floor on their knees. Two of the men who had been wounded were now dead; one was badly hurt and wouldn't survive. Two had small wounds and three had no wounds.

"Stand that one up. The one with the bruises on his face," Grady said pointing to one of the men. "This is the bastard that shot Brian."

"Yeah. He's that witch's brat," Franklin confirmed.

As Grady walked toward the man, the man pushed one of the guards into Grady and ran toward the barn door. Jacob's other men pointed their guns to shoot him, but Grady yelled, "I'll take care of him," And ran after the man. Approximately, fifty feet from the barn, Grady tackled the man from behind. Both men fell forward onto the snow-covered dirt.

The man's face scrapped along the ground and Grady turned him over straddling him. He put his hands around the man's neck and started to squeeze. The man hit Grady in the side of the head, but Grady didn't seem to feel it. Grady's eyes were intently looking into the man's eyes, as he pressed harder and harder. The man's eyes began to bulge and his face was beet red. Finally, the man's arms fell to the ground. Grady continued for several more minutes and then stood up. He pulled his gun and shot the man seven times. Then he pulled his ankle gun and emptied it into the man's chest. He stood there looking down at the bloodied body for several minutes, then looked up into the night sky, the light snow blowing around his face and said, "Rest in peace, brother." Then he slowly walked back to the barn.

Several of Jacob's men were standing at the barn's entrance and parted as Grady walked into the building, not noticing them. Jacob put his hand on Grady's shoulder and guided him to a man kneeling on the ground. Mike was standing behind him with his .45 pointed at the back of his head.

"Grady, let me introduce you to Danny Hanigan," Jacob said. Danny Hanigan looked up at Grady, who was still holding his ankle gun in his hand, and then lowered his eyes to the ground.

"I know him," Grady said in disgust.

"Then you know Shorty here," Jacob said grabbing Shorty's hair and lifting Shorty's head.

"Yep," Grady said.

"Well, Shorty was just telling us an interesting story. He says, and his buddies over there," Jacob said pointing to the other assassins, "agree with him. He claims the Hanigan brothers didn't like Mike's solution to Barry Brenan's crew not following the rules. So when the Johnson family tried to kill me and failed, he contacted them and joined forces," Jacob said then kicked Danny Hanigan in the face," You fucking motherless whore. My kids were at that parade with me."

Mike picked Danny from the ground and placed him in a kneeling position again.

"Shorty, what else do you want to tell us? Where's Jerry Hanigan?" Jacob said.

"They said if we didn't work with them they would kill us. We had no choice," Shorty said.

"Is that so? And you thought we would be less scary than Jerry? I don't think you're that stupid Shorty. I need to know where Jerry is."

"I don't—"

Jacob interrupted, "Shut the fuck up Shorty," Jacob motioned to Mike to step away from Danny Hanigan. When he did, Jacob pulled his Colt .45 and shot Danny in the head. As Danny fell backward, he shot him again in the heart.

Shorty fell backward and yelled, "We don't know where he is. He took three guys and said he was he was going to visit the castle."

Jacob's eyes widen as he realized what Jerry Hanigan meant. He yelled, "Grady, take care of the Don and keep these guys," pointing to the surviving attackers, "alive. Nate will help you. The rest of you come with me." Then he ran out of the barn and into the driver's seat of the first car he saw. Franklin, jumped in the back with Mike, as the other men found cars. Tony Amato slid into Jacob's car.

"Tony, we got this. Stay here. Take care of your father," Jacob said.

"Fuck that!"

Jacob drove off with Tony. Three cars followed him across the dirt field and then on to Roosevelt Boulevard and south. The cars disappeared in the now heavily falling snow.

# 30

**THE SEVEN BYRNE** family members and Catherine gathered in the living room. Mercy's nerves were on edge and every thirty minutes she looked out the front window to be sure the guards were still there blocking the street. Then she would go to the yard and look up and down the alleyway to check on the men Jacob had placed at both entrances to the alley.

"Sit down Mercy. You're making me nervous, Charlie said.

Earlier, Mercy had persuaded Charlie to go to the vault and get her a couple of guns. Jacob had some weapons placed in the safe room, but Mercy wanted to be armed in case they couldn't make it to the room. Mercy had been shooting with Jacob more than a few times and she was comfortable with the Colt stub nose revolvers Charlie choose. They were small and the recoil was less than larger weapons.

"Give me one of those Mercy," Catherine said.

"Have you used guns before?" Mercy asked.

"Army brat. Chased my dad around the world for eighteen years."

Catherine took the gun from Mercy, checked to see if it was loaded, put her foot on a hammock and lifted her skirt to reveal a blue garter. She tucked the gun in the garter and lowered her dress. Charlie, Jake and Jimmy looked at each other and smiled.

"You wearing, Mercy?" Catherine asked. Mercy shook her head no. Catherine put her other leg on the hammock. Charlie, Jake and Jimmy looked at each other again. Instead of lifting her dress, Catharine put her hand up her dress and pulled out an identical blue garter, slid it down her leg and handed it to Mercy. Mercy put her leg on the same hammock and began to lift her dress. All three Byrne boys quickly turned away. Mercy slid the garter to just above the knee and put the stub nose gun in the garter.

"I'm gonna check the guards in the alley," Charlie said.

"I'll help you, Jake said.

Catherine smiled as the boys left the room.

Charlie and Jake walked through the kitchen and into the small yard.

"Holy shit, did you see those gams?" Jake said.

"Yeah, Charlie said as he peered over the fence and looked toward Front Street. There was no guard. He turned and looked toward Howard Street. There was a guard leaning against the fence of the first house.

"That's odd. I don't see Sammy," Charlie said.

"Maybe he's taking a piss," Jake said.

"Taking pisses is why God made alleys," Charlie said.

"Let me look," Jake said as he pushed Charlie out of the way.

Jake looked down both sides of the alley and didn't see either guard.

"In the house, something's wrong."

Charlie and Jake ran through the kitchen and into the living room.

"In the safe room, now," Jake said.

"Why?" Rose said.

"No time," Charlie said and grabbed Rose's arm and started to guide her to the trapdoor.

"Molly went down the steps first and Mercy handed Gerard to her. Then she took Georgie by the arm and said, "Okay, you now."

"No! I'm staying to help Jake," Georgie yelled.

Jimmy picked Georgie up and placed him on the steps and Mercy forced him down as he descended the steps. Rose followed. Catherine pulled her revolver and was pointing it at the kitchen doorway.

"You're up Anna Oakley," Jimmy told Catherine.

"You boys okay?" Catherine asked.

"Fine. Go ahead."

Catherine went down the steps and Jake closed the door. He heard the latches being set in place and rolled the throw rug over the trapdoor. Jimmy and Charlie lifted the heavy sofa and placed it on the rug.

"I'm going to get the other guards," Charlie said.

"No, don't open the front door. What if our men have been taken out?" Jimmy said. "Get your rifles and load them."

Charlie and Jake did as Jimmy commanded and all three stood at the doorway to the kitchen waiting.

Jerry Hanigan had selected three men he knew had the experience he needed, and it was working out just the way he had planned. Sammy Edelman was trusted by Mike Kelly and was on guard duty at the alleyway entrance on Front Street. Barry Brenan had been a friend of Sammy's before Mike Kelly wacked him and was all too happy to help take Mike, Frank and all the Byrnes family down. John Wiley had been with Jerry when the Byrne gang took out the Italian boss, Frankie Capaci, in 1920. Davey McMillan was part of the crew that dealt with Johnson's back in 1933. These were tough men, who knew what to do and were willing to do it.

Sammy walked around to Howard Street via Allegheny Avenue and surprised the guard by shoving an eight-inch knife through his throat. While Sammy was taking care of the guard, Hanigan, Wiley and McMillan climbed to the roof and waited for him. When Sammy arrived, Hanigan pulled out several sticks of dynamite, placed them on the roof just above the back bedroom of the Byrne home and lit the fuse.

"When this goes off, all hell with break loose. So let's get in and out as fast as possible," Hanigan said. "I want Mercy and Molly Byrne alive. The rest I don't care."

Hanigan was one of the original Irish thugs hired, in the early 1920s, to help Byrne Construction to keep the Italian Mob in line. He quickly became a valued soldier in Jacob and Franklin's gang. Over the years, he had become resentful of Mike Kelly's rise in the family. He always thought that he should have been in an upper leadership position, rather than just a crew leader. The killing of Barry Brenan had been the last straw and his opportunity to get internal support. He connected with the Johnson family and secured an alliance with them. If all went well, by the morning, he'd be running the K&A Gang and the Johnsons would have their revenge.

# 31

**THE BLAST FROM** the dynamite was bigger than Hanigan thought it would be. It caved in most of the bedroom roof and sent debris flying for a couple hundred feet. The dust was so thick that, at first, he couldn't see where the hole was. When it cleared he said, "Okay let's go!" Hanigan, McMillan and Wiley grabbed the ropes they had fastened to pipes and lowered themselves into the room. Sammy Edelman stayed on the roof and ran to the front of the house. The guards from both Howard and Front Street were running toward the Byrne home front door. Sammy pointed his Thompson machine gun and opened fire. The guards quickly took cover behind several parked cars, and began shooting back.

Jimmy was expecting an attack from the backyard door, and was surprised when a blast shook the whole house. Plaster from falling ceiling created a cloud of white dust that made it hard to see. He didn't have to see. It was clear that whoever was coming for them had blown a hole in the roof and would be coming at them from upstairs. There were two staircases in the home, one that led to the living room and one that was in Jacob's office. The upper door to the stairway leading to Jacob's office was normally locked, so Jimmy was sure they would come from the main staircase.

"Charlie, go to Pop's office and watch for anyone coming down that staircase. Kill them if they do. Jake, you and I will stay here," Jimmy said.

Charlie grabbed a couple for clips from the bookcase where he hid them, fixed one in his rifle and ran to Jacob's office.

"Jake, we need some cover. Help me drag the dining room table in here," Jimmy said.

Jake and Jimmy took the two leaves out of the table, closed it and dragged it to a spot near the staircase in the living room.

"Is this going to stop bullets?" Jake asked.

"The wood's about one and a half inches thick and is maple. So... I have no fucking idea," Jimmy said.

"Great, mister military man," Jake said.

"We didn't have many dining room tables in the fucking desert Jake. Grab the table leaves and put them against the backside of the table," Jimmy said. "I hope that does it."

"Open the table a little. We can shoot through the opening in the center," Jake said.

Jimmy pulled on one side and Jake on the other side of the table until the opening was several inches wide.

"Clever Jake, Clever," Jimmy said.

"No Jimmy, I just don't want to kick the bucket before I get my first piece of ass," Jake said.

"If we get out of this alive, I'll take you somewhere to fix that problem," Jimmy said then yelled, "Charlie anything happening?"

"I heard someone trying to open the door a few seconds ago, but that stopped now," Charlie yelled back.

"Get ready Jake. This is the only way down," Jimmy said. A second later, they heard the undeniable chatter of a Thompson machine gun and the reports of pistol fire outside.

"Sounds like our boys are trying to get in," Jimmy said.

Jake looked through the opening in the table and quickly pulled back. "Someone's coming down the steps," Jake whispered. Several seconds later, there was a deafening blast from a shotgun, then another. A split second later, the blast pushed the table back toward Jake and Jimmy.

Jake quickly stuck his M1 barrel through the opening and rapid fired five rounds. There was a scream and the noise of a person falling down the steps. Jimmy took a quick look through the opening and saw Davey McMillan lying at the bottom of the staircase, writhing in pain. There were several bleeding wounds in his legs. The shotgun was lying next to him. Jimmy stuck the barrel of his M1 threw the opening, sited on McMillan's head, and pulled the trigger. The bullet hit him in the upper part of his head leaving a small hole and came out the back taking half his skull with it.

"Fuck!" Hanigan yelled. "Get back."

Wiley moved back up the stairs with Hanigan close on his tail. Hanigan had seen a table upturned about fifteen feet from the bottom of the stairs. The shooters were behind that, he was sure. He judged that the ceiling above the table was the floor of a small bedroom to the left.

"Wiley, go to that bedroom and put everything you have into the floor," Hanigan said.

"What?"

"Remember the Capaci job?" Hanigan said.

"Right! When we shot through the ceiling."

"So what the fuck are you waiting for?" Hanigan yelled.

Wiley rushed to the room, upturned the bed on its side and said, "Okay, motherfuckers," and pulled the trigger of his Thompson. Immediately, the Thompson responded and began rapidly pumping bullets into the floor. Just as rapidly, the bullets started to bounce back into the bedroom, smashing through the ceiling and walls. One ricochet bounced up through Wiley's shoe tearing off his big toe.

Wiley screamed and fell to the floor dropping the Thompson and holding his foot. "What the fuck?" he yelled.

Hanigan rushed to the room. Wiley had his shoe off started to wrap his foot with a tee shirt he found under the bed next to a Sears catalogue. The carpet was shredded and splinters from the wood flooring were scattered around Wiley. Hanigan pulled off a piece of loose carpet creating a bigger hole, and then he pried a piece of wood from the floor.

"That bastard! That fucking smart bastard," Hanigan yelled. "He reinforced the floors with steel. Son of a bitch!"

Hanigan ran to the bathroom, opened the medicine cabinet and searched for alcohol. He found it and a clean hand towel and brought it back to the room. He poured the alcohol on the towel and handed it to Wiley. Wiley screamed in pain.

"Here, wrap this around your foot. That filthy yellow-stained tee shirt will kill you," Hanigan said.

Wiley did as he said and stood up. He limped around the room and said, "Okay, I can walk."

"We're going to bust that other door down and get downstairs," Hanigan said.

Hanigan sprinted to the door and Wiley limped behind him. He pulled his handgun, motioned to Wiley to stand back, and said. "The fucking bastard probably has steel in the doors too." Then he shot at the lock, blowing it apart and the door opened slightly. As soon as it did, a rapid volley of bullets hit the door splintering it.

Hanigan jumped to the side of the door stepping on Wiley's foot with the missing toe. Wiley screamed in pain. Hanigan pushed him forward down the hall. "Out the back window," he yelled.

There was a hard-backed chair in the hallway. Hanigan picked it up and threw it through the window. "Okay, you go first," Hanigan said. Wiley scrambled out the window and jumped down two feet to the shed roof. He landed on his wounded foot, screamed, fell down, rolled to the edge and then off the roof. He landed in the yard.

Hanigan just looked at the roof not believing what just happened. He jumped down, went to the edge of the roof and looked down. Wiley was on the ground unconscious and he left leg was at an unnatural angle. His right leg was halfway on the step.

"Fuck me!" Hanigan said then sat down, turned around, hung off the roof and jumped to the yard.

Hearing the noise Wiley made falling off the roof, Jimmy, Jake and Charlie ran toward the yard. Hanigan heard them coming, pointed his gun at the shed window and shot four times. Then he turned to run into the alley. As he did, he heard men running down the alley. He frantically looked around for a way to escape, but saw none. Then he noticed that Wiley was halfway on a door to the basement. It had a large lock on it. He quickly pushed Wiley off the door and shot at the lock. The lock blew apart. He pulled the door open and went down the stairs.

The basement was dark with just the light from the open door coming in. He went back and pulled the door shut. He found a light switch and turned it on. The only thing in the basement was a black cabinet and a large safe.

Jimmy fired a couple of shots threw the kitchen window into the yard. There was no response, so he cautiously looked out the window. No one was there. He motioned to Jake and Charlie to follow him. When he opened the door and stepped out, he fell over Wiley leg that was halfway on the step. Wiley screamed in pain, and fearing it was an ambush, Jake fired two rounds from his .45, hitting Wiley twice in the heart.

The yard door burst open. Jimmy, Charlie and Jake all pointed their weapons at the door ready to fire. Two men stood in the door with their weapons pointed at the trio.

"It's okay boys; point the weapons down," Jacob said.

# 32

*NO USE TRYING* to hide, Hanigan thought. *They would know by the broken lock that he was in this basement.* Hanigan felt like a rat in a trap. The only door in the basement was the one he came through. There was a small window at the front of the house that was used to fill the coal bin, but it wasn't big enough for him to get out. *This is it,* Hanigan thought. *You fucked up big time Jerry.*

He ran to the back cabinet with the idea of using it to block the door. He dragged it to the door entrance and placed it on the steps. That would at least give him a little time to fight off anyone coming through the door. *If I'm going to die today, they'll be a lot of Byrne's family coming with me*, he thought.

As Hanigan turned back to take cover behind the safe, he noticed that moving the cabinet revealed a door. For a second, his hopes soared. He ran to the door, tried the handle, but the door was locked. His hopes sank as he realized the door was made of metal. In frenzy, he smashed his fist into the door several times then sank to the floor in despair.

Then he heard what sounded like a muffled female voice coming from the door. He quickly got up and put his ear to the door.

"Jimmy, is that you?" the voice said.

Taking a chance, he said, "It's Jacob. It's okay. It's safe now. You can open the door."

After a few seconds, he heard the latch open and at the same time another voice yelled, "No, don't open it!"

Hanigan pushed hard on the door and knocked Molly to the floor. Hanigan came into the room with his weapon ready to fire. Mercy ran to get one of the rifles Jacob had placed in the safe room. Hanigan saw her and yelled, "Don't do it. I'll kill the bunch of you. I swear."

Mercy stopped and Hanigan motioned her to sit down. "All of you together over there."

"Why are you doing this Jerry? We've known you for twenty years," Molly said.

"As it turns out Molly, it was a lapse of judgment. I rolled the dice and lost," Hanigan said.

"It's not too late, Jerry," Rose said. "I knew your ma and dad. They were good people. I'll talk to Jacob for you. We can work something out."

Hanigan smiled and said, "No, that boat has sailed already. My only chance is all of you. Jacob lets me go and I don't kill you."

Rose was holding baby Gerard and pulled him tighter to her chest. Hanigan noticed this and said, "I'm no baby killer. I won't hurt the kids." Rose just stared back at Hanigan.

There was a noise from the ceiling, like someone dragging something. Then someone knocked on the trapdoor. Hanigan shot twice at the door. The bullets bounced off the steel plating. "What the fuck is with you people and all this steel?" Then Hanigan yelled, "I got your family down here. They're dead if you try to come in."

There was no response for a minute or so, and then a muffled voice said, "We can work this out. Don't do anything rash."

"I want some cash and a car, or I start shooting people, starting with Molly," Hanigan yelled.

"Okay. Give me fifteen minutes," the voice said.

"Park it on Howard Street near the alley," Hanigan said. "Is that you Jacob?"

"Yes," Jacob said.

"I guess my brother's dead then?" Hanigan said.

"No he's okay," Jacob lied. "We have him and the others locked up in the barn."

"I want him here too."

"That's going to take more time," Jacob said.

"I don't care. Get him here or Molly dies, then the others."

"Okay, don't do anything rash. I'll get you whatever you need," Jacob said.

"Are these the only weapons?" Hanigan asked Mercy pointing to several rifles in the corner.

"No, there are two pistols in that table drawer," Mercy said.

Hanigan pulled the pistols out of the drawer and put them in his suit pockets. He then walked over to the rifles and smashed two of them. The third he leaned on a chair and then sat down.

"Who's this?" Hanigan asked pointing to Catherine."

"Why, you writing a book?" Catherine said.

Hanigan got up from his chair, walked over to Catherine and said, "You're a feisty one, aren't you?" Then he grabbed her hair and pulled her head back. He stuck the muzzle of the gun on her forehead and said, "Now, who are you?"

"She's Franklin's friend. Her name is Catherine." Mercy said, "Leave her alone."

"Now was that hard? No. Next time I ask someone something, just answer," Hanigan yelled.

Forty-five minutes passed before there was a knock on the trapdoor. "We have the car and your brother's in it. There's ten grand in the glove box. Let my family out and you can go to the car," Jacob said.

Hanigan laughed. "Doesn't work that way Jacob. I'll be taking some protection with me. I'm going to open this basement door in a couple of minutes and I better not see anyone there."

Hanigan grabbed Molly and put his arm around her neck, pulling her tightly to his chest. He put his pistol to her head, and said, Mercy, you and Catherine get behind me and put one arm on each shoulder. You walk when I do or I kill Molly."

Mercy and Catherine did as Hanigan ordered.

"Unlatch the door Molly and push it open slowly," Hanigan said.

Molly opened the door and Hanigan moved forward, saw no one was in the basement and started walking slowly to the basement exit. He noticed the cabinet was off the steps. Jacob's men probably did it when they came in the room. Just as they reached the first step, Georgie ran out of the safe room and yelled, "Leave my ma alone."

Shortly startled, Hanigan turned and in doing so moved the gun away from Molly's head.

In an instant, Mercy put her free hand up her dress and pulled the snub nose revolver out of her garter. She pointed it at the side of Hanigan 's head and pulled the trigger. At the same time, Catherine retrieved her snub nose and shot Hanigan in the side of his neck. Hanigan dropped his gun, released Molly and fell to his knees.

Both Mercy and Catherine pointed their guns at him and fired.

# 33

SAMMY EDELMAN HAD seen Jacob's men enter the house and knew that Hanigan didn't get the job done. His only hope was to get to the yard of the corner house on the Front Street alley, and pretend he had been knocked out. He ran across the roof to the last house and then climbed down into the yard. He sat there for a minute building courage and then smashed his gun into the side of his head. It hurt like hell, but he needed more, so he did it a second time.

He fell to his knees and then to the ground, unconscious. As he began to come to, he heard gunfire. After ten minutes, he heard people coming down the alley. He forced himself up and opened the yard door. Two of Jacob's men were walking down the alley toward Front Street. When they saw Sammy open the door, they pulled their weapons and pointed them at him.

"Sammy, what the fuck happened to you?" one man said.

"I don't know. One minute I was in the alleyway and the next I woke up in here," Sammy lied.

"You're bleeding. Come with us. We'll get you fixed up. I'm sure Jacob will want to talk to you."

Both men took Sammy by the arm and helped him walk to Jacob's house. When they arrived, Mike Kelly was at the front door. Mike questioned Sammy and then sent him into the house so he could bandage his head. By the time Sammy had seen to his wound, Franklin was assessing the damage done. He questioned Sammy again, and Sammy told the same story.

Walk with me upstairs," Franklin said to Sammy. "Why do you suppose they killed Joey McGill but only knocked you out?"

"I don't know Frank. Lucky I guess," Sammy replied.

"This is where they came in," Franklin said pointing to the missing roof of Jake's bedroom.

"Holy shit! That dynamite did a job," Sammy remarked.

"Yeah, it sure did," Franklin said as he glanced back. "Sammy, did they take your piece?"

"Yeah.

"You sure? You still groggy? Let me help you check," Franklin said as he patted Sammy down.

"What the fuck Frank?"

"It's okay Sammy. Just helping. Come on. Let's go downstairs," Franklin said.

"Sit over there Sammy. I got a few more questions, but I got to talk to Mike for a minute first," Franklin said.

Mike was at the front door talking to the guards who had battled the shooter on the roof. Franklin walked over to him and said, "Mike, we need to get the bodies up at the barn taken care of. Take Sammy with you. There something fishy about his story, so be careful. I think he may have been in on it. We'll talk to him at the barn."

"Sure, what about the bodies here?" Mike asked.

"No. Leave them for the cops. They'll be here any minute. This was self-defense all the way," Franklin said.

"Hey Sammy, I need some help up at the barn. You're with me," Mike said.

"Frank said he wanted to talk to me," Sammy said hesitating.

"No, it's okay. He said you could come. He'll talk to you later."

It was a couple of hours before Frank could get back up to the barn. The police had come and questioned him, but since it was Jacob's house, they had let him leave. He left his house keys with Jacob and the family would stay there until they could get the damage to Mercy Row fixed.

Franklin asked Catherine if she could get a leave of absence and stay with the family until the danger had passed. She agreed. Franklin was surprised and somewhat impressed that Catherine seemed unaffected by her killing of Jerry Hanigan. She told him that God forgave you for killing someone who was trying to kill you or your family. It was the first time he had any inkling that she even believed in God. He had a lot to learn about Catherine and he was excited by the prospect.

When Franklin arrived at the barn, he saw that Grady had things under control. Grady had his men start digging a one hundred by one hundred foot, six-foot deep hole using the equipment they had left there from digging the ditch. They would finish it the next day, but what they had done so far would make a good burial place for the men killed during the attack.

Grady's idea was to finish the hole, backfill it and lay a solid foundation of concrete. Later, they could build an industrial building, a gas station or two rows of homes similar to Mercy Row on the slab.

Once Franklin was satisfied that the scene was cleaned up, he had the surviving attackers, including Sammy Edelman, brought to the out building where they had stored the bodies of the dead attackers.

I want you to tell me why you shouldn't join your friends here," Franklin said. There was no reply from the men.

"What do you think Mike?" Franklin continued.

"I think they should all go on the same trip. Fucking traitors," Mike said and spit on Sammy.

"Mike, I didn't do anything," Sammy cried. "It's not my fault they clubbed me."

"Jesus Christ Sammy. Do you think we're completely stupid?" Franklin said.

"No, bu—" Sammy stopped short as Franklin hit him in the stomach with the butt of a rifle.

"First of all, you smell like a gunpowder factory. Secondly, you said they used dynamite. Nobody said anything about that. Worst of all was that fucking stupid story about being bopped on the head. It has as many holes in it as you'll have in a couple of minutes. So just shut the fuck up," Franklin yelled. Sammy lowered his head.

Franklin waved his hand and Mike, Grady and two others took positions behind the surviving attackers. One attacker was crying, two others and Sammy just had their heads bowed. The final attacker had his head high and stared directly at Franklin. Franklin had to admire his courage. He had to be only nineteen or twenty. The others were all in the forties or older. He nodded to the shooters and each one cocked their weapon, raised them to point to the ceiling and fired.

Two of the attackers collapsed to the floor whimpering. Sammy just stared wide-eyed at Franklin. The only one who had no reaction was the kid.

"So here's the deal. We decided not to kill you. Instead, you're going to move to the west coast. First thing in the morning, Grady and some of his men will take you to the train and travel with you to Los Angeles. That will be your new home. Later, if you want your families with you, that's up to you," Franklin said. "But, you will never come back to Philly. If you do, you're dead." Franklin said and paused.

"Once you get settled on the west coast you'll start sending us tax every month. If you miss any payments, I'll send Mike out to see you. Got it?"

All of the men, except the kid, nodded yes.

"Sammy, I have one more question for you and if you don't answer it, stutter or try to bullshit me, I'll kill you here and now."

"Anything Frank, anything you want," Sammy said.

"Who was Hanigan working with in Don Amato's gang?"

"Galanti," Sammy said without hesitation.

Franklin looked at Tony, and Tony nodded. Franklin looked at the kneeling men in disgust and said. "Get these fuckheads out of here Grady."

One of the men looked up and said, "Thanks Frank, we're sorry we got into this. We're sorry."

"Don't thank me. It was Jacob's idea. If it was up to me you'd be laying with your friends over there," Franklin responded. "Kid, come over here."

The young attacker stood up and walked over to Frank. "What's your name?" Frank asked.

"Mickey."

"How'd you get messed up with these fuckups?" Franklin asked.

"My, Pop over there," Mickey said pointing to one of the attackers. "The one that shit his pants."

"How old are you?"

"Seventeen. Be eighteen in May," Mickey said.

How would you like to join the Army?" Franklin asked.

"Yeah, I wanted to but my Pop wouldn't let me," Mickey said.

"In the morning Mike's going to take you to join up. You can write a note to your mom and Mike will deliver it," Franklin said.

"No need. She's dead."

"When the war's over, stop by and see me," Franklin said.

Mickey nodded to Frank and walked off with Mike.

# 34

AFTER THE FAILED attempt to murder the Amato's and the K&A Gang leaders Nicky Galanti, his brother Al, and cousin Joe decided it was in their best interest to leave town. Having friends with a home in Miami, they stole a 1940 Lincoln and drove the twelve hundred miles in three days. Nicky had an X gas ration sticker that he boosted from the house of an industrialist in Bala Cynwyd, that allowed them to purchase an unlimited amount of gasoline.

On the evening of December 22nd they arrived at the Miami home near South Beach, and drove up the long driveway. Nicky had purchased several bottles of wine, whiskey and some groceries. *It'll be like a vacation. When it cools down, we'll go home and finish the job,* Nicky thought as he parked the car close to the home's entrance.

"Joe, the key's under the plant on the right. Al, help me with the food," Nicky said.

Joe tipped up the planter and yelled, "What the fuck?" and jumped back.

Nicky turned, drew his weapon and pointed at the pot. "What?"

"A fucking cockroach as big as a fucking cat," Joe said.

"For Christ sake, like you never saw a roach," Nicky said.

Joe used the toe of his shoe to push the two-inch insect out of the way and grabbed the key. He shrugged his shoulders, shivered and said, "I hate those fucking things.

"Get used to it. We're in Florida," Al quipped. "Open the door, will ya?"

Joe unlocked the door, looked for a light switch, turned it on and said, "This is some joint."

The home was decorated in the deco style so popular in Miami. The large foyer had a curved staircase that led to the upstairs bedrooms and a curved doorway leading to the kitchen and another to the main living room. The three men took the groceries to the kitchen and Nicky opened a bottle of whiskey.

"Joe, grab a few glasses. We'll relax for a few minutes. Then I'll cook some macaroni and marinara," Nicky said.

Joe opened several cabinet doors before he found the glasses, picked out three and put them on the table. Nicky poured a large measure of whiskey in each glass, picked his up and said, "Salute." The three drank from the glasses. "Let's go sit for a while," he continued.

They walked through the doorway into the dark living room. Nicky felt the side of the wall for a light switch, found it and turned it on.

"Hello Nicky. How you doing?" Tony Amato said.

All three men went for their weapons, but stopped when three of Tony's men sneaked up behind them put guns to their heads.

"You scared the fuck out of me, Tony," Nicky said pretending innocence.

Tony's men frisked them and took their guns and two knives they had in their coat pockets.

"What's going on, Tony?" Nicky asked.

"Come on Nicky, stop the bullshit. You know why I'm here. The three of you sit down over there," Tony said pointing to a large sofa.

Tony was sitting in a high-backed chair holding a .45 on his lap. "This is great. I always wanted to do this. I saw a movie once where a guy sat in a dark room waiting for another guy to come in the room. He surprised him. The only difference was that in the movies the guy in the chair killed the other guy right away."

"How'd you know we were here?" Nicky asked.

"Nicky, you need to get some better friends. As soon as he hung up with you, Collins called me," Tony said.

"Now what," Nicky asked.

"You said something about making some macaroni and marinara. I'm hungry. How about you guys?" Tony asked his men.

"Yeah, I could eat," one of Tony's men said.

"You have enough for seven, Nicky?" Tony asked. Nicky nodded yes.

Nicky filled a pot with water and placed it on the stove. When it was boiling, he blanched the Italian plum tomatoes.

"I don't like those canned tomatoes. My mother would kill me if I used them," Nicky said and hesitated, smiled and continued. "Bad choice of words."

Nicky then poured virgin olive oil into a large saucepan and placed it on the stove. While it heated up, he peeled and crushed some garlic cloves. When the oil was hot enough, he added the garlic to the pan. He sliced the tomatoes and took out the seeds.

"Ya gotta take out the seeds. That's the secret for a good sauce. You call it sauce, Tony, or gravy?" Nicky asked.

"Sauce, only low lifes call it gravy," Tony answered.

"I call it gravy," Joe said.

"I see what you mean," Tony quipped. They all laughed.

Nicky carefully placed the tomatoes in the pan, added some salt and pepper and after five minutes or so, he broke up the tomatoes with a whisk. When the sauce was simmering, he filled a large pot with water and brought it to a boil. He added the dry macaroni. Then he put oil in a frying pan and added four slices of veal.

"I hope you don't mind, we don't have enough meat. I wasn't expecting company," Nicky said."

"It's fine Nicky," Tony said.

"Tony, can I ask you something?" Nicky said.

"Go ahead."

"How'd you get here so fast?"

"They got this new thing called an airplane," Tony said and laughed.

"Yeah. I heard of that," Nicky said smiling.

"Al set the table. We're ready to eat.

Nicky put the food on the table and said, "Boun Appetito."

"Nicky, you guys take the meat," Tony said.

"You sure?" Nicky asked.

"Yeah, go ahead."

The seven men enjoyed their meal and drank three bottles of the wine Nicky had bought. Nicky made coffee and they discussed the old days. Nicky had supported Don Amato after the Don cut Frankie Capaci's throat and took over the South Philly Mob. Tony and he worked together on some jobs to help enforce the Don's will.

Tony stretched his arms in the air and said, "Nicky that was a fine meal, but it's getting late."

"Glad you liked it Tony. Tony, if you don't mind, I'm not cleaning up this mess. Let that fucking rat Collins do it," Nicky said.

"Yeah, that's okay Nicky," Tony said as he put his hand in his lap and pulled the .45 up and shot Al Galanti in the forehead. He then shot Joe Galanti in the head.

"Nicky, I was gonna shoot you in the stomach and take you to the Everglades and let the alligators eat you alive. But, for old times' sake and for this meal," Tony waved his hand over the table. "I'm going to do it quickly," Tony said.

"I appreci—" Nicky was interrupted when a bullet entered his forehead and into his brain.

One of Tony's men then shot each man in the heart once. They cleaned up the blood, but left the unwashed dishes. Then they drove the bodies to the inland bay and sunk them with weights.

When they were finished, they drove to the airport, boarded their chartered plane and returned to Philadelphia to enjoy the Christmas holiday with their families.

# 35

JACOB, MOLLY, MERCY, the baby, Rose, the four Byrne's boys, plus Bonnie and her five puppies all temporally moved into Franklin's mansion on Broad Street. At Franklin's request, Catherine Avril had also moved in. It was a full house, but it was also a big house and there were enough bedrooms if the boys shared.

Georgie was sitting on the floor playing with Bonnie's puppies, while Bonnie sunned herself by the living room window. Jacob, sitting on a comfortable stuffed chair near the burning fireplace, marveled at how calm it was. After the last several months, he wasn't sure it would ever be calm again. He was happy that he decided to wait until after the holiday's to deal with the Johnsons. They were beat now and he didn't expect any trouble from them in the near term. Still, until old lady Johnson was silenced, he wouldn't feel that his family would be safe. Killing an old woman was not something he relished doing.

Franklin was sitting in a chair near Jacob, thinking about Catherine. It had been nice having her around, fulltime, for the last several days. He looked over at Georgie playing with the puppies and thought how much it looked like a cover of The Saturday Evening Post.

"Another?" Franklin asked Jacob holding up a bottle of Irish whiskey.

"Sure," Jacob said, holding his glass out. Franklin poured two jiggers in Jacob's glass.

Just as Franklin finished pouring the whiskey, he heard one of the puppies yelp and he turned to see what had happened. It was running, more like hopping to the doorway, where Catherine had just entered. The puppy ran up to Catherine and rubbed herself against Catherine's leg. She picked the puppy up and hugged it.

"Can I keep it, Frank? Jake told me I could have one of his puppies. It looks like this puppy picked me," Catherine said.

"Of course. It suits you." Franklin said. "What will you name her?"

"Bunny. I love the way she hops around," Catherine said.

"One more to go," Jake said as he entered the room.

"One more what?" Jacob asked.

"Puppy! I found homes for all but one," Jake said. "Charlie has Ginger, Catherine has Bunny, Mercy has Simone and I have the only boy, Zack. One more to go."

"What about the mom, Bonnie?" Jacob said.

"That's the family dog. She's the mom," Jake said.

"Well, it looks like Zack has left you a little present over there," Jacob said and pointed to a yellow puddle near the doorway."

"He didn't mean it. I'll get something to clean it up," Jake said and picked Zack up. "No peeing in the house Zack. Hear me?"

The doorbell rang.

I'll get it," yelled Rose.

"Wait. Let me see who it is first," Jacob said as he walked to the window.

"The guards would have checked whoever it is out, Jacob," Franklin said.

"I know. No harm double checking," Jacob said looking out the window. It's okay; it's Mr. Schechter.

Rose opened the door and let Schechter in.

Good afternoon Alan," Rose said. "Can I get you a coffee or something else?"

"No, thank you Rose. I'm here to see Frank. Is he here?"

"He is. He's in the living room. Let me take your coat and hat."

Schechter took off his overcoat and hat and handed them to Rose. Then he walked to the living room.

"Hello everyone," Schechter said.

"Mr. Schechter. Alan, it's good to see you," Franklin said. "This is Catherine Avril, my Gi— ah, friend.

"Good to meet you Miss Avril," Schechter said holding out his hand.

Catherine took his hand, shook it lightly and said, "It's my pleasure."

"Alan, have a seat," Jacob said. "Whiskey?"

"Yes, thank you. It will help take the nip out of the air."

Jacob poured Schechter a glass and handed it to him.

"Well, Franklin. I have some good news and some bad news. Which would you like first?" Schechter said.

Franklin looked at Schechter for a minute and said, "The good news."

"The warrant has been expunged."

"That is good news," Franklin said. Catherine hugged him and Jacob shook his hand.

Franklin looked at Schechter and said, "Thanks Alan. I know you worked hard on it. Now what's the bad news?"

"There is no bad news. I always say that. It makes the good news even better," Schechter said smiling.

One of the puppies walked over to Schechter squatted on his shoe and peed. Everyone laughed, including Schechter. "I deserved that. Who is this pretty little girl?" Schechter said as he picked up the puppy.

"That's your new puppy," Jake said walking back in the room, with a pale of water and some rags.

"Mine. No, I don't know. Not sure the misses would approve," Schechter said.

"Do you have kids, Mr. Schechter?" Jake asked.

"Yes, three."

"Don't you think they would like a puppy?" Jake asked.

"I am sure they would, bu—"

Jake interrupted Schechter saying, "Good, then I have a few questions for you. First, do you promise to keep the dog in the house when it's cold or too hot?"

"Yes, of course. Who keeps a dog out in the cold?" Schechter replied.

"Will you feed her three times a day?"

"Yes."

"Will you promise to never hit her? To love her? To take care of her? Bring her for visits to see her Mom?" Jake said.

"Yes, I promise. I wouldn't hit an animal."

"What will you name her?" Jake asked.

"Well, I don't know. The children will name her I guess," Schechter said.

"Okay, Mr. Schechter, then she's yours."

Schechter held the puppy up to his face and said, "I don't know what just happened little girl, but I guess you're coming home with me." Everyone laughed.

"I hope you all have a merry Christmas," Schechter said.

"And you and your family a happy Hanukkah, Alan," Jacob said.

Jake walked out with Schechter to help him take his new family member to the car. When he returned, he said excitedly, "It started snowing."

Georgie ran to the window to see the snow and all the puppies ran after him. "I love the snow," Georgie yelled. "Yippy!" The puppies started barking.

"What's all this noise?" Rose said as she walked into the room. "Quiet! The lot of you. I have something to say." Everyone fell silent even the puppies.

"Frank..." Rose paused. Frank looked at her with a concerned face. "Your kitchen, or what you call a kitchen, is a mess. You have no proper pots and pans. Your fridge is dirty. The plates are mismatched, and the one tablecloth you have is wine-stained."

"I—" Frank said and was interrupted.

"Let me finish," Franklin nodded okay. "Tomorrow, Molly, Catherine and me are going shopping for a proper kitchen. And while we're at it, we're buying Christmas decorations. This place looks as festive as Mulligan's Funeral Home," Rose said.

"Catherine clapped her hands and said, "Yea!"

"Thank you Catherine. Even though we have no proper kitchen, Molly, Mercy and me have put together a passable meal. It's ready now, so go wash up and come to the dining room. Jake, put the puppies away and clean up that mess first."

Jake, Jacob and Franklin all stood to attention, saluted and said "Yes sir, General Patton."

Fifteen minutes later, the whole family was seated at the dining room table. Jacob was at one end of the table, with Molly next to him.

Franklin was at the other end of the table, with Catherine next to him. Mercy and the baby were next to Molly, Georgie was on the other side of Jacob. Charley and Jake were at opposite sides of the table. Jimmy was on the other side of Franklin. Rose was in the kitchen and wasn't sitting at her place next to Jimmy. The puppies were in their makeshift crate and Bonnie was lying next to the puppies.

Rose placed a bowl of mashed potatoes on the table and took her place.

"Catherine, would you like to say grace?" Molly asked.

"Of course," Catherine said. "In the name of the Father, Son and Holy Ghost.

*Blessed are You, loving Father,*
*For all your gifts to us.*
*Blessed are You for giving us family and friends*
*To be with us in times of joy and sorrow,*
*To help us in days of need,*
*And to rejoice with us in moments of celebration.*
*Father,*
*We praise You for Your Son Jesus,*
*Who knew the happiness of family and friends,*
*And in the love of Your Holy Spirit.*
*Blessed are you forever and ever.*
*Amen."*

"How nice Catherine. Thank you," Rose said. "You all may eat now."

The family enjoyed a meal of meatloaf, mashed potatoes, boiled carrots, string beans and fresh baked rye bread from Rose's favorite bakery. Desert was a choice of cherry or apple pie. Jake had both. The adults, which now included Charlie and Jake, had coffee with condensed milk.

"I have something to say," Charlie said. Everyone became quiet. "My birthday's coming up January eighth. My eighteenth and..." He paused. "And I am joining the Marines. Molly dropped her coffee cup on the table.

# 36

THERE WAS CONSIDERABLE pressure on Charlie to change his mind and not join the Marines. Arguments ranged from he's too young, he needs to finish high school to the family needs him. For each argument his family had, Charlie had a logical and well thought-out answer. By Christmas day, Molly, Mercy and Rose had accepted that whether or not they liked it, when Charlie turned eighteen he was joining the Marines. Because of that, they were determined to make this Christmas special.

Jacob, although he didn't voice this opinion, was proud that Charlie wanted to fight to protect his country's values. He had been too young to join up for the first war and now he was too old for this one. If he had been Charlie's age during the first war, he would have done the same. Charlie had proven himself this past week. He was courageous and smart when it came to tough situations. Jacob was sure he would do well.

The family had attended Christmas midnight mass at Saint Hugh's church, which was in the parish where Mercy Row was located. On Christmas morning, the snow from two days prior was still on cars and along the side of the roads, but the streets and sidewalks were clear. The pristine white color of the fresh snow had been replaced with a combination of the black specks from tires and asphalt, and the gray ash people used, from their furnaces, to help make the ice less slippery. As Jacob peered out the front window of Franklin's home at Broad Street, he found himself wishing for a white Christmas.

The kids were all napping or in their rooms playing with their gifts. The smell of a roasting turkey and baking pies filled the house. The food smells mixed with the aroma from the evergreen Christmas tree. It made for a festive atmosphere. Bonnie and her puppies were asleep, curled up near the fireplace. The radio was playing the latest Christmas songs. Jacob loved this time on Christmas day when the hubbub of the holiday gave way to peace and quiet. In an hour or two, it would all change. This year, Molly invited the Amato's, Mike and Grady's family and Nate, who had no one at home this year. It would be nonstop bedlam until they all went home at the end of the night, but for this moment, it was quiet.

"A penny for your thoughts, Papa," Mercy said.

"Here, sit down," Jacob patted the seat of his oversized chair.

Mercy sat down next to Jacob, kissed him on the cheek and said, "Well?"

"Well what?"

"A penny for your thoughts?"

"Oh, nothing really. Just taking advantage of the quiet before all hell breaks loose," Jacob said.

"You love the bedlam," Mercy said.

"Yeah. I guess I do."

Franklin walked into the room carrying two glasses of eggnog.

"Mercy, I didn't know you were here or I would've brought you an eggnog," Franklin said.

"That's okay Uncle Frank. Eggnog is, well, not my cup of tea," Mercy said and chuckled.

"Something else then?"

"No thank you. I'm fine. And may I say you're looking very dapper today," Mercy said.

Frank was wearing a dark blue pinstriped double-breasted suit, with black shoes and a lighter blue printed tie.

"Thank you Mercy. You like?" Franklin said as he spun around like a fashion model.

"Yes I do."

"Catherine got me this for Christmas," Franklin said.

"Sit down before you spill the eggnog," Jacob said.

Franklin handed Jacob a glass and took a seat in the chair across from Jacob.

Franklin held his glass up and said, "Merry Christmas Jacob, Mercy."

"Merry Christmas Uncle Frank," Mercy said.

Jacob held his glass up, touched it to Franklin's and said, "Merry Christmas Frank."

Franklin and Jacob both drank. "Wow! Jacob said. "This is more whiskey than nog."

Mercy spent the next few minutes in light conversation, waiting for the best time to bring up the subject she wanted to address with her father and Franklin. Since the attack on Mercy Row, she knew they would have to do something about the Johnsons. Even though her father had deferred any action until after the holidays, she knew the Johnsons were still a threat to the family. She also knew how threats to the family were resolved, but this was an old woman. It was different. If they did nothing they would look weak. They couldn't afford any more internal problems so looking weak was out of the question. If they killed the old women they would be seen as too ruthless to their political and legal connections and could lose favor.

"Papa, have you and Uncle Frank thought about how you're going to deal with the Johnsons?" Mercy said.

"Of course, but were kind of in a hard place with this. Damned if we do and damned if we don't," Jacob said.

"You don't have to worry about this Mercy. We'll handle it," Franklin said.

"I have an idea," Mercy said, and continued, not waiting for any comments. "The Mercy Row foundation has worked with Byberry in the past on some fundraising and I have a good relationship with a director."

"Byberry, the nut house?" Franklin asked.

"Well, they like to be called the Philadelphia State Hospital at Byberry, but yes, the nut house," Mercy answered.

"Go on, "Jacob said.

"I think with a large donation I can get him to have the old women declared mentally ill and committed to Byberry," Mercy said.

"You mean a large enough bribe," Jacob said.

"Bribe, donation. Same thing. Whatever you call it, the old women would be out of the way and we would have done nothing anyone could fault," Mercy said.

Jacob looked at Franklin who smiled. Jacob kissed Mercy on the forehead and asked, "How did you get so smart?"

"I have good role models, Mercy answered. She kissed her father then Franklin and said. "I have to get back and help Mom with the stuffing. Think about it."

Christmas dinner was a feast. The Amatos brought with them dishes that were traditional for Italian families including cannolis. Catherine made a wonderful beef burgundy dish and there was the traditional turkey with stuffing, sweet potatoes and cranberry sauce. There was also a minced meat pie, a pumpkin pie and a French apple pie. And, of course, Irish soda bread, rolls and rye bread from the German bakery on Front Street.

Since she had done such a good job saying grace several days before, Molly asked Catherine to say grace for Christmas dinner. She read a prayer she chose because of Charlie's decision to join the Marines. She said "*In the name of the Father, Son and Holy Ghost.*

> *Almighty God*
> *We stand before you in supplication,*
> *Asking Your Divine mercy and protection,*
> *To envelop with Your invincible armor,*
> *Our loved ones in all branches of the service.*
> *Give them courage and strength*
> *Against all enemies,*
> *Both spiritual and physical,*
> *And hasten their safe journey,*
> *Back to their homes and families.*
> *Amen.*

Molly was crying by the time Catharine finished the prayer. Seeing his mother crying, Charlie leaned over and kissed her cheek. Then he whispered in her ear, "Mom, I promise you, no Jap's going to kill me. I'll be home when the war's over, I swear. I love you Mom."

After the meal, the dishes were cleared and Rose placed a large pot of fresh brewed coffee on the table. Molly, Mercy and Catherine each brought a pie to the table and Mrs. Amato followed them with the cannolis. There were many oohs and aahs from the guests. Jacob went to the den and brought back a tray with a decanter of Port, a bottle of Sherry, and a bottle of brandy. He poured glasses for those who wanted it and offered a toast.

"Here's to family and friends. There is nothing as important. May nineteen forty-four be happy, healthy, and prosperous for all of you. May we see the end to our wars with Germany and Japan, and the return of our troops. Many of whom are, right now, taking their Christmas dinner in foxholes. And, here's to Jimmy, who fought the war and returned, and to Charlie who will defend our freedom as a Marine. May he come home safely."

"Here, here," Franklin said and everyone drank.

"You may not believe this, but from my viewpoint I can see out of the large window in the back of the room. I can tell that we now have an official white Christmas," Jacob said.

Everyone turned to look through the window. The children ran to the yard door, threw it open and rushed outside. The snow was whirling around their little heads as their mothers ran after them with coats. Bonnie and her puppies were racing after all of them.

*What a picture-perfect evening this has been*, Jacob thought. *Enjoy it while you can boyo. Tomorrow you have to decide how to handle the Johnsons.*

# 37

MERCY'S MEETING WITH the Byberry director had gone well. Mercy left him with two envelopes. One envelop for a donation to the institution and one for his personal use. He agreed that if they could get Mrs. Johnson to the hospital, he would be able to do the paperwork that would keep her there for the rest of her life. That was the dilemma facing Jacob and Franklin. How would they get old lady Johnson from Oxford to Philadelphia?

"Look, Frank, we have to do this right. No violence and no cops, "Jacob said." We don't know anything about her. She may never leave her house. The house is guarded. I'm not sure how we can get her to Philly."

"I have an idea Papa," Mercy said.

The next day, Catherine drove past a sign that said *Kennett Square—the mushroom capital of the world*. She wasn't sure why she agreed to go to Oxford. She had told herself it was to save an old woman's life, but this old woman was responsible for having many people killed and imprisoning and torturing Franklin. With that woman out of the way, Franklin and all of the Byrne's family would be safe and that was a good enough reason for Catherine.

After a few hours at the Chester County library, she had learned enough about Oxford for her to pretend she was writing about it. Actually, the cover was she was writing about the Baltimore and Pennsylvania Railroad that went through Oxford, which was the half waypoint on the route. Catherine hoped she could pull it off and was a bit nervous and a whole lot excited about her prospects of success.

Catherine's first stop was Dickey's Bookshop. She had found Dickey's in a copy of the oxford telephone directory at the library. Her plan was to buy a few books about Oxford and establish her cover story. When she was a young girl, she had seen a movie about Mata Hari, a female German spy during the First World War. Now, she felt as if she was sort of living the story. She was hoping the ending would be different, because the French executed the real Mata Hari.

As Catherine entered Dickey's Bookshop, she was greeted by a roly-poly man who looked to be in his late fifties. "Afternoon Miss. Welcome to Dickey's. Can I help you with something?"

"Good afternoon. Yes I'm looking for books about Oxford," Catharine replied.

"Not many books about this bloody place," the man said.

Realizing the man spoke with a British accent, she asked, "London, right?"

"Why yes. Have you been there?" the man asked.

"Two years at Oxford," Catherine lied. She had been in London, but not to study. It was a fling after college with one of her professors.

The man put his hand out," Reggie Chambers. And you are?"

Catherine took his hand, shook it and said, "Mary Ford, Good to meet you Mr. Chambers."

"Call me Reggie please," Chambers said still holding Catherine's hand.

"Be careful young lady. He's a lecherous old coot," a women said who had come through a doorway to a backroom."

"Ahh, my golden tongued misses. Please let me introduce you," Chamber's said as he, still holding Catherine's hand, came around the counter and presented her hand to his wife. "My wife, Mrs. Emily Dickey Chambers."

Catherine took Emily's hand and said, "Mary Ford."

"My pleasure Miss Ford. Now, let's see. I heard you say you were looking for a book on Oxford," Emily said as she guided Catherine to one of the shelves of books.

"Yes, I'm writing about Oxford and I wanted to learn more about its history," Catherine said.

Emily looked surprised and said, "About Oxford?"

"Actually, the book's about the Baltimore and Pennsylvania Railroad. Oxford was the halfway point on the route to Baltimore from Philadelphia," Catherine said.

"Still is Mary," Reggie said.

Emily took a book from the shelf and said, "This is the only book I have about Oxford. It's a used first edition, written by Jeffery Johnson in 1905."

Catherine took the book from Emily, opened it to the first page, and said, "Jeffery Johnson. I read about one of the original Oxford families was named Johnson. Is he one of them?"

"No sweetheart. He would turn over in his grave if he heard that. He was a scholar from Kennett Square. Worked for the DuPont family chronicling the various towns in Southeast Pennsylvania and in Delaware," Emily said.

"Why would he turn over in his grave?" Catherine said.

"Well, the Johnson's you're talking about have a sullied reputation. People say they ran guns to the south during the Civil War and got into moon shinning during Prohibition. Even had connections to gangsters, some say," Emily said.

"That's interesting. Do any of the Johnson's still live here?" Catherine asked.

"Unfortunately, they do. The family has a farm a few miles out of town," Emily said.

"Do you think someone in the family would talk to me? Say, the matriarch or patriarch?" Catherine asked.

"Oh no sweetheart. You stay away from them. They're bad people. They won't see you anyway," Emily said.

"Not even to discuss me writing about her family?" Catherine said.

"Like I said, very private. They only time we see Mrs. Johnson is on Sundays at church. She never misses."

"Mrs. Johnson? Is she the elder in the family?" Catherine asked.

"Yes and she is as mean as a woman can be," Reggie said.

"I'd really like to talk to her," Catherine said.

"If you really must, you might be able to meet her at the Oxford Café. After church, she always goes there for breakfast. She normally has her two sons with her, although I haven't seen the younger one the last couple of weeks. Maybe he went in the service," Emily said.

"I might just do that Emily," Catherine said.

"Mary, please be careful with these people," Emily said.

"Em it's about tea time. Mary, would you like to join us?"

"Him and his tea. I can make you coffee if you prefer Mary," Emily said shaking her head.

"Tea would be fine," Catherine said.

"Well, there you go. Tea it is. And we have some wonderful scones Emily just baked," Reggie said putting his arm around Catherine's shoulders and leading her to the back room.

Emily Dickey Chambers just shook her head, looked up and followed them to the back room.

# 38

ON SUNDAY JANUARY 2nd, 1944, Catherine drove back to Oxford. She was not feeling her best because she and Franklin had spent New Year's Eve in New York City. They had hoped to see the ball drop at midnight, but as was the case in 1942, it was canceled and replaced by a moment of silence. They celebrated until eight in the morning, caught a train back to Philly and had dinner with Jacob's family at six on New Year's Day. Then she had to get up at five in the morning to drive to Oxford.

When she arrived at Oxford, she went directly to the Oxford Café and waited for Mrs. Johnson. She ordered black coffee, ham and eggs with hash browns and toast. By the time Mrs. Johnson arrived, Catherine had drunk three cups of coffee and was feeling a little better. Johnson was with a man who looked to be in his mid-thirties. She presumed it was her son.

Mrs. Johnson and her son ordered their breakfast. Catherine waited until they were served their meal and nodded to a man who was standing outside the restaurant. He took his hat off, wiped his brow and put the hat back on. She then got up from her seat, opened and palmed the small bottle of cholera hydrate Franklin had given her. Then she walked over to the Johnsons.

"Mrs. Johnson. I was wondering if I could talk to you for a moment," Catherine said.

"Who are you?" Johnson's son asked.

"My name is Mary Ford and I am writing a book about Oxford and—" Mrs. Johnson cut off Catherine, "We're not interested."

An instant later, there was a loud screech of tires and a crunching of metal on metal. Mrs. Johnson, her son and the other patrons looked out the window to see two cars. One car had steam coming out of the engine area and the other car's passenger side door was crushed. While everyone was looking at the accident, Catherine quickly emptied the choral hydrate into Mrs. Johnson's coffee.

Mrs. Johnson's son turned back and said, "Stupid jerk. People need to learn to drive."

When Mrs. Johnson turned back to the table, Catherine asked again. "I just need a few minutes Mrs. Johnson.

The son got out of his seat and said, "My mother said we're not interest. Scram."

"Okay. Okay I'm sorry," Catherine said. She walked back to her table, paid the bill and left the restaurant. As she was starting to get into her car, she heard the distinct sound of an ambulance. She smiled and drove out of town on her way back to Philadelphia.

Mrs. Johnson finished her breakfast and drank her coffee. Her son paid the bill and they both walked to the door. Mrs. Johnson's son opened the door for his mother and she walked out. She stumbled, fell against the wall, then to the ground outside of the restaurant door. Her son rushed to her and yelled, "Ma, you okay?" There was no answer. "Ma, Ma. What's wrong?" Meanwhile, several people walking by the restaurant stopped to see if they could help.

A man in a white coat who had been attending one of the drivers in the accident ran to Mrs. Johnson and said, "I'm a doctor. Let me see." He examined Mrs. Johnson for a minute or so and said," It's her heart. I need to get her to the hospital. Help me carry her to the ambulance."

The doctor and Mrs. Johnson's son carried her to the ambulance and placed her on a gurney. A man was lying on the other gurney. His head was bandaged and blood was seeping through the white cloth.

"It's lucky we were here," the doctor said as he closed the one of the doors.

"I'm going with her," Johnson's son said.

"No room. We're taking her to the Chester Hospital. We'll meet you there. We need to go now. The doctor jumped in the back and closed the other door. The ambulance began to drive away, the siren blasting.

Johnson's son ran to his car, got in and started the engine. He put it is gear, started to move forward and felt something was wrong. He got out of the car and saw he had two flat front tires.

The ambulance turned off Limestone Road onto US 1 on their way back to Philadelphia. two and a half hours later, they pulled into the Philadelphia State Hospital at Byberry. While she was unconscious, the doctor, who was actually one of Jacob's men, had put her in a straight jacket and gagged her. She woke up just as they reached the Philly city limits.

The Philadelphia State Hospital at Byberry was located in Northeast Philadelphia, off Roosevelt Boulevard. It was established in 1907 as a work farm for the mentally ill. By 1944, Byberry was a series of large red brick buildings that housed close to two thousand patients from the mentally challenged to criminally insane. Byberry had the reputation of a facility with very poor living conditions, where patients were regularly given lobotomies and shock treatments against their will.

The ambulance turned in to the entrance and pulled up to the rear of the building, where the director of the hospital was waiting. Mrs. Johnson was still on the gurney. When the director of the hospital examined her in the ambulance he said, "We're going to take good care of you Mrs. Breyer. You had a little nervous breakdown. You're safe here." Mrs. Johnson looked at the director, eyes wide and started shaking her head no.

"Why'd you pick Breyer as her name," Jacob's man asked.

"I like Breyer's ice cream," the director replied.

# 39

"WHAT TOWN'S THIS?" Jake asked Jimmy.

"Jenkintown."

"Why so far away?" Charlie asked.

Jimmy didn't say anything and turned right off Old York Road onto Greenwood Avenue. He passed the old car dealership that was now a Moose Lodge and stopped in front of a large stone house.

"Is this it?" Jake asked.

"Yep, this is it. The best whorehouse in all of Pennsylvania," Jimmy said.

Both Charlie and Jake became aroused in anticipation of what was about to happen. As they walked to the door, both boys adjusted themselves so they didn't appear too eager. In Jake's case, this was a difficult task as he was very well endowed, defying the old myth that Irishmen have small penises.

Charlie rang the doorbell. A minute later, a very attractive woman, in her early thirties opened the door. Upon seeing Jimmy, she screamed, "Oh my God! Jimmy. It's so good to see. I thought you would be away until the war ended. I couldn't believe it when I got your call." She hugged him tightly and kissed him on the lips.

"It's good to see you too Sally. It really is," Jimmy said.

"And is this Charlie and Jake?" Sally asked.

Yeah, my brothers Charlie and Jake. I brought them today so they can further their education," Jimmy said.

"Well, come in boys. We have some fine teachers," Sally said looking at Jake's bulge." By the looks of this one, I think he's ready for class right now," She took hold of Jake's arm and pulled him gently though the door.

The foyer of the home was large and included a spiral staircase leading to the second floor. A door on the left led to a spacious room, where several men were sitting at a large cherry wood bar drinking, and laughing with three of Sally's employees. To the right was a double doorway. Sally opened one of the doors and led Jimmy, Charlie and Jake into the room. It was a private sitting room with a large sofa and several oversized chairs. There was a table on the right wall, with a tray of various kinds of liquor.

"I thought we would use my private room, if that's okay with you Jimmy?" Sally said.

"You know I love this room," Jimmy said.

"I know Charlie. How about a drink boys?" Sally said.

Sally went to the table, filled three glasses with Scotch and started to hand one to Jake, and pulled her hand back. "Are you old enough to drink?" Sally said laughing.

"I'm old enough to do a lot of things," Jake answered.

"I bet you are," Sally said and handed the glass to Jake.

She gave a glass to Charlie and the other to Jimmy.

"How about you Miss Sally?" Charlie asked, "You not drinking?"

"Charlie, I learned my lesson a long time ago. I stay away from booze. But I'll have a drink with you," Sally said as she walked over to the table and poured some soda into a small glass. "That better?"

"Sure," Charlie said.

"Okay then. Here's to your health."

The four clinked glasses and drank.

"So Charlie, Jimmy tells me it's your birthday next week. I hope you appreciate the present your brother's giving you," Sally said.

"Charlie's leaving for the Marines after his birthday, "Jimmy said.

"Oh! Then we need to make this a very special day for you, Sally said as she pushed a button on the wall.

A few minutes later, two women entered the room from a side door. One was dressed in a mock women's Marine uniform. Her long blonde hair lay partially over her jacket that was half-open revealing her ample bosom. She wore short shorts that showed all of her very long legs.

The other woman had her hair in a bun and wore glasses. She was a slender brunette wearing a sheer white blouse that revealed her large red nipples. She was carrying a ruler that she dropped on the floor as if by accident. Then she turned her back to Jake and Charlie and bent over to pick it up. When she did her, very short black skirt rode up to show her beautifully round pink bottom. She was not wearing panties.

Charlie and Jake sat staring at the women, as if in a trance. The woman dressed as a Marine walked over to Charlie, took him by the hand and led him to the door and up the stairs. The women dressed as a schoolteacher went to Jake, took his head in her hands and kissed him on the lips. She then took his hand and led him to the door and up the stairs. As they walked up the stairs, she lightly smacked Jake on his behind with the ruler, several times.

"Thanks Sally. That was great," Jimmy said.

"My pleasure. You know I would do anything for you," Sally said moving closer to Jimmy on the sofa. She bent forward and kissed him. As she did, she ran her hand up his pant leg to his crotch. She massaged gently.

Feeling no reaction, Sally said disappointedly, "Jimmy, do you want a different woman?"

"No, no never! You know how I feel about you. It's just...," Jimmy said but paused. "I haven't told anyone this and you have to promise me you won't either."

"I promise. What is it?" Sally asked becoming concerned.

"When I was wounded it did something to me. The docs told me they couldn't find a medical reason why this should happen," Jimmy said.

"What did it do, Jimmy?" Sally asked.

"I can't get it up. The docs called it erectile dysfunction," Jimmy blurted out.

"You scared me. I thought it was something serious," Sally said.

"What? Jesus Christ Sally, I can't get my dick hard. I can't fuck anymore! I think that's serious," Jimmy said sliding away from Sally.

"Do you know how many men come here and have that same problem? You're not the only one Jimmy. We can fix that. It just takes time. Doctor Sally can cure you," Sally said.

"How?" Jimmy asked.

"I want you to visit me two to three times a week. If you can't make it here, I'll come to you. We'll work on this together starting now," Sally said as she knelt in front of Jimmy, unzipped his trousers, pulled out his flaccid member and bent over.

# 40

**ON THE DAY** of his induction into the Marines, Charlie asked that Jacob be the only one to drive him to the induction center at Thirteenth and Market Streets. It was just too difficult for him to have the entire family there. As he said his farewells, Molly, Mercy and Rose tried to keep it to together for Charlie's sake, but in the end, all three cried.

Jake shook his brother's hand, leaned in and whispered, "Kill those motherfuckers."

Charlie hugged Georgie and said, "It's your job now to keep tabs on Jake. Are you ready for that?"

"Yes," Georgie said tentatively and hugged Charlie again. "I'll miss you Charlie."

"It's okay; I'll be home in no time. Here, shake," Charlie said, "It's the way men say goodbye." Georgie took Charlie's hand, shook it hard, and smiled.

Jimmy and Franklin were sitting by the fireplace waiting for everyone to say their goodbyes. As Charlie started to walk toward them, they both rose from their chairs and saluted. Jimmy shook Charlie's hand and said, "Charlie you're a smart guy. Stay smart when you see action. It will keep you alive. I know you'll do us proud."

Franklin embraced Charlie, and said, "Keep your head down kid and don't volunteer for anything. Hear me."

Charlie kissed baby Gerry on the head, hugged his mother, Rose and Mercy again and then left the house with Jacob.

During the ride to the induction center, Charlie was very quiet. Jacob didn't say anything, thinking Charlie was just overwhelmed by leaving. The truth was Charlie was bone tired. Two nights before, Jimmy, Grady and Mike invited Charlie to their weekly get together, where they discussed world politics, told dirty jokes, smoked cigars and drank a lot of beer, a whole lot of beer. It was the first time Charlie had smoked a cigar or anything for the matter. He swore it would be the last time.

The night before he was to leave, the family held a combined late birthday and farewell party for him. The Amatos had attended as well as several of his school friends. They drank too much and stayed up way too late. He had barely been able to wake up and take a bath before it was time to go.

The trip to Thirteenth and Market Streets was short. Jacob found a spot and parked the car a couple hundred feet from the entrance. Charlie had only a small travelling bag with necessities in it. The Marines would give him everything he needed. Jacob took the bag from the trunk and handed it to Charlie.

"Pop, thanks for the ride," Charlie said.

"I'll walk you down."

"No, it's okay. I got it from here," Charlie said not wanting to have the other inductees see him escorted by his father.

"Well, then. I guess this is it. Charlie, the whole family's proud of you. Do me a favor and please be careful," Jacob said.

"I will Pop. I will."

"I guess you're too big for a hug from your old man," Jacob said.

"I wouldn't want the other guys to see me," Charlie said and stuck out his hand.

Jacob grasped Charlie's hand with both of his and said, "Come back to us son."

"I will Pop," Charlie said, turned and walked to the induction center doorway.

Jacob stood watching until Charlie entered the building. Then he got back in his car, sat there for a minute, rubbed a tear from his eye and drove back to Franklin's house.

Charlie waited in the induction center for an hour before he was called for an interview. After the interview, a Marine doctor examined him and he was pronounced fit for induction. Several hours after he entered the building, Charles Byrne recited the oath of enlistment:

*"I, Charles Byrne, do solemnly swear to bear true allegiance to the United States of America, and to serve them honestly and faithfully, against all their enemies or opposers whatsoever, and to observe and obey the orders of the President of the United States of America, and the orders of the officers appointed over me."*

With this oath, Charlie became a private in the United States Marine Corps with the pay of fifty dollars per month. Shortly after taking the oath, Charlie was on a bus with thirty-nine other privates and one sergeant, headed for Parris Island, South Carolina. It took fifteen hours to reach Parris Island and when they did every man on the bus was tired, hungry, excited and scared.

The bus stopped and a tall, muscular sergeant with a grizzly look entered and yelled, "Ladies, stop talking and listen." When several of the men kept talking, he yelled, "I said stop fucking talking. When I give you an order, you obey. In a minute, you will leave this bus and form two lines facing south. Sit the fuck down you," he yelled at one of the men who got out of his seat ready to leave. "You wait for my order. Face south ladies. Now get out. Hurry."

Everyone stood up and rushed out of the bus. They formed two lines, but facing north. "Did you not hear me? What are you, fucking morons? I said facing south. About face," the sergeant yelled. All but two men turned. "Jesus H. Christ, I said about face," The sergeant yelled again and kicked one of the men in the ass. "Turn around." The two men turned, "That's better. Now all of you face me. That's a right face." The men turned and faced the sergeant.

"In a few minutes, you'll run over to that building," The sergeant pointed to a Quonset hut, "Where you'll get your shots, see a medic, have your heads shaved and get your uniforms. When you wear your uniform for the first time, you're going to think you're a Marine. You're even going to look like a Marine. But, you won't be a Marine. You'll be lower than the smallest piece of whale shit at the bottom of the ocean. If, and I say if, you make it out of basic training you'll become a Marine. You'll be part of a unique fighting force. A force, with a proud reputation for kicking ass. You'll be a killer! A well trained killer. And your job will be to kill Japs. My job is to train you to stay alive so you can kill Japs. And I take my job seriously. The last man to reach the building will clean the latrine for a week. Go!"

For eight weeks of basic training, the sergeant never spoke in a normal voice. Every statement, every command was yelled. They ran everywhere, learned to march, take commands, and they learned to become killers. Charlie excelled during basic training. He became muscular, confident and mature. He became a Marine. After a ten-day leave, Charlie left the United States to take his post in the Pacific with the 1st Marine Regiment.

# 41

**PAVUVU, RUSSELL ISLANDS,** *South Pacific*
*July 12, 1944*
*Dear Mom and Dad:*

    *I'm writing this letter sitting under a coconut tree, looking out at the Pacific Ocean. Can you believe that? Of course, it's not as nice as it sounds. The black oil from sunken ships washes up on the sand and if you get it on you, it's hard to get off. We have air raids from time to time, so there are a lot of trees lying on the beach.*

    *Philly should be getting pretty hot now. You guys are lucky, because it's nothing like where I am. No! I can't mention where I'm at but it's hot and very, very humid. One hundred ten degrees some days, ninety-five most days. It rains a lot, which can be good because it cools things down. But, being wet all the time is no fun either.*

    *I just received a letter you wrote a few weeks ago. Mail is slow, so I hope I get some more soon. I was happy to hear that baby Gerry and Mercy are doing well. Hard to believe he's seven months old. Eight months now, I guess.*

    *We have mosquitoes the size of humming birds and I saw a spider the other day that was as large as my palm. I'm not kidding! Not my favorite thing, spiders, as you know.*

    *Our days are spent training and scuttlebutt has it that we will be seeing action soon. Most of us can't wait. The sooner we beat the Japs the sooner we come home. My friend, Ed Marsten, says his parents wrote* and told him they heard the war would be over by Christmas. They live in Washington, DC so maybe they know something. I hope so. Don't get me wrong. I'm not sorry I joined up, but this is a lot harder than I thought it would be.

Mom, you and Rose would be proud of me. I wash my own clothes, make my bed and clean up around my bunk. We don't cook for ourselves, and the food isn't very good. Half the time we eat C-rations and the other half are hot meals. Sometimes the C-rations have chocolate fudge, which isn't bad. My favorite candy is Hersey's chocolate.

My dungarees are finally worn out enough that I don't look like a new recruit. The old salts like to pull tricks on the new replacements so it's better to look like you've been around for a while. The other day a corporal sent a young replacement to get some Shinola. They told him it was an explosive like nitro and to be very careful with it. The supply sergeant, who was in on it, gave him a bag of dog (excuse me Mom) shit. He carefully carried it back and handed it to the corporal who dropped it to the ground. The recruit hit the deck and covered his head thinking it would explode. We all stood around laughing. Then the corporal opened the bag and poured out the dog stuff and said, "You don't know shit from Shinola." I know, pretty stupid, but we try to get our laughs however they can. Now that guy's nickname is Shinola. I'm trying to avoid any nicknames.

I write Jake often and he seems to be doing okay. He says he hates school and wants to quit and work in the family business, but what's new? He still talks about joining up when he's eighteen. I hope the war's over before that. I know you worry about me already and adding him would really be tough on you.

Tell Uncle Frank and Catherine I said hello, Uncle Mike and Grady also. Can't believe Uncle Frank and Catherine are still together. It's a record for Uncle Frank. Kiss Grandma Rose for me. I miss her, Mercy and Georgie too. I wrote Pop Pop Amato and Tony a couple of weeks ago. I'm sure they'll write back. Give my little Ginger a hug and Bonnie too.

Jimmy wrote me and said he was dating someone. He didn't say who. Do you know? He said he was working with the construction business and helping Rose and Mercy with the foundation. Sounds like he's keeping busy.

Well, I have to go, so please write again soon. If you can, send me a razor and some shaving cream. The one's they have here are not so good.

I love and miss you all.

Love, Charlie

# 42

NOT A DAY passed that Molly didn't wait for the mailman in anticipation that he would have a letter from Charlie. If there were a letter, her mood was bright and happy. When there were no letters, she became sullen. Today she was bright. A letter arrived from Charlie and it only took ten days for her to receive.

When the family was living in Franklin's home, Charlie left for the marines and used that address to write. So, Charlie's letters were being delivered there for two months after they moved back to Mercy Row. During that period, Molly would drive over to Franklin's house every day and wait for the mail carrier. Often, Catherine, who had moved in permanently with Franklin, was there and Molly and Catherine became close friends. Molly, Catherine, Rose and sometimes Mercy often got together for lunch or coffee. These gatherings mostly occurred at Mercy Row since Rose still refused to ride in a car. "When the war's over," she said.

Jake called them the old hen's club, which, of course, the women didn't appreciate. That made Jake happy. He loved to rile people, all in good fun of course. More than once, Rose took him by the ear and walked him out of the room. That made Jake even happier.

It took six months to repair the damage done to the Broad Street mansion. Mercy Row was an easier job and was completed in two months. When it was completed, Jacob decided instead of taking Georgie in an out of school they would stay at Mercy Row until after

Labor Day, when school restarted. That way, he could continue to go to Saint Hugh's School.

Molly had just read Charlie's letter aloud to Mercy, Rose and Catherine, when Jake walked into the living room.

"Mom, have you seen Pop?" Jake asked as he entered the room.

"He's in the dining room meeting with Nate. Do you need him for something?"

"It can wait," Jake said and then saw the letter Molly was holding. "Is that a letter from Charlie?"

"Yes. Just got it," Molly said.

"What's he say?"

"Here, take it. We've finished," Molly said and handed the letter to Jake. "Be sure your father gets it after his meeting."

"Will do," Jake said. "What's the old hen's club up to today?"

"Don't you make me get up. You won't like it," Rose said pretending to get up.

Jake threw up his hand and ran out of the room. The old hen's club members smiled.

Nate Washington didn't often ask to meet with Jacob. He knew his job at the house and as leader of the Negro faction of the K&A Gang. So, Jacob was surprised when he asked for a few minutes on a personal matter. They set the meeting for just after lunch, as Jacob had to prepare some bids for building housing for returning military families when the war was over. Just the fact that the government was asking for bids made Jacob feel that the country's leaders felt the war would be over in the not too distant future. He had suggested that the land he owned in northeast Philly, off Roosevelt Boulevard, might be a good site for a housing project. With, of course, one exception, a small area close to the boulevard that already had a cement foundation.

Jacob finished his calculations and waited for Nate to arrive. While he waited, he worked on a letter he had started for Charlie. He worried a lot about Charlie. The war in the Pacific had been very tough. This was especially true for the marines who seemed to be the tip of the spear in so many battles. He saw an unofficial article that stated there were over six thousand causalities during the battle for

Guadalcanal, three thousand in Tara and two thousand in the Marshall Islands. He couldn't fathom what Charlie was experiencing.

Nate knocked on the side of the entrance to get Jacob's attention.

"Come in Nate. Sit down. Can I get you a drink?" Jacob asked.

"Whiskey, thanks," Nate answered.

Jacob poured two glasses, handed one to Nate and said, "To your health."

Nate clicked Jacobs glass and said, "And to yours."

Both men drank and Jacob filled the glasses again and said, "How can I help you Nate?"

Jacob, you know I don't ask for much. It's not my way. But we need your help," Nate said.

"We?" Jacob asked.

"I mean my people," Nate said.

"Go on."

"It's about the PCT and them hiring Negro motormen and conductors. Have you read about that?" Nate asked.

"Sure. Who hasn't? I thought that was settled. The PTC agreed to train some Negro men for those jobs," Jacob said.

"They did, after the government made them. Eight of our boys start training on August first. Problem is, some white boys at the PTC are pissed off. Some asshole reporter printed the names of our men and now they're being told to quit or else," Nate said.

"I never understood what the problem was. We need drivers for trolleys and we can't find them. It makes sense to hire Negro drivers, especially those already working for the PTC. There's a God damn war going on for Christ sake!" Jacob said.

"These men need protection, at least until they get started training," Nate said.

Jacob sat back, thought for a minute and said, "They need a place to hide out. A place no one would suspect. And I have the perfect place," Jacob said and paused." My house on Broad Street."

"Your house? Are you sure?" Nate said.

"Sure. It's empty." Jacob reached into his pockets and held a set of keys out to Nate. "Wait until late tonight and get them in the house. They can bring their families if they want. It will be tight but safe. See

Mike and tell him I said to post two of his men in the front and back of the house."

Nate took the keys, put his hand out and said, "I'll never forget this Jacob."

Jacob shook Nate's hand and said, "Nate, you've always had my back. Now it's my turn. Let me know if you need anything else." Nate turned to go and Jacob asked, "By the way, how's your boy doing?"

He's fine. Flying planes over there in Europe. Don't know where, exactly," Nate said.

"You religious Nate?" Jacob asked.

"Yes sir. Baptist."

"Well, I'll light a candle for him next time I'm in church," Jacob said.

"That would be very kind of you Jacob," Nate said and started to leave again. He stopped, turned around, walked back to Jacob and said, "Can I ask you a question?"

"You know you can. What is it?" Jacob said.

"Do you suppose we'll go to heaven when we die?" Nate asked.

"Of course. Why not?" Jacob said.

"Well," Nate said and paused. "We have bruised a few of the Ten Commandments."

"Did you beat your wife, Nate?" Jacob asked.

"No."

"Do you love her and your boy? Did you protect your family?" Jacob asked.

"Sure. That's what men are supposed to do."

"Do you believe in God?"

"Yes."

"Do you love your country?"

"Yes I do. Like to see some changes through," Nate said and smiled.

"Did you ever hurt someone who didn't deserve it?" Jacob asked.

Nate thought about it then answered, "Not that I know of."

"Me either, so I think we're both good," Jacob said.

Nate smiled, waved goodbye and left.

# 43

**ON THE MORNING** of August first, Nate and several of his crew drove to Jacob's Broad Street home and picked up the eight PTC trainees. Jake and Jimmy had insisted that they wanted to help and they became part of the team that would provide security for the eight men. Nate made them promise not to bring any weapons.

At 7:45am, they parked near the entrance to the PTC offices where the trainees were to report. Angry union employees, who decided to go on strike rather than allow Negro conductors, blocked the entrance. Early in the morning, a committee representing the PTC employees announced that the entire workforce was striking, in defiance of the union leader's decision not to strike. Philadelphia public transportation was paralyzed, making it impossible for large numbers of people to get to work.

Jake and Jimmy stood in front of the trainees and Nate's men were on each side, as they made their way through the hostile crowd. Everyone on the security team was wearing a suit and hat in an attempt to look as official as possible. That didn't stop the jeers and taunts of the strikers who were waving signs with racial slurs and *Go Back to the South* written on them. Someone threw an egg that hit Jake in the back and it was all Jimmy could do to keep him from smashing his fist into the first protester he saw. They finally got the trainees to the door and in the building. Jimmy sighed in relief and led the security team back through to protestors.

As Jake passed through the crowd, one of the protesters yelled at him, "Fucking scab bastard." Jacob turned on the man and said, "What the fuck's wrong with you? There's a war going on and you're fucking things up."

"Fuck the war," one man yelled.

"You fucking Nazi prick," Jake yelled. The man threw a punch at Jake's face, which Jake easily blocked. With incredible speed, Jake punched the man three times in the face and chest. The man fell back into the crowd unconscious. Seeing this, the crowd of protestors attacked Jake and the team and an all-out donnybrook ensued. It was eight men against at least forty protesters.

One striker, taking Jimmy by surprise, smashed him in the face with a thick sign stick. Jimmy fell to his knees, but quickly recovered, grabbed the man's legs and pulled. The man fell to the ground. Jimmy got up, found the stick and beat the man unconscious. He then started to swing the stick wildly into the crowd of strikers.

Nate saw one of his men get hit with a baseball bat and fall to the ground. He ran to the man and as he did, several protesters blocked his way. One had the bat. Nate punched the man with the bat in the solar plexus, and grabbed the bat as the man fell to the ground gasping for air. He quickly swung the bat at the second man, hitting him on the side of the head. The man fell to the ground.

After he dragged his injured man to safety, Nate turned to see that ten strikers had Jake pinned against the wall. Jake had taken a defensive position, crouched with his hands and arms protecting his face and upper body, as the strikers pounded on him. Nate ran to him and started smashing the bat into the backs of the attackers. Two fell and the others turned on Nate, who swung the bat wildly to keep them at bay. This allowed Jake to move away from the wall. As he did, he smashed his fist into the back of one man's head and kicked another in the back of his legs, making the man fall to the ground. Jake then stomped the man in the face.

The police department had assigned a team of ten police officers to stand across the street from the PTC building with hopes their presence would deter violence. They had orders not to interfere with the strikers unless necessary.

It was ten minutes before sergeant in command finally decide to break the fight up. The police pulled Jake and the team away from the crowd and stood in front of them, holding their nightsticks at the ready. Ten of the strikers were lying unconscious on the ground. The police sergeant yelled at Jimmy, "Get the hell out of here!"

Nate picked up his man and they all ran to their cars. Jake, Jimmy, and Nate got into of their car as the other men took Nate's car. A protester, holding a baseball bat, went around the police and ran up to the car that Jimmy was driving. He started to swing the bat at the passenger side window where Jake was sitting. Jake quickly pushed the door open and hit the man knocking him down. He jumped out of the car, kicked the man several times and jumped back in the car. Jimmy hit the gas and sped off.

After a few minutes, Jimmy looked over at Jake and seeing several lumps on Jake's forehead and his nose bleeding said, "Looks like they rearranged your face some. You actually look better."

"Yeah you're looking good too," Jake said. "You might want to get a steak for that eye of yours. Jimmy's right eye was swollen shut, and was bleeding above the eyebrow.

Nate yelled, "I think I broke my fucking hand."

They all began to laugh.

The Philadelphia Public Transportation Company strike lasted six days. Because Philadelphia was one of the most important hubs for weapons and ammunitions manufacturing, the federal government deemed the strike a national security issue. On day four of the strike, President Roosevelt ordered the Secretary of War to take over the PTC. The general in charge sent troops to operate the streetcars and the elevated trains and set up a process for mediation with the strikers.

On day six, the strikers still refused to go back to work. Frustrated by the striker's lack of patriotism and willingness to negotiate, the Secretary of War made an ultimatum to the strikers. Any employee not reporting to work by August 7th would be fired, their draft deferments negated and they would be put on the top of the draft list. Employees exempt from military service by age or medical reasons would be denied job availability certificates for the duration of the war. The ultimatum had the desired effect and on August 7, 1944, the strike ended. The eight Negro trainees resumed their training.

A month after the strike, The War Manpower Commission issued a report that estimated that the strike cost over four million work hours in Philadelphia war plants. That loss of work hours equaled the production of two hundred sixty flying fortresses or five destroyers.

# 44

Private First Class Charlie Byrne adjusted his helmet strap, checked his M1 rifle and waited to board the landing craft. The sea was choppy and climbing down the rope ladder to the LCVP would be difficult. He had practiced this many times, but he was still apprehensive. He would worry about the Japs when they hit the beach. Right now, he just didn't want to make a fool of himself by falling off the rope ladder.

Charlie was so absorbed in thought that he didn't hear the command to start loading. The marine behind him gave him a shove and Charlie snapped out of it and moved forward toward the edge of the ship, and then over unto the rope ladder. It was a difficult decent into the boat, especially with and extra fifty pounds of weapons and field pack. When he finally reached the boat, he took his seat and looked up at the men still climbing down the rope ladder. He was relieved to see that it was just as hard for them as it was for himself.

The sergeant told his men it would take fifteen to twenty minutes to reach the beach. It was the longest twenty minutes in Charlie's life. Five minutes into the trip, the Japanese artillery started to pound them. Charlie felt helpless in the open top boat. It like being a fish in a barrel. All you could do was pray one of the shells didn't hit your boat.

As the LCVP got closer to the beach, the artillery barrage got worse and the Japanese started firing the machine guns they had placed in protected bunkers. A shell exploded about fifty feet to the left of Charlie's boat, sending a salt-water spray over the craft. Another shell hit the LCVP to the right and wood splinters, blood and flesh landed on top of Charlie's helmet. He saw nothing because he and every other man in his boat were hunched over with their hands on the top of their helmets.

The door dropped and the sergeant yelled something Charlie didn't understand, but knew it meant get out of the boat. The first marine out of the door was hit by machine gun fire. The force pushed him back into the LCVP and onto several other marines, knocking them down. They pushed him away and continued to disembark. Charlie knew instinctively and by training that the safest place to be was on the beach and he was eager to get off the boat.

As he leaped into the shallow water, Charlie tripped over another Marine who was lying in the water, and fell forward. As he fell, several bullets hit the man behind him in the chest. Charlie crawled over the marine he tripped over and in doing so turned him over. Charlie looked into the man's face, which was now just a bloody pulp of flesh and blood.

Charlie continued to crawl for another ten feet then got up, crouched over and ran as fast as he could to a forward area where several other marines had taken shelter. He dove into a position next to his sergeant, Joe Phelps. "Put some fire into that bunker up there Byrne," Phelps ordered pointing toward a concrete and steel bunker about fifty yards up the ridge. Keeping as low as he could, Charlie pointed his M1 at the bunker and started to fire rapidly. He did that until he ran out of ammo, reloaded and did it again. He had no idea if he had hit anyone and neither did any of the other men who were shooting at the open steel doors. They were as close to the ground as they could get and still be able to fire their weapons.

"Byrne, you think you can put a grenade into those open doors?" Phelps asked.

"I can try," Charlie said.

"Do it," Phelps said and threw Charlie the grenade attachment for the M1.

"I need to get up on that ridge to fire this," Charlie said. "I need cover."

"Smith, Gormley, on three, fire everything you got into that bunker. One, two, three," Phelps yelled.

The three men pointed their weapons at the bunker and opened fire. At the same instant, Charlie scrambled up to the ridge, planted the butt of his M1 on the ground, aimed and fired. The grenade exploded on top of the bunker. Charlie had missed. He loaded a second grenade, as bullets peppered the ground around him. Phelps, Smith and Gormley reloaded and started firing at the bunker again. Charlie fired again. This time, the grenade went through the opening in the bunker and exploded.

A Japanese soldier crawled out the opening and started running. He was on fire. Phelps took aim and shot the man, then yelled, "Good job. Now let's do the same to the next bunker. By nightfall, they had put three more bunkers out of commission, but the 1st Marine Division still only held the beaches they landed on. The Japanese continued to shell the marines, making sleep impossible. After several more days, Charlie's company started to move inland.

Charlie wasn't sure how long they had been on the island. He just knew it was longer than he wanted it to be. The heat and humidity were unbearable. Making things worse was the shortage of water. Lack of sleep, food and water was taking its toll. Dave Smith, one of the men that helped Charlie and Sergeant Phelps destroy bunkers on the first day, developed heat stroke and was evacuated to the hospital ship. Phelps sent Gormley back to the beach to fill their canteens, but he hadn't returned in over an hour.

"Hey Sarge, how long we been in this hell hole?" Charlie asked.

"Let me get my appointment book out," Phelps said facetiously. "How the fuck do I know. Feels like a month," he continued.

"If I don't get some water I'm going to croak. Where the fuck is Gormley?" Charlie said.

"You keep asking questions I can't answer Byrne. Try to get some shuteye," Phelps said.

Charlie leaned back, pulled his helmet over his eyes and fell asleep. Fifteen minutes later, he woke up to someone banging the top of his helmet.

"What the hell?" Charlie yelled as he sat up.

"Here," Gormley said as he tossed Charlie his full canteen. "Don't say I never gave you anything."

Charlie greedily opened the canteen and took several long gulps. He let the next gulp linger in his mouth. He spit it out and yelled, "You trying to poison me. This tastes like oil."

Phelps opened his canteen, smelled the water and said, "Shit! The water has oil in it. Where did you get this crap Gormley?"

"They got big barrels on the beach. Some guy told me they brought it in from the ships," Gormley said."

"Did you drink any before you filled the canteens?"

"Well, no. I met some Navy guys and they had a few bottles of pop. A gave them five bucks for two bottles and drank that," Gormley said.

"Fuck! You poisoned me," Charlie yelled and spit on the ground.

"Shut up! You'll live Byrne. Gormley, take these back and this time check the water first," Phelps said handing Gormely the canteens.

"Gees Sarge, how'd I know?" Gormely said.

"Just do it and hurry. No more screwing around on the beach."

Gormley took the canteens, poured out the water and started back toward the beach. He stopped, fished around in his pocket and pulled out something. "I forgot. I got you guys something. You owe me two bucks each." He threw one item to Phelps and another to Charlie and started off to the beach again.

"Holy shit! Good and Plenty's," Charlie said in amazement.

"Never heard of them. What are they?" Phelps asked.

"Candy licorice candy. They make them in my hometown, "Charlie said as he opened the box, took out a white candy, leaned back and put it in his mouth. He rolled it around letting the candy coating melt and then chewed the black licorice. "Heaven, just heaven," Charlie said.

Charlie took another candy from the box and put it in his mouth. A shell exploded just to the right of the foxhole he and Sergeant Phelps occupied. The noise was deafening and dirt covered Charlie. He brushed away the dark foul soil from his face and saw a box of Good and Plenty's lying on the bottom of the Foxhole. He looked over at Sergeant Phelps and he was staring straight ahead.

"Sarge! You okay?" Charlie asked. Phelps didn't answer. "Sarge," Charlie said again. No answer again. Charlie reached over and pulled on Phelps' arm. Phelps fell toward Charlie. Then Charlie saw the hole in Phelps' helmet. He made the sign of the cross, pulled the sergeant's dog tag and placed it in his pocket. Then he picked up the Good and Plenty's from the bottom of the foxhole and put them in the same pocket.

# 45

*PELELIU ISLAND, SOUTH* Pacific
*Battle of Bloody Nose Ridge*
*September 22th, 1944*

The eight days they had been on Peleliu had been a complete hell for the 1st Marines. It seemed that every foot of ground they won was bathed in their own blood. Charlie Byrne had lost his sergeant and several close friends, but he had no time to mourn them. The last five days had been a particularly bad time. They attacked what the marines now called Bloody Nose Ridge, and took enormous causalities.

Now the marines were trapped in a ridge and had been for several days. During the day, the Japanese shelled the location with mortars and at night, they sent infiltrators into their lines and attacked the marines in their foxholes. Most marines now shared a foxhole so one could sleep while the other kept a lookout.

"How hot do you think it was today?" Sarge.

"Who the hell knows? Hot! And it's still hot," Gormley answered.

"Scuttlebutt is we might get relieved soon," Charlie said.

"News to me. I wouldn't hold my breath."

"We can hope," Charlie said.

"I'm hoping you shut the fuck up so I can get some sleep," Gormley barked.

"Okay, Sarge. Sorry. Go ahead."

Sergeant Gormley pushed himself as low in the two-man foxhole as he could and tipped his helmet over his eyes. He was snoring a few minutes later. Charlie smiled. He liked Ed Gormley, who was originally from Los Angeles. Gormley's father was a movie editor and Charlie loved hearing the stories Ed told about meeting various movie stars.

Charlie looked up at the night sky. It was shimmering like a field of diamonds. He had never seen so many stars until he came to the South Pacific. *I wonder how far away those stars are?* Charlie thought. *Are there planets like earth up there?* He wondered. *Is heaven up there? The nuns said it was. Is there really a heaven and hell? Is there really a God that takes care of all of this?* For the first time in his life, Charlie doubted what his family believed and what he had been taught about God. *If God was all-loving, how could he let people suffer the way Charlie had seen? How could God let men die in agony holding their own guts in their hands? If there is a God,* Charlie thought, *I think he just put us on Earth and said go make your own paradise. Boy, did we fuck up.*

There was a noise. It sounded to Charlie like shoes scraping on the ground. Sarge, Sarge wake up," Charlie whispered and shook Gormley's shoulder.

Gormley sat up quickly and asked, "What is it?"

"I heard something at about eleven o'clock," Charlie said. Gormley looked in front of him and to the left and said, "I don't see anything. Get your bayonet out."

Charlie pulled his bayonet and started to fasten it to his rifle. At that moment, he heard a fast paced shuffling and he looked up. There were two Japanese soldiers running fast toward their foxhole, their rifles with bayonets pointing straight at Charlie. The first Jap hit Sergeant Gormley hard. The momentum pushed both of them out of the foxhole. Within a second, another Jap soldier smashed into Charlie as he parried the man's bayonet away from himself. He brought the butt of his rifle up attempting to smash the soldier's jaw, but the man pushed his rifle away. Both men fell into the foxhole and scuffled for footing.

Charlie's bayonet had fallen to the ground when the Jap soldier hit him. Holding onto the Jap soldier with one arm, Charlie searched for the bayonet with his free hand. The soldier rolled Charlie over, but couldn't use his rifle or bayonet because it was tightly held between the two men's torsos. Charlie rolled the soldier back so that he was on top of him. He found the bayonet at the bottom of the foxhole, picked it up and brought it down toward the soldier's eye.

The Jap soldier grabbed Charlie's hand before the blade could pierce his eye. Charlie pushed hard, but the soldier was strong. The Jap soldier pushed the blade downward away from his eye. This gave Charlie advantage and he pushed hard again. The blade of the bayonet slid into the soldier's throat. He gurgled for a minute and then died.

Charlie looked to see how Gormley was doing. He saw the Jap soldier standing over him with his bayonet ready to stab Gormley in the chest. Charlie quickly picked up the dead Jap soldier's rifle that had broken on the impact with Charlie. Using the rifle like a spear, Charlie threw it at the man with all his strength. The rifle hit the soldier in the leg and bounced off harmlessly. The soldier looked over at a wide-eyed Charlie. This gave Gormley enough time to knock the bayonet away and bring his own bayonet up and threw the man's jaw and into his brain.

Charlie fell back into the foxhole gasping for air. He sat there for a minute listening to gunfire as the marines repelled the Japanese attack. Suddenly, he heard a strange metal on metal click and then he saw a black cylinder hit the edge of the foxhole and fall in. He yelled "Grenade," and started to jump out of the foxhole.

Sergeant Gormley hit the ground and flattened himself. Charlie was on the lip of the foxhole when the grenade exploded. The concussion threw him forward five feet and he landed next to Gormley. Gormley picked up his rifle and fired at two more Jap soldiers as the attempted to cross the foxhole. He killed both.

Blood was seeping from several wounds on Charlie's back and Gormley yelled for a medic. Then he rolled Charlie over.

Charlie looked at him, then up at the sky, and said, "I just saw a shooting star. I can make a wish right?"

"Yeah Charlie you can," Gormley said.

"Okay, I wish…" Charlie stopped as his vision faded to black.

Medic. I need a Medic," Gormley yelled again.

# 46

IT HAD BEEN over a month since Molly received a letter from Charlie. In his last letter, he said he wouldn't be able to write for a while, but that didn't lessen Molly's worries. She wasn't sure where Charlie was, but she had seen the newsreels and read some articles about the marines battling Japanese forces on some islands near the Philippines. General MacArthur made a promise to return to the Philippines and she thought Charlie might be involved in that battle.

"Hey Mom. How do you like my costume?" Georgie said breaking Molly out of her melancholy.

"Very nice, Georgie. What are you supposed to be?" Molly asked.

"A mummy," Georgie said proudly.

"Oh," Molly said not sure what a mummy was. "Where did you get those wrappings from?"

"Jake got them and helped me get wrapped," Georgie answered.

"Don't worry Mom. I used one of the old sheets that were in the fire," Jake said walking into the room. "Anything from Charlie?"

"No. Not yet. I'm so worried about him."

"Don't worry Mom," Jake said and kissed Molly on the head. "He's fine. He's a Byrne. The Japs wouldn't dare hurt him. Come on Georgie. You got your pillowcase?"

"I'll go get it."

"Are you going trick or treating with Georgie?" Molly asked surprised.

"Yeah. I heard there were some kids stealing candy from the smaller ones. Anyway, maybe Georgie will give me a couple of the penny Grade A chocolates people give out," Jake said smiling.

When Georgie came back with his pillowcase, he and Jake walked to the front door. Rose was there giving candy out to the kids. She dropped a couple pieces in Georgie's bag. Jake grabbed a couple of Tootsie Rolls from the bowl and Rose lightly slapped his hand. Then Georgie walked down the steps holding his arms in front of him, acting like the mummy from a recent movie he saw. Jake started down the steps behind him and looked toward Front Street. He saw a Western Union boy on a bike turn onto Wishart Street.

Jakes eyes widened and his heart beat faster. The boy on the bike slowly peddled up the street. The closer he got the faster Jake's heart beat.

"Jake, what are you waiting for?" Georgie asked.

Jake didn't reply. He just watched the boy on the bike get closer and closer. Then the boy stopped in front of Jake. Jakes heart skipped a beat.

"Hey buddy," the Western Union boy said.

Jake couldn't answer. "Hey buddy," The boy said again a little louder.

"Yeah," Jake said tentatively.

"Is this East Wishart Street?"

Jakes shoulders slumped in relief. His mouth was dry so it took him a few seconds to answer. "No. Turn around. It's on the other side of Front Street.

"Thanks."

Jake sat down on the step, and sighed.

"Jake. What's wrong with you? Let's go. They're gonna give away all the good candy," Georgie said.

Jake said, "Okay. Sorry. Let's go. We'll start on Allegheny Avenue. When I was a kid they gave out the best stuff." Jake and Georgie walked toward Howard Street, turned right and then one block to Allegheny Avenue. It was the only street in the neighborhood where the homes had porches and a small lawn.

Rose watched as Jake and Georgie walked up the street. She had also seen the Western Union boy and was holding her chest trying to slow her heartbeat. She had seen too much death. *Way too much,* she thought. *The older you get the more death you see. First, my husband, then my own Ma and Pa. Sean my youngest son died so young.* Rose wiped a tear from her eye. *Mr. Byrne and George. I couldn't take it if Charlie was killed.*

"Trick or Treat," a kid dressed as a hobo said.

Rose looked down and smiled, picked out two pieces of candy and dropped them in the hobo's sack. "Here you go sweetheart," Rose said.

"Thank you Mrs.," the hobo said.

*And life goes on,* Rose thought.

Molly was still in the living room. She turned on the radio hoping to hear some news about the fighting in the Pacific. She dialed through the station and couldn't find any news so she left the radio on the Benny Goodman Show. She liked his music and was hoping it would cheer her up.

Jacob walked in the living room, saw Molly and kissed her on the cheek.

"What're you listening to?" Jacob asked Molly.

"It's the Benny Goodman Show," Molly answered.

"Didn't we see him years ago?" Jacob asked.

"Yes him, Glenn Miller, the Dorsey Brothers. We saw them all. You were a pretty good dancer back then," Molly said.

"Still am, I think." Jacob said and took Molly's hand. "Let's see." Jacob helped Molly to her feet and they began to dance.

"Not bad," Molly said.

Jacob swung Molly out and around and then back into his arms.

"Okay. Pretty good," Molly said smiling.

Jacob pulled her closer and they danced around the room.

"Ummm, what's that I feel? Are you happy to see me?" Molly said.

"Let's go to our room and find out, shall we?" Jacob said and led Molly toward the stairs.

The phone rang.

"Leave it," Molly said.

"I'll only be a minute," Jacob said and walked over to a small hallway where the phone was.

Molly stood by the stairs waiting. A few minutes later, Jacob walked back into the room. His face was ashen and he was shaking his head.

"What wrong Jacob," Molly asked, alarmed.

Jacob took Molly in his arms and said, "Don Amato's dead."

# 47

GERARDO AMATO'S REQUIEM mass was held at the Cathedral Basilica of Saints Peter and Paul. After the mass, the beloved Don's body, followed by over two hundred cars, was driven to Holy Cross Cemetery in Yeadon, Pennsylvania for interment. After the gravesite ceremony, close family and friends were invited to the Amato home for lunch. The entire Byrne family, Rose, Franklin, Mike Kelly and Grady arrived thirty minutes after Tony's family.

Tony Amato, his wife Carmella, their two daughters and Gerardo Amato's only living brother greeted each guest as they arrived. The food served was a feast of Don Amato's favorite dishes. Jacob was sitting with Carmella Amato and Molly when Tony asked him to come with him to his office.

"Thank you Jacob, for coming and for the beautiful flowers," Tony said.

"I can't believe he is gone, Tony. I just can't believe he died," Jacob said.

Tony's eyes glazed and he shook his head. "He didn't die. He was murdered," Tony said and hit the desk with his hand.

Surprised, Jacob said, "You said he had a heart attack."

"We thought that until we saw the autopsy report. He was poisoned," Tony yelled.

"Who? Why?" Jacob asked.

"That fucking snake Nicky Galanti was being backed by Dominick Delucia."

"North Jersey? I thought you had good ties to them," Jacob said.

"Me too. It can't be just them. Somebody important in New York has to be backing them. They wouldn't do this alone," Tony said.

"How bad?" Jacob asked.

"Very," Tony replied.

"What about internal? Somebody had to give your father the poison."

"Their bodies are probably already in the Delaware Bay," Tony said in a low voice.

Jacob sat back in his chair and said, "I think I need a drink."

"Sure," Tony said as he walked to a cabinet, opened it, took out a bottle, and poured two drinks. He handed one to Jacob. "To my Pop," Tony said. Both men clicked glasses and Jacob hesitated.

"Go ahead, Jacob. Not on the carpet please," Tony said.

Jacob walked over to the tiled area by the fireplace and poured some of the drink on the floor. He walked back to Tony clinked glasses again and drank. Jacob sat down, put his hand to his head, rubbed his temples and said, "How can I help?"

"I have to go to New York and try to iron this out. Can you take Carmella and the girls to your place until I get back?"

"Sure. Of course," Jacob said.

Tony took out an envelope from his desk drawer and handed it to Jacob.

"What's this?" Jacob asked.

"Information you'll need to take care of my family if I don't come back," Tony said.

"You need some muscle to come with you?"

"No. Hopefully, I'm meeting with friends. I'll talk to them and see what I can do. We're good earners and two of the families make a lot of moolah from us. I'm going to need permission to go after Delucia," Tony said.

"We're here for you. Just give me the word," Jacob said.

"Thanks Jacob" Tony said, "And Jacob, everyone thinks Pop died from a heart attack. I need it to stay that way for now."

That evening, Jacob took Carmella and her two daughters Maria, and Sophia to his home. The next morning Tony Amato and his consigliere Vincenzo DeBello left for New York City.

Tony Amato, the new leader of the South Philadelphia Mafia entered the restaurant feeling uneasy. He was meeting friends. Friends of his father's and friends he had known all his life, but he still felt unsure of the result of this meeting.

The New York Italian mobs and in turn most of the other organizations in the country had experienced recent turmoil in the ranks. Charlie Luciano was imprisoned in 1936, but was still able to lead his family from his jail cell and had great influence on the commission. Recently, however, rumor had it Luciano would be released after the war and most likely deported back to Italy. Frank Costello, it was said, was worried that he could lose his leadership position in the family and with the commission. Many leaders of the Chicago outfit were indicted and faced jail time. Frank Nitti was dead. In Louisiana, Carlo Matranga recently died and left a power gap. Some people who once had power were no longer as influential as they once were. This worried Tony. If he were wrong about his father's friends, he and Debello might never leave this restaurant, alive that is.

A man stopped Tony and Debello in front of the private room set aside for their meeting and indicated that he needed to search them.

"It's okay Lorenzo. They are friends," A man in the room said.

Lorenzo showed Tony and Debello into the room.

Two elderly men sat at a large table set for four people. Tony approached the closest man, who did not stand up, and kissed him on both cheeks.

"Don Rossetti," Tony said. "Good to see you again." Then he walked around the table and kissed the second man on both cheeks, and said. "Don Belotti, you get younger looking every time I see you."

Don Belotti smiled and said, "Tony, please sit."

"Don Belotti, Don Rossetti, this is my consigliere Vincenzo Debello," Tony said.

Debello, being from the old school, bowed and shook each man's hand.

"Please sit," Don Rossetti said.

A waiter who had been in the corner came to the table and poured each man a glass of wine. Belotti waved a hand and Lorenzo and the waiter left the room and pulled the door closed.

"Please accept our sympathies for your father's passing. He was a dear friend and he will be missed," Don Rossetti said. "I am sorry we could not speak to you at his funeral, but we are here now, so how can we help you?"

"My father didn't die from a heart attack. He was poisoned," Tony said.

Both Don Belotti and Don Rossetti reacted in surprise. "Who would do such a thing?" Don Belotti said.

"Dominick Delucia," Tony said.

"And you know this how?" Don Rossetti asked.

"The autopsy showed that my father was poisoned. We found the man who put the poison in his food and convinced him to tell us who ordered him to do this. He told us Dominick Delucia paid him and promised he would have a good position in the organization. This man, this putrid fuck, was working with two others in my organization," Tony said.

"And where are these men now?" Don Rossetti asked.

"Somewhere in the ocean off of Cape May by now," Tony said. Tony went on to tell the Dons about the attempt on his father and his life by Nicky Galanti and Nicky's ties with Delucia.

"We believe one of the New York families is backing Delucia," Tony said.

"Don Belotti and Don Rossetti looked at each other and then at Tony. Don Belotti said, "And what do you want from us?"

"My family's in danger. I'm in danger. Delucia has to go. I need your support," Tony said.

Don Belotti rubbed his hand across his forehead and said, "Things are not as they are supposed to be with the commission. There are people who are not happy and who seek more power. One of these men has New Jersey under his thumb," Belotti looked at Don Rosetti. Rosetti nodded.

"We will talk to the commission about this man, because we loved your father and because we trust you. It is also in our best interest that this man does not become powerful. Tomorrow evening I will call you and let you know our position on this matter," Don Belotti said.

Tony and Debello stood up and Tony said, "Thank You Don Belotti, Don Rossetti."

Both men nodded and Rossetti said, "Sit down Tony. Let's eat." He knocked on the table three times and the door opened. The waiter came in with bread and olive oil and placed it on the table.

# 48

**AT SEVENTEEN YEARS** old, Maria Amato had blossomed into a beautiful young woman. Her hair was raven black, her eyes deep brown with long lashes and she had the classic Italian high cheekbones. She was a slender girl with just the right curves for her body type. Maria and Jake had often played together when they were children. The last time he saw her was at Christmas, but he was too shy to talk to her. That was the first time he has seen her in over three years, when she left for boarding school in Connecticut.

For some reason, that Jake couldn't fathom, he had become shy around Maria. He had known her for a long time and Jake was not a shy person. Carmella had often visited Molly and Maria would come with her. When they were children, Jake enjoyed trying to scare her with snakes or insects. Once he talked her into going in the attic. When she did, he closed the attic door and locked it. She was locked in the attic for thirty minutes before Molly heard her screaming and let her out. Now, he was petrified of saying or doing something that would make him look like a fool. So, he did the only thing he could think of. He ignored her.

Jake was sitting at the kitchen table, eating a donut when Maria came into the kitchen.

"What's that you're eating Jake?" Maria asked.

"Donut," Jake answered.

"What kind of breakfast is that? Let me make you some eggs and bacon."

"No," Jake said.

"Why not?"

"No," Jake said again.

Exasperated, Maria said, "Have it your way," then asked, "You going to mass this morning?"

"No," Jake said.

"Okay. That's it! What is your problem?" Maria said.

"What do you mean?" Jake asked.

"You haven't said ten words to me since I've been here. We used to be good friends. Now you treat me as if I have leprosy. So I ask again. What is your problem?" Maria said.

"Nothing. I don't have a problem," Jake said twitching in his chair.

Maria just stared at him, pursed her lips, cocked her head and waited.

"Oh crap," Jacob finally said. "It's just that you've changed."

"I've changed? How?" Maria said angrily.

"Well," Jake said and paused, "You... you're... ahh... you're beautiful."

Maria sat down in a chair next to Jake and said. "So because I'm attractive you hate me?" Maria asked.

"I don't hate you. I..., I'm... I'm attracted to you," Jake finally blurted out.

"So you treat me bad because you're attracted to me?" Maria said knowingly leading Jake along.

"No. No. I just don't want to make a fool out of myself," Jake said.

"Too late," Maria quipped. Then she stood up, walked behind the still seated Jake, put her arms around his neck and kissed the back of his head. "You are a silly boy Jake Byrne. I've had a crush on you since I was eight years old."

"Me?" "Jake said.

"Is your name Jake Byrne," Maria said.

"Yes," Jake said.

"Then yes, you," Maria said and lightly tapped Jakes head. "So, here's what we're going to do. First I'm going to make you a good breakfast, and then we're going to mass."

Two hours later, Maria, her thirteen-year-old sister Sophia, and Jake were in the backseat of Tony's black 1941 Chrysler heading to Saint Hugh's church on Tioga Street. Tony's man was driving and another man was in the passenger seat holding a shotgun. Mike Kelly and Grady were following in a separate car.

As the New Yorker turned off Allegheny Avenue onto Howard Street, a blue sedan cut off Mike Kelly's car, sped up behind the New Yorker, and smashed into the back bumper. Jake fell forward hitting the passenger seat. He recovered and pushed Maria and Sophia to the floor as the driver of the New Yorker sped up the narrow street, the blue sedan following.

Two men in the backseat of the blue sedan opened fire on Mike Kelly and Grady. The bullets hit the front right headlamp and tire. Unable to steer any longer, Mike stopped and he and Grady jump from the car and took cover behind the parked cars on each side of the street. Running up the street, still behind the parked cars, Mike tried to shoot the back tires out on the blue sedan. Having to run and shoot at the same time, he missed.

Tony's man in the passenger seat of the New Yorker leaned out of the window and blasted the blue sedan with his shotgun. He missed. The men in the blue sedan returned fire and hit Tony's man in the head. He fell back into the car dropping the shotgun between the door and the passenger seat.

"Take a right on Westmorland. There's a police station a couple blocks over," Jake yelled as he tried to pull the shotgun to the backseat. It was wedged in, but when the driver turned onto Clearfield Street, it loosened enough for Jake to pull it free.

Mike and Grady were still running after the blue sedan when it turned to follow the New Yorker. The driver of the New Yorker saw the police station on the left, drove up on the sidewalk, and stopped. He jumped out of the car and starting firing at the blue sedan. They fired back and hit him in the leg. Jake, seeing the driver fall, pushed his door open, leveled the shotgun at the now close blue sedan and fired. The blast hit the passenger side window shattering it and the passenger's face. The blue sedan's driver lost control and hit the rear of the New Yorker. Jake fired again at the driver, killing him instantly. Just as the two men in the backseat of the blue sedan turned to Jake,

Mike and Grady came up behind them and shot through the rear window killing both men.

Jake threw the shotgun back into the front seat and said, "Maria. You okay?"

Both girls were crying and Jacob first helped Maria off the floor and then Sophia. Several police officers ran from inside the station, guns drawn, to the New Yorker. Mike and Grady put their guns on the ground and raised their hands.

# 49

TONY WAS JUST about to leave New York City when he called Jacob and heard about the attack. Breaking every speed limit, Debello drove from New York to Jacob's house in record time. Debello pulled up outside the house and Tony jumped out and ran to the door. The guards at the door knew Tony and opened the door for him. He ran in yelling Maria and Sophia's names.

On hearing their father, both girls ran to the foyer and hugged him. He hugged them back and said, "Thank God you're okay." Both girls started to cry. Carmella came into the foyer and put her arms around the girls and Tony.

Tony spent some time with the girls and then asked Jacob if they could meet. Jacob asked Grady, Mike and Jake to explain what exactly happened. When they were finished, he thanked them for saving his girls and asked if he could speak to Jacob alone.

After the others left the room, Tony filled Jacob in on his meeting with Don Belotti and Don Rossetti. After he finished, he yelled, "I'm not waiting for their approval. Fuck that! That bastard Delucia tried to take my girls. My girls! He's dead. Dead."

"He'll be dead, Tony. I promise you that. But, we need to do it right. Let me send a couple guys to Newark and keep tabs on him. Find out where he goes. We wait a day until you get your support from the commission. Then we take him out and anyone else in his gang you want."

Tony, sighed, twisted his head several times to relieve the tension in his neck and said, "Okay, Okay. Who you going to send?"

"Nate. We'll send Nate," Jacob said.

"He's a good man," Tony said and paused, "Where's Franklin? I thought he would be here."

"He and Catherine are in Cape May. Something about celebrating their one year anniversary of something or other. I called him and told him what happened. He'll be back tomorrow morning."

"Good. You know Jacob, that son of yours is a real warrior," Tony said.

"I know," Jacob said and shook his head. "I had hoped he might be more inclined to be part of the construction company."

"Maria told me what he did. We need men like Jake to protect our families," Tony said.

"He's just a kid Tony," Jacob said.

"Same as you were. Same as me at his age. It didn't stop us," Tony said.

Jacob shook his head as if to get the thought out of his head. He took a piece of paper from his desk and handed it and a pen to Tony. "Before you leave, write down some places you think Delucia might be in Newark. Tony took the paper, wrote down several addresses and slid it across the desk.

"You know, before he left for the navy, Tony Junior told me he didn't want to work in the family business, Tony senior's eyes glistened, "Said he had some idea for his own business."

"I know, Mercy told me," Jacob said.

"I was proud of that. I wanted him to do his own thing," Tony said.

"He was a good man and he was a good husband. He would have been a great father," Jacob said.

"Thank you Jacob. Now I have to get my family home. Tomorrow, one way or another, we go to New York," Tony said and rose from his chair. Jacob stood up and Tony kissed him on each cheek and left the room.

Jacob picked up the phone and dialed Nate. He briefed Nate on what had happened and what was going to happen and asked him to go to Newark. Two hours later, Nate and Willy Williams drove to Newark.

"Willy, Jacob don't want any trouble up here. We just find out where this Delucia hangs out and what he does," Nate said as he parked the car on Seventh Avenue across from Maddalena's restaurant. "Got it?"

"Yeah, I got it," Willy said. "Why are we dressed like we work in a factory?"

"Willy, sometimes I just want to beat you over the head," Nate said and knocked on Willy's head with is knuckles.

"Hey, watch it."

"What do you thinks gonna happen if we started walking around this neighborhood in hundred dollar suits?" Nate said and smacked Willy's head again.

At about 8pm, Delucia parked his car in front of the restaurant and he and two of his men entered Maddalena's. Nate noticed that two other cars parked nearby.

"Stay here. I'll be right back," Nate told Willy. Nate left the car and walked over to the restaurant and through the door. He asked the hostess if the owner was around.

"Stay here. I'll get him," the hostess said.

She came back with a short Italian man in a tailored suit. The irritated owner said, "What do you want? Deliveries are in the back. Go to the back."

"No delivery sir. I'm looking for work. I can wash dishes, sweep up, whatever you want," Nate said.

"No. No work here. Now go," the owner said.

"Sorry sir," Nate said as backed out the door.

"As Nate left the restaurant, the owner said to the hostess, "Fottuti moulinyans senza valore." It was a something Nate had heard before.

Nate and Willy waited for Delucia to leave the restaurant. One of the cars that was waiting pulled out first, then Delucia's car, then the second waiting car followed. Nate and Willy followed them to a building several blocks south on Seventh Avenue. There were two guards at the door and when Delucia walked up, they opened the door.

At midnight, Delucia left the building. Once again, one of the waiting cars went first and the second car followed behind Delucia. The three cars drove to a residential area and Nate followed. Nate parked a block away from Delucia's home and waited.

"Willy, get some sleep," Nate said. "Hand me one of those sandwiches you brought first."

Willy pulled out one of the sandwiches and handed it to Nate. Nate unwrapped it and took a bite. He quickly spit it out. "What the fuck. This is liverwurst. I hate fucking liver," Nate said.

"That's all we got," Willy said. Nate threw the sandwich at him.

"You eat it," Nate said.

Willy rummaged around in the bag, pulled out two candy bars, and threw them on Nate's lap. "Chocolate bars. That's it?" Nate asked. Willy shrugged his shoulders.

"Just go to sleep, I'll wake you in a few hours," Nate said as he took the wrapper off a chocolate bar.

At about 10am, Delucia left his house. He stopped at a bakery and then on to the same building he had left from the night before. Again, the two cars took their posts outside the building.

"Willy, you stay here. I'll go find a phone and call Jacob."

"Okay," Willy said and got out of the car.

Nate found a payphone in a gas station and called to report to Jacob what he had seen.

"He goes to his office in the morning, has lunch delivered and then at 8pm he gets dinner at a restaurant. I don't know if he does this every day. Give me a couple more days and I'll find out," Nate told Jacob.

"No, Tony doesn't want to wait. We'll just have to take our chances. What do you think is the best place to hit him?" Jacob asked.

"Not the office. Too many men." Nate paused and then said, "Maybe his house?"

"How about the restaurant?" Jacob asked.

"Two cars, with two men in each, outside. Two men with Delucia at the table, that I saw, Nate replied.

"We'll need to take out the men in the cars first," Jacob said.

"I have an idea," Nate said. "I need you to bring me something special."

# 50

DON BELOTTI CALLED Tony with his approval at 11am not long after Nate reported to Jacob. Tony Amato called Jacob and had Jacob and Franklin meet him at noon. By 1pm, Tony was leading three cars and seven men, including Jacob and Franklin, to Newark, New Jersey. They met Nate at the Cathedral of the Sacred Heart on Ridge Street. When Tony entered the church, Nate and Willy were sitting in the last pew. Tony, Jacob and Franklin sat down beside them.

"What do you think about this church Nate?" Tony asked.

"It's pretty. Only thing is..." Nate paused and said, "The money they spent building this place could have fed a lot of people."

"You're Baptist, right?" Tony asked.

"Yep," Nate answered.

"Don't Baptists have big churches?"

"No. Not like this," Nate said and paused. "Tony, excuse me but I have to talk to Jacob. That okay?"

"Sure."

Jacob, you bring that special thing I asked for?" Nate asked.

Jacob handed Nate a brown paper bag and said, "It's all here."

"Thanks I'm starving," Nate said and opened the bag, pulled out a hoagie and handed it to Willy. Then he took another hoagie from the bag, held it up and said, "Just oil, no mayo, right."

"No mayo," Jacob said.

Nate took a large bite of the hoagie, chewed it well and swallowed. He looked up at the cathedral's roof and said, "Heaven." He then put his hand back in the bag and pulled out two silencers.

Nate finished his hoagie and said, "Maybe we should go outside. I don't want God to hear what I got to say."

As Tony, Jacob and Franklin left the pew each genuflected and made the sign of the cross. When they walked out of the door, they each dipped their fingers in holy water and made the sign of the cross again.

When they were all outside the cathedral, Nate asked, "Do you have to do that every time you go into church and leave?"

"Pretty much," Jacob answered.

"Lotta work just to go to church," Nate said. Jacob smiled.

"Let's go somewhere out of the way until it's time to say hello to Delucia," Tony said.

The group drove across town to a small restaurant Tony knew. It was far enough from Newark's Little Italy that they wouldn't be seen but close enough so they could get to Maddalena's quickly. The owner greeted Tony and Jacob who had entered first, but when he saw Nate and Willy, he said, "We don't serve Negros here."

Jacob put his hand on his hips making sure his suit coat opened to reveal the two .45s he carried. The owner waved them all in. They ordered food and Nate told them the rest of his plan. At 6pm, Nate and Willy left for Delucia's office and parked nearby.

At 7pm, Tony, his men, Jacob and Franklin drove to Maddalena's. One car parked at Seventh Avenue and Cutler Street, and the other at Seventh Avenue and Wood Street. Jacob, Tony and Franklin pulled their car behind the car on Cutler Street and waited.

Nate pulled up behind Jacob's car at 8:10pm. He told Willy to wait in the car while he talked to Jacob. Nate opened the back door of Jacob's car, sat down and said, "He's here."

"Okay." Jacob said. "Try to keep them alive." Nate nodded and he and Willy crossed Seventh Street and walked up toward Wood Street. As they passed the first Delucia guard car, Willy broke right and Nate tapped on the driver's window.

"Mister," Nate said.

"The guard yelled, "Get the fuck out of here."

Nate put his hand to his ear and said, "Sorry sir, I can't hear you."

The guard rolled down his window and said, "What the fuck do you want?"

Nate pulled the .45 with the silencer attached and pointed at the guard and said, I want you to get out of the car." The second driver reached under his jacket for his gun. As he did, Willy pulled open the door and put his .45 against the back of the guard's head.

"Both of you out, and bring the keys," Nate said. Both men did as they were told. Willy opened the trunk and said, "Get in. On your stomach." Willy tied both men's hands behind their backs. He then tied their feet together and taped their mouths.

"Keep quiet and you'll be fine," Nate said and shut the trunk lid.

Nate and Willy continued down Seventh Avenue to where the second car was parked. Willy acted as if he was crossing the street and Nate tapped on the passenger's window and said "Hey mister."

"What?" the man said.

"Can't hear you," Nate said touching his ear.

"Tough shit, keep going," the man yelled.

Nate shook his head, pulled his .45 with the silencer attached, and said, "Get the fuck out." The driver saw this and went for his gun. Willy pulled on the driver's door, but it was locked and wouldn't open. The driver got his gun out and Nate seeing it, shot through the window. The bullet shattered the window and hit the driver in the head. The passenger was hit with fragments of glass.

"Get out." Nate said. The passenger opened the door and got out. Nate took his gun and walked him to the back of the car. While he was doing that, Willy came around and pulled the dead man out of the car, dragged him to the trunk and threw him in. Willy pulled the rope out and started to tie the dead man's hands.

"What the fuck are you doing? He's dead. He ain't going nowhere," Nate said and shook his head in frustration.

Willy tied the other guard's hands, tapped his mouth and pushed him in the trunk with the dead guard. Nate closed the lid.

"Willy, what the fuck?" Nate said.

"Ain't my fault. I'm nervous," Willy said.

Nate and Willy walked back to where Jacob was parked and told him it was clear. Tony and Jacob walked a short distance down Cutler Street and turned into a small alleyway. There was a door slightly opened to let the hot kitchen air out. It was just the way Nate said it would be. Jacob pulled his gun, opened the door wider and walked into Maddalena's kitchen. He pointed the gun at the chef and said, "Quiet. We're not going to hurt you. Sit over there and keep your mouth shut." The chef sat on a chair near the door. Tony tied his hands to the chair and taped his mouth.

While Tony and Jacob were walking down the alley, Nate and Willy started walking back to Maddalena's front door. Franklin pulled onto Seventh Avenue and slowly drove toward the restaurant. Tony and Jacob waited a few minutes, and then entered the main dining room.

The dining room was long and narrow. It held twelve tables, but only four were occupied. Sitting at the third table from the front, on the left was Delucia and two of his men. Delucia was the first to see Tony approaching and he yelled a warning. Jacob stood facing the other diners, his hat low on his face and his guns pointed at them. At the same time, Nate burst through the front door and pointed his gun at the diners.

On hearing the warning, Delucia and his men went for their guns. Tony shot the man on Delucia's right first. The bullet ripped a hole in his chest and the man fell forward on to the table. Tony's second shot a split second later, hit the other man on Delucia's left in the head. He fell back against the wall, bounced off and crashed onto the table. Delucia froze as Tony pointed the gun at his head. Other diners began to scream. Nate yelled, "No one will get hurt. Keep your seats."

"Put the gun on the table," Tony said. When Delucia placed his gun on the table, Tony picked it up and said, "Get up. Come around here."

Delucia pushed his man and he fell to the floor. He then stepped over him to where Tony was standing. Tony said, "Out."

As Delucia started toward the door, Tony followed behind him. Jacob followed them walking backward as he passed the other diners. Nate stood just inside the doorway. A man sitting at the first table next the door, reached under his coat, pulled a .45, pointed it at Nate and fired. The bullet hit Nate in his upper left arm. At the same time, Nate fired three rounds at the man. Two hit him in the center of his chest. He fell back against the wall and slid down.

Delucia, seeing an opportunity to escape, ran forward trying to get out the door. Nate held his good arm out straight and Delucia ran onto his hand jaw first. The blow knocked Delucia off his feet and he hit the floor on his back. He was unconscious. Nate and Tony grabbed Delucia and dragged him to the car Franklin was driving. They opened the trunk and threw him in. Tony jumped in the backseat and Jacob followed him. Nate and Willy ran to their car as Franklin sped away. Nate followed and Tony's men in the two other cars followed Nate.

From the time Tony and Jacob walked into the dining floor of Maddalena's to putting of Delucia in the car trunk took less than three minutes. It took the police twenty-five minutes to respond to Maddalena's owner's call. When they arrived, there were only the three dead Delucia mobsters and the owner still there. The owner was sitting at a table bent over with his hands on his head. When questioned, he claimed to have seen nothing.

# 51

"DELUCIA'S AWAKE," TONY said.

"I hear him," Jacob said.

Franklin pulled over at a gas station and filled the tank. He gave the attendant five dollars and told him to bring out anything he had in the station to eat. When the attendant left to get the food, Franklin banged his fists on the trunk lid and yelled, "Shut the fuck up or I'll shut you up."

The attendant returned with a bag full of candy bars, nuts and a six-pack of cola and handed them to Franklin.

"That's it?" Franklin said.

"Sorry sir. That all we have," the attendant said.

Franklin handed the man a twenty-dollar bill. "This is for the three other cars behind me. Fill them all up. Keep the change."

"I can't use you X sticker for their cars. Sorry sir," the attendant said.

"They all have X stickers," Franklin said.

"Are you the police?"

"Something like that," Franklin said. "Now, go fill up the cars."

Thank you sir," the attendant said, smiled and went to the pump behind Franklin and started to fill Nate's car with fuel.

Franklin took several candy bars from the bag and gave the rest to Jacob. He grabbed two colas and walked back to Nate's car. Willy rolled down the driver's side window. Franklin handed him the candy and colas. "Follow us when we leave. I'm sending the others home. How's your arm?"

"It's okay. I'll have it looked at later. Where we headed Frank?" Nate asked.

"The Barrens," Franklin said and walked back to the other cars.

"Did he say the Pine Barrens," Willy asked.

"Yeah," Nate answered.

"Why we going there?" Willy asked.

"Do I have to explain every fucking thing to you? What's in the Pine Barrens?" Nate asked.

"Nothing but Pine trees," Willy answered.

"Right!"

"Oh," Willy said and paused said in a low voice, "You know the Jersey Devil's supposed to be in there."

"The only devils in the Barrens tonight will be us," Nate said.

An hour and a half later, Franklin pulled up to a desolate road not too far from Medford Lakes. There was no moon out and it was very dark. Jacob turned on his flashlight and walked to the back of the car.

"Open it Frank," Jacob said.

Frank opened the trunk and jumped back. "That smells awful. He shit himself."

"Out," Jacob said.

Delucia slowly climbed out of the trunk and stood unsteadily in front of Jacob and yelled," Do you fucking Micks know who I am? Who I'm connected too?"

Jacob shined the flashlight on Delucia's face.

"Oh yeah, you're the guy that was in the trunk. Am I right?" Franklin asked looking at Jacob.

"Yeah, he looks like the guy that was in the trunk," Jacob answered.

Who you working for in New York, Delucia?" Tony asked.

"Fuck you. I ain't saying nothin. Just shoot me now and get it over with," Delucia said.

"Why do they always make it so hard?" Franklin said and shot Delucia in the foot.

Delucia screamed and fell to the ground. Franklin shot him in his other foot. Delucia screamed again.

"Easy or hard, Delucia?" Tony said.

Delucia spit at Tony. Jacob shot him in the hand. Delucia was lying on the ground whimpering when Jacob shot him in his other hand. Delucia passed out.

Franklin leaned down and smacked his checks to wake him up, but Delucia stayed unconscious.

"Willy, can you get me a bottle of the cola?" Franklin asked. Willy went to the car, took a bottle out of the car and handed it to Franklin. Franklin opened it and poured the contents on Delucia's head. Delucia sputtered and slowly opened his eyes. Jacob pulled him to a sitting position and leaned him against the trunk of the car.

Franklin stuck his gun in Delucia's crotch. "Now tell me who you're working with in my gang and in New York," Tony said.

"Okay, Okay. Galanti," Delucia said.

"I know that, who else?" Tony asked.

"You killed them all," Delucia yelled.

"Who you working with in New York?"

"Nicolini," Delucia said.

"Motherfucker," Tony yelled.

"Did he give the order to have my father murdered?"

"Yeah."

Tony put his hands on his temples and rubbed them. He reached in his pocket, pulled out a switchblade knife and opened it. Then he leaned down, put the blade on Delucia's neck and said, "My father told me to never waste a bullet on a piece of shit." Tony cut Delucia's throat. Delucia grabbed his throat in a vain attempt to stop the bleeding. As he sat choking and dying, Tony undid his fly and pissed on Delucia.

They carried Delucia's body a few hundred yards into the woods. They leaned him against a tree and Tony put the knife in his right hand and said, "Just in case the animals don't eat him before someone comes by."

"Not much chance of that here, especially in November, "Jacob said.

They all walked back to the car. Jacob sent Nate and Willy home to get Nate's arm looked at, and then drove Tony home. During the ride, Tony was quiet and visibly upset, so Jacob and Franklin didn't say anything. As they pulled up to Tony's home, Jacob asked, "Tony, who's this Nicolini?"

Tony looked at Jacob, shook his head and said, "He's my wife's uncle, the godfather to my daughter Maria.

# 52

"**YOU HAVE EXCHANGED** your promises and given and received rings in my presence. By these acts, you have become husband and wife. According to the laws of the Commonwealth of Pennsylvania, I hereby pronounce that you are husband and wife. You may now seal your union with a kiss," the judge said.

Jimmy took Sally in his arms and kissed her.

"Congratulations Mr. and Mrs. Byrne," the judge said.

"Thank you your Honor, It was a fine ceremony," Jimmy said.

Taking Sally's arm, Jimmy guided her to the office door and into the hall. Jake followed arm in arm with the Maid of Honor, Mary Block. When they were in the hallway, Mary kissed Jimmy and Sally. Jake kissed Sally, shook Jimmy's hand and said, "Congrats brother. You too sis."

"Thank you Jake," Sally said and kissed Jake on the cheek.

"So when are you going to tell Mom and Dad?" Jake asked.

Jimmy blanched and said, "Soon."

Molly busied herself making coffee and arranging the pastries just right on the dish. The girls were coming over and she wanted everything to be perfect. When one of the Danish broke in her hand, she threw it on the table, sat down and started to cry. It wasn't the broken pastry that bothered her. It was that she hadn't heard from Charlie in over two months. Everyone tried to tell her that in battle it was difficult for men to write letters, but this didn't make her feel any better. She reasoned if he was fighting, then he was in extreme danger. She couldn't help thinking the worst had or could happen. It was driving her crazy. She couldn't sleep well, she couldn't concentrate and she was irritable.

Rose walked into the kitchen, saw Molly crying, put her arms around her and said, "What's the matter sweetheart?"

"No letter from Charlie again. I can't help thinking the most horrible things," Molly said and sobbed.

"I know. I'm worried too," Rose said. "Has Jacob heard anything from Senator Stevens?"

"Nothing. I called the Red Cross as well, but no word yet."

"All we can do now is keep praying. How about later we go light a candle for Charlie's safe homecoming? We'll ask Saint Christopher to pray for him," Rose said.

"I would like that," Molly said.

"Catherine's waiting for us and Mercy said she would have coffee with us. Hand me that broken Danish," Rose said.

Molly picked the two pieces of the Danish off the table and handed them to Rose. Rose placed them on the plate and said," I'll eat that one."

Catherine and Mercy were sitting at the table when Rose and Molly entered the dining room. Rose placed the platter of pastries on the table and Molly filled the cups she earlier put on the table, with coffee.

"That smells divine," Catherine said. "I'm so happy they took coffee off the ration list last year.

"It's Red Circle coffee. I ground it myself in the store," Molly said.

"Ladies, I want to say a prayer for Charlie," Rose said. "In the name of the Father, Son and Holy Ghost." The other women did the same.

> *"Almighty and eternal God,*
> *those who take refuge in you will be glad*
> *and forever will shout for joy.*
> *Protect Charlie as he discharges his duties.*
> *Protect him with the shield of your strength*
> *and keep him safe from all evil and harm.*
> *May the power of your love enable him to return home*
> *in safety, that with all who love him,*
> *they may ever praise you for your loving care.*
> *We ask this through Christ our Lord. Amen"*

Jake, Franklin and Jacob walked into the room while Rose was reciting her prayer for Charlie. They bowed their heads until she was finished and then walked over to the table.

"Well, look at this, it's the old hens club meeting again," Jake said as he reached to pick up a pastry. Rose hit his hand with a fork.

"Oww, that hurt," Jake yelled.

"It was meant too," Rose said as she picked the tray up and held it out for Jake to take a pastry. "Take the broken one."

"Where's Jimmy?" Jacob asked.

"I don't know," Mercy said.

"That's odd, he told Jake he wanted to see us in the dining room," Jacob said.

"What about? Molly asked.

Jake took a bite of the Danish and scrunched his shoulders, indicating he didn't know. He swallowed and said, "I know you aren't used to having men at the hen's club meeting, but can we sit down?" Jake pulled the end chair out and sat down. Jacob took a chair next to Molly. Franklin sat next to Catharine and took her hand in his.

"How are Uncle Tony and Carmella?" Mercy asked Jacob.

"They seem okay. There are a few things Tony has to work out, but I think they'll be okay," Jacob said.

"I miss Pop Pop Amato," Mercy said.

"We all do," Jacob said.

"Any letters from Charlie?" Franklin asked. Catherine kicked him on his ankle indicating that this was not a good subject.

"No. Nothing," Molly said tears welling up in her eyes.

"There will be. I remember when I was on the frontline. I didn't have time to take a crap let alone write a letter," Franklin said. Catherine kicked him again.

"What?" Franklin asked looking at Catherine. She mouthed back, "Shut up."

"How about those Eagles? Jacob said trying to change the subject.

"You mean Steagles," Jake said.

"That was last year. Now the Steelers and Eagles are back playing on separate teams." Jacob corrected Jake.

Jimmy and Sally walked into the room just as Jacob was giving Jake a history lesson about Philadelphia baseball and football. Jimmy walked over to his mother, kissed her, kissed Rose, Catherine and then Mercy.

"I think you all know Sally," Jimmy said. Everyone said they did.

"I wanted to have you all in one place so I could tell you something. That way I only have to say it once and take any flack you want to give me," Jimmy said. Jimmy paused then continued, "Sally and I have known each other for a long time. This year I discovered that I love her dearly. And, more surprisingly, she loves me. So yesterday we got married."

Everyone in the room, except Jake, sat open-jawed starring at the couple.

"Where? Where did you get married," Jacob said.

"City hall."

"I know you guys are mad, but it was my idea so be mad at me, not Sally," Jimmy said.

Molly got up from the table and walked over to the couple. She looked at Jimmy, smiled and said," We're not mad. Just surprised. I'm happy if you are, Jimmy."

"I'm very happy."

Mercy then hugged Sally and said, "Welcome to the Byrne family, for better or worse."

"Isn't any of your brats going to get married in a church, the proper way," Rose said and then went to hug Jimmy and Sally.

Each person hugged and kissed the couple and gave their congratulations."

Now that that is over with, we women have a lot of planning to do," Rose said.

"For what?" Jake asked.

"The party, Rose replied. Now shoo. You men are not invited."

"Jimmy and Sally started to leave and Rose stopped them. "Not you Sally. You're a Byrne woman now. You're with us."

Sally walked back to the table, smiled and took a seat. Jimmy, Franklin, Jacob and Jake left the room. As Jake walked out, he said in a loud voice, "Cluck, Cluck, Cluck."

The phone rang in Jacob's office just as he and Franklin walked through the door. Jacob picked up the phone, "Jacob here."

"Jacob, its Tony. Can you meet with me this afternoon? I need your help again."

# 53

TONY ASKED JACOB to bring Franklin, Mike and Grady to the meeting. They arrived at Tony's home at 4pm and were shown to Tony's office by a guard. Tony greeted each man with a kiss on the cheek. He offered them a drink and they all accepted. Tony poured four whiskeys and a wine for himself.

"To your heath," Tony said.

Each man clicked glasses and Tony said, "Please sit. Thank you for coming. I've asked so much of you I hesitate to ask this one last thing."

"Tony, come on. You're family and all you've done for us, so please ask," Jacob said.

"I have a big problem. Don Nicolini, the man behind my father's murder, the man who tried to kidnap my daughters, is still a danger to my family. I've explained this to Carmella and she understands. She's furious with her uncle. I'm bound by our tradition to take action against this man for killing my father. My father cannot rest peacefully unless this man pays with his life. Problem is, he's a boss of a family represented on the council," Tony explained.

"So your rules say you can't kill him?" Franklin said.

"True, but I have talked to Don Belotti and Don Rossetti and they promise to stand up for me with the commission. I believe this will be enough. The problem is, they say the assassins must come from outside my family and not be Italian. I cannot be directly involved in the murder of a boss," Tony said.

"And that's where we come in," Jacob said.

"That's where you all come in. I need your help and this needs to be done personally by the four of you. I cannot afford to have strangers or people I don't have close relationships with do this."

"Tony, we're here for you," Jacob said.

"Don't be so fast to accept Jacob. Don Nicolini will be no easy mark. He has a small army of men. He has survived his sixty years by being cautious. This will be dangerous."

"Gerardo was like a second father to me. I feel the pain of his loss and I miss him. I'm in, but I'll let the others speak for themselves," Jacob said.

Of course, I'm in," Franklin said.

Mike nodded his affirmative and Grady said, "Don Amato told me an old Italian saying once. It really helped me after Brian was murdered. He said all is forgiven to those who take revenge in the pursuit of justice. I will never forget that. I'm in."

"Thank you," Tony said and stood up. "I'm going to thank you the Irish way." Tony walked to each man and shook his hand. "Now, if you don't mind, I'll go check on our lunch."

As Tony was walking out of the room, Jacob said, "I'll come with you. I want to check on Jake."

"Jake came with you?" Tony asked.

"Yes, he wanted to see Maria. To be sure, she's okay, he says. I think he's a bit smitten with Maria."

"She's been talking a lot about him also. Ah young love," Tony said.

When Tony and Jacob walked into the kitchen, Maria was showing Jake how to make meatballs. He had several, on a piece of wax paper that were more ragged ovals than balls. Maria was laughing and Carmella was by the stove stirring the sauce.

Maria jumped up when she saw Jacob and said, "Uncle Jacob." Then she kissed him on the cheek. Jacob walked over to Carmella and kissed her on the cheek.

"That smells incredible," Jacob said.

"Lunch will be ready in thirty minutes, that is, if Maria starts making the meatballs herself," Carmela said and laughed.

"I was just checking. Let us know when you're ready, "Tony said. Carmella nodded.

On the way back to Tony's office, Jacob said, "Tony, that saying your Father told Grady. What was it?" Jacob thought for a few seconds. "All is forgiven to those who take revenge in the pursuit of justice. I never heard that before. How do you say it in Italian?"

"I never heard it before either. He probably made it up. He was always making up his own sayings and telling people they were ancient Roman or Italian proverbs," Tony said.

Jacob smiled and said, "Well, I like it."

Forty-five minutes later, everyone was sitting at the dining room table enjoying an Italian feast.

"Jake, how'd you make out making those meatballs?" Jacob asked.

Jake held up a misshapen meatball in his spoon. "Pretty good I think." Everyone laughed. "So, Pop, if it's okay with Aunt Carmella and Uncle Tony, can I take Maria to the movies? She really wants to see Meet Me in St Louis."

"Sure, as long as you behave yourself Jake," Carmella said. Jake turned red. "I'm kidding Jake. How about you? What movie do you want to see?"

"Well, Captain America's playing, but it's not about me. It's about Maria," Jake said.

"I like this kid. He knows what's important," Carmella said smiling.

Jacob, who was in the middle of eating a meatball, put his fork up and nodded. He swallowed and said," Okay, "I'll send a car for you later."

"No need, I'll send him home with one of my men when the movie's over," Tony said.

If it's okay, we need to leave now. The show starts in fifteen minutes," Jake said.

"If it gets done early, maybe we can stay and see Captain America. It's the second feature," Maria said.

"And I like this girl. She knows what's important," Jacob said. "Do you need a ride?"

"No, it's just two blocks away. We'll walk," Maria said.

"Take Mario with you," Tony said.

"Do I have to have a guard?" Maria said.

"I'll take care of her," Jake said.

Not wanting to make Jake feel bad, Tony said, "Okay. No guard."

When Maria and Jake left, Tony walked to the door and told Mario, "Follow them, but not so close they see you. Wait until the movie is done and follow them back."

After lunch was finished, Tony, Jacob, Franklin, Mike and Brian resumed their planning. It was decided that Nicolini's office, in the heart of Little Italy, was too well guarded. His home in New Rochelle was out because his wife, daughter and two grandchildren lived there. Nicolini often ate at different Little Italy restaurants but these were too risky as well. They finally decided that their best opportunity would be an apartment where Nicolini kept his mistress. During the week, he stayed at the apartment. On most weekends, he went to the New Rochelle home.

"I've met with him in the apartment before. He keeps guards in the lobby and back entrance but none in or outside the apartment. It's on the fifth floor and there is only one other apartment on the floor," Tony said.

"Fire escape?" Franklin asked.

"No, just the elevator and back stairwell. That's where the guards hang out," Tony said.

"We've done something like this before. I think we can come up with a plan," Jacob said. A picture of George Graham holding Angelo Adone in the air by his neck until he died passed through his mind. He missed George.

"Grady, go to New York and check out that building. I want to do this fast," Jacob said.

"Sure. I'll go in the morning."

"Make it tonight," Jacob said.

"Anything else we need to know, Tony?" Franklin asked.

"As I hear more I'll let you know," Tony said.

"Tony, why are Rossetta and Belotti backing you on this? Jacob asked.

"I'd like to think it was because they were friends with my Pop. But, what they really want is control of north New Jersey. When Nicolini is gone they can take Jersey and it's one less powerful man they have to deal with."

Jacob patted Tony on the shoulder and said, "You watch out for the family and in a few days this will be all behind you. I promise," Jacob said.

# 54

JAKE PAID FOR the tickets and he and Maria walked into the movie theater. The movie was about to start so they bought some popcorn and a couple of sodas from the soda machine. Jake put a nickel in the slot and the cup dropped and started to fill with cola.

"When I was little I use to go to the Wishart movie theater around the corner from Mercy Row. They had a machine like this one. One time I stuck my hand up the dispenser and was able to pull out about fifteen cups," Jake said.

"You must have been a little stinker," Maria said.

"I was, but that's another story. I took the cups home to my mother to show her. I was sure she was going to be proud of me. Instead, she yelled at me, took me back to the movie and made me give the cups back. And, I had to apologize to the manager."

"You must have been mortified," Maria said.

"I might have been, if I knew what that meant," Jake said.

"It means you were embarrassed."

"I wasn't embarrassed. I was pissed off. Next time I went to the movie I took thirty cups," Jake said and laughed.

Maria guided Jake to the middle of the last row of seats. The news film that played before every movie was showing scenes from the battle of Peleliu in the South Pacific.

"My brother Charlie's somewhere over there. I hope he's not on that island. Looks horrible," Jake said.

"I know," Maria said.

"Hey, why are we sitting way back here anyway? It harder to see, "Jake said.

"I like it back here. It's dark and nobody wants to sit here. See, it's empty, except for that couple kissing over there," Maria said as she took Jake's hand in hers.

"Do you sit in the last row a lot?" Jake asked.

"This is my first time," Maria answered.

Jake and Maria stayed for both movies. When Captain America finished, the theater lights came on. Maria took a handkerchief from her bag and said, "Let me get that lipstick off your mouth."

"You could do with a touchup yourself," Jake said smiling.

Maria took a small silver compact from her purse and reapplied her lipstick. "Okay. Ready."

Jake and Maria left the theater hand in hand. When they were a hundred yards or so down the street, Mario started following them. The walk was short and as they turned onto Maria's street, they noticed a stranger standing at their door. He was holding a Browning rifle.

"Maria, go back the way we came. Mario's following us. Tell him to hurry. Don't come back with him," Jake whispered.

"But...."

"Do it. Go," Jake said urgently

Maria started running back down the street. Jake hid behind a parked car. Crouching, he quietly ran up the street toward Maria's house. The man had come back down the steps and was standing on the sidewalk facing the door. The door was open.

Jake leaped from between two parked cars and hit the man square in the back with a body blow. The man went forward hitting his face on the steps. There was a crunching sound of bone breaking. He grabbed the man's head and smashed into the steps five more times. Jake picked up the rifle and searched the man for a handgun. He found it and put it in his waistband.

By this time, Mario was halfway up the street to the house. Jake put his finger to his lips indicating that Mario be quite. Mario slowed down and came up to Jake.

"How many?" Mario whispered.

"Don't know. Where are the other guards?" Jake said.

"Dead, I guess," Mario said.

"We need to go in," Jake said.

"Tony's got a safe room," Mario said.

"Where is it?"

"Second floor in the back," Mario answered.

"Okay, let's go," Jake said.

Mario held him back and said, "I'll go first."

"Take this," Jake said and handed him the Browning.

Mario walked into the foyer and saw one of his men lying in a pool of blood. Jake followed him. There were voices coming from the second floor and Jake hoped that Tony, Carmella and Sophia had been able to get into the safe room. Mario motioned to Jacob to take the backstairs and he would go up the front stairs.

Mario waited several minutes to be sure Jake was at the back stairway and then he slowly walked up the front stairs. The voices got louder as he got closer. The men were arguing about how to get into the room. *The Amatos must be in the safe room*, Mario thought with relief.

The back stairway was adjacent to the safe room and it had a door on the second floor. Jake couldn't open the door with the men there, so he crouched just inside the doorway. Mario lifted the rifle, stepped out into the hall and rapidly started firing the Browning.

One man fell back against the door and slid down leaving a trail of blood. The other three fired back at Mario. Mario quickly moved back to cover. The three men frantically looked for a way get out of the hallway. There were two doors, one on the left and one on the right. While the other two continued to shoot at Mario, one of the men opened the door on the left. It was a closet. The man motioned another man to open the door on the right. All three continued to shoot at Mario as they lined up to go through the door.

The man opened the door and Jake fired twice into the man's torso. The man fell forward toward Jake. Jake pushed him up and over himself. The man tumbled down the steps. The second man was still shooting at Mario. Mario fell to the ground, leaned out and fired the Browning. He hit the third man and he went down. The second man turned and rushed into the stairway running into Jake. Both Jake and the man toppled over each other as they fell down the steps.

They landed on the first man's body, with Jake on top. Both Jake and the man had lost their guns during the fall. Jake started hitting the man in the face. The man pushed back, but Jake threw his weight on him so he couldn't move. Jake hit the man again and continued to hit him until Mario came down the steps and said, "He's dead kid."

Jake looked at Mario and then the man and stood up, "Where's Maria?"

"Safe," Mario said.

"The family?" Jake asked.

"Safe."

# 55

BECAUSE OF THE attack on the Amatos, the timetable for the Nicolini hit became more urgent. Grady had returned from his surveillance of Nicolini in New York City and confirmed that the apartment was the best choice for the hit. Because Tony wanted to keep his involvement secret, Franklin, Grady, Mike and Jacob would do the job alone.

Two o'clock the afternoon of the day after the attack on Tony's family, Jacob pulled a 1941 black Cadillac sedan in front of his Broad Street home, parked, and waited. Franklin was the first to arrive. Ten minutes later, Grady and Mike parked behind them. Mike opened the trunk, took out fifteen ammunition clips and three hand grenades and put them in the trunk of the Caddy.

"Pays to know people at the Frankford Arsenal," Mike told Grady.

"Last time I used one of those babies it almost killed me," Grady said pointing at a hand grenade.

"I remember. You couldn't sit straight for a week. Don't worry. If we need them, I'll pull the pin," Mike said and laughed.

Two hours later, they were on the Upper East Side of Manhattan, where Nicolini's apartment was located. Jacob parked the car a block away and the four men found a delicatessen nearby. They took seats at a booth in the rear of the Deli. A waiter wearing a pristine white apron tied around the waist came to the table and asked, "What can I get you?"

"Four coffees to start," Jacob answered. "Grady, what do you want?"

"I'll have a hoagie, no mayo just oil," Grady told the waiter.

"What's a hoagie?" the waiter said.

"A hoagie. You know! Lunchmeat on a long Italian roll, lettuce, tomato, onions," Grady said.

"You mean a hero sandwich," the waiter said.

"What's a hero? Never heard of it." Grady asked.

The waiter rolled his eyes and said, "Lunchmeat on a long roll, with lettuce, tomato and onions."

"It's the same fucking thing. Give me one of those," Grady said.

"We don't sell heroes. We're a Jewish delicatessen," the waiter said.

"Why the fuck did you tell me about it then?" Grady said as the waiter just looked at him tapping his pen on the order pad.

"All right. I'll take a ham sandwich," Grady said.

The waiter looked up to the ceiling and said, "We're a Jewish delicatessen," and waited.

Grady looked at Jacob then Franklin and said, "Is this guy fucking with me?"

Franklin quickly asked the waiter, "What do you recommend?"

"The Rueben," the waiter replied.

"What's in a Rueben?" Grady asked.

"Who gives a shit? Just give us four of them," Franklin said to the waiter.

As the waiter left to place the order he mumbled, "Fucking tourists."

The deli was located on the corner of Seventy-Second Street and First Avenue. It was close to Nicolini's apartment, which was located at Seventy-third Street and First Avenue. At precisely 5pm, Grady and Mike left the deli and walked up First Avenue. When they reached Seventy-Third Street, they found a small restaurant, took a table by the window and waited for Nicolini to show up. Jacob and Franklin drove the car to Seventy-third and York Avenue, parked, and waited.

Jacob sat in the car staring out of the front window saying nothing for the first ten minutes.

"What's up, Jacob?" Franklin asked.

Jacob turned and looked at Franklin and said, "Nothing. Why?"

"You're sitting there looking like your trying to take a crap but you can't, Franklin said.

"Sorry. I was thinking about Charlie."

"Nothing from the senator yet?" Franklin asked.

"No. Nobody seems to know where he is. Molly called the Red Cross, but they can't find anything out either. Frank, I'm getting worried," Jacob said.

"He'll be fine. Things get confusing in battle. It's just the way it is," Franklin said trying to be encouraging, but he was beginning to believe something very bad had happened to Charlie.

"I hope you're right Frank."

*Me too*, Franklin thought.

At 8:07pm, Mike walked up to Jacob's car, opened the back door and got in. "He's here. Just came with four men. They walked in to the building together. Looks like Tony was right," Mike said.

Grab the ammo," Franklin said.

Mike opened the trunk and took out the three hand grenades and the clips. He handed a grenade and several clips to Franklin and then to Jacob. He put the rest in his pockets.

"Okay. Let's go," Jacob said. The three men walked back to the restaurant where Grady was waiting.

"Here," Mike said and handed Grady four clips for his .45 Colt and a hand grenade. "Just in case."

"Thanks. See you in a few," Grady said and walked out of the restaurant, crossed the street and walked down Seventy-third Street to a small alleyway at the rear of Nicolini's building. He took out a small handheld crowbar, forced a window open and climbed through.

The basement of the building had a musty odor and was pitch black. Grady opened his lighter and lit it. A minute later, Mike dropped down from the window and said, "Everything okay?"

"So far," Grady said and started walking. Mike followed him. Grady opened a door and light spilled into the room from an overhead light in the hallway.

"The back doorway should be just above us. That's where Tony said two of the bodyguards hang out," Grady said.

"Where's the elevator?" Mike asked.

"Middle of the building. The other bodyguards stay at the front door."

"Right. Let's find the elevator," Mike said.

Mike and Grady pushed the button and waited for the elevator to reach the basement. They entered the elevator car and Mike pushed one. When the doors opened, Mike said, "Ready?"

"Yeah. Let's go," Grady said as he pulled an eight-inch stiletto. Mike did the same.

Mike and Grady walked down the hall to the back entrance. As they approached the door, they saw a man sitting in a chair off to the side.

"Hey buddy, where's the front door? We're lost," Mike said as he and Grady continued to walk toward the man.

"It's the other way," the man said and stood up.

Mike and Grady continued to walk toward the man. They were about fifteen feet from the man when Mike started to run toward him. The man put his hand in his suit jacket and tried to pull his gun. Mike hit him full force before he could get his gun out. The man fell back against the wall with a thud. Mike put the knife at the man's throat and said, "Not a fucking word," and he pushed the knife slightly in so the man could feel it. The man said nothing.

"Where's the other guy?" Mike said.

"Pissing," the man said hoarsely.

"Sit down," Mike ordered.

The man did as Mike said.

Mike pulled his .45, put muzzle on the man's forehead and said, "When your friend comes back, you say nothing. Just let him walk up to you. If you even grunt, I'll blow your head off. Got it?

The man nodded yes. Mike and Grady stood behind him out of site from the hallway.

Fifteen minutes after Mike followed Grady down Seventy-third Street, Franklin and Jacob, paid the restaurant bill and walked across the street to the main entrance of Nicolini's apartment building. They expected to see Grady and Mike, but instead, there was a doorman.

Jacob walked up to the doorway and said, "We're here to see Mr. Casey.

"We don't have no Mr. Casey in our building sir," the doorman said.

"Is this fourteen oh one, First Avenue?" Jacob asked.

"No sir. That's down the block," the doorman said pointing down the street.

As the doorman pointed, Franklin put his gun to the man's side and said, "Be quiet. I'm not going to hurt you unless you make me. I want you to act like we belong here. When you open the door, you go in before us. I'll have my gun on you and if you say anything you're dead."

The doorman did as Franklin ordered and opened the door. He started to lead Jacob and Franklin to the elevator. Franklin dropped back a few paces and allowed Jacob to go before him. As they passed the guards, Jacob turned and smashed the first guard in the face with his fist. The guard staggered back and Jacob followed his stiletto in his hand.

Seeing this, the second guard started for his gun. Before he could draw it, Franklin shoved his knife in the man's throat. The guard gurgled as Franklin pulled the knife to the right severing the man's windpipe and carotid artery. The guard fell to the floor, blood spurting from his throat.

Jacob pushed the first guard to the wall and stabbed the man in the heart. The man stood upright for a few seconds and then crumbled to the floor.

"Where's a closet?" Jacob yelled at the doorman, who was staring at him wide-eyed. The doorman didn't answer.

Where's the fucking closet!" Jacob yelled.

"That door over there," the doorman pointed to a door behind a desk.

"Open it," Jacob said.

The doorman walked to the door, took his key out, opened it and stood back. "In," Jacob ordered. The doorman walked into the room.

Franklin dragged the man he had killed to the closet. Jacob did the same.

"Give me your belt," Jacob said to the doorman.

The doorman took off his pants belt and handed it to Jacob. Jacob tied his hands behind his back. Seeing a scarf on a hanger

Jacob grabbed it, told the man to lie down and tied the doorman's feet together.

"You have any tape or something I can gag you with?" Jacob said.

"In the custodian's tool box, over there. Please mister, don't gag me. I won't be able to breathe," the doorman pleaded.

"Use your nose. Believe me, this is much better than the alternative," Jacob said, pointing to the two dead guards. He walked over to the box and opened it. There was a roll of gray duct tape in the box. He took it and wrapped it around the man's head covering his mouth. He was careful not to block the man's nose.

"Listen to me. Stay quite. Don't try to get lose and you'll be all right. After an hour, you can do whatever you have to. Understand? One hour," Jacob said. The man shook his head that he did. Jacob took the man's wallet, took out his driver's license and dropped the wallet on the floor.

Jacob held up the driver's license and said, "I know where you live. You know nothing. Right?"

The doorman nodded yes, and Jacob left the closet, pulled the door shut behind him and locked it with the doorman's key. He then locked the front door to the building.

"Where the fuck is Grady and Mike? They should have been here," Franklin said.

Frankie Piccolo pulled his pants up, buttoned his fly and fastened his belt. Then he rolled up his copy of Esquire magazine and put it in his back pocket. He took his suit coat from the hook, slipped it on and walked out of the stall. *Whew. Wouldn't want to be the next person to come in here*, Frankie thought.

Frankie walked to the sink looked at himself in the mirror, patted a few hairs down and walked out of the men's room. As he came closer to the backdoor, he saw Joey Greco sitting in the chair. "Hey Joey. You gotta see the babes in Esquire this month," Frankie said as he pulled the magazine from his back pocket. "There's one with the biggest bazoo—" Frankie was interrupted when Mike pushed his stiletto into his throat. Frankie's eye opened wide with surprise as blood pumped from his neck. Frankie dropped the magazine and collapsed.

"What do we do with this one?" Grady said pointing to Joey.

"Tie him up," Mike answered. "Make it tight."

Grady and Mike walked to the elevators and saw Jacob and Franklin waiting.

"Everyone ready?" Jacob asked and everyone nodded yes. "Let's go."

# 56

HAVING JUST WALKED up five flights of stairs, Jacob, Franklin, Mike and Grady paused on the fifth floor stairwell to catch their breath.

"Tell me again, why we couldn't use the elevator," Grady said.

"What's the matter Grady? You been eating too many soft pretzels?" Mike said and smiled.

"What's my motto Grady," Jacob asked.

"Let's see." Grady paused and said, "The boss is always right."

"Better safe than sorry," Jacob reminded Grady, "We don't know who's in the hall, and I don't want to be in a little metal box if that who has a gun pointed at us."

Franklin opened the door a crack and looked out to the right. Not seeing anyone, he opened it wider and looked to the left. "It's clear. No one's in the hallway." Franklin walked out into the hallway and the others followed.

There were only two apartment doors to the left and two to the right of the elevators. Jacob presumed that each apartment had two entrances, one for the help and the other for the owners. He chose the one that had a more elaborate door. It was possible that Nicolini was sitting in the living room, which most assuredly would be near the owner's doorway. If he was, they could make the hit and be back down the steps in minutes.

Jacob motioned Mike to kick in the door, and then thought better of that decision. Instead, he tried the doorknob and it was unlocked.

He slowly pushed the door open and saw that the entrance opened into a foyer. There were three open doorways, one to the right, one to the left and one straight ahead. Jacob peeked into the doorway on the left. It was the living room and no one was there.

He moved to the door on the right and before he could look into the room, he heard a chopping sound. *It must be the kitchen*, Jacob thought. He motioned to Frank to get behind him and he tiptoed across to the other side of the door, taking a quick glance in the room as he did.

Mike and Grady readied themselves to rush into the room. On Jacob's signal, Grady ran crouched into the kitchen. Nicolini was standing behind a table cutting onions. Grady fired twice, but missed. Mike came in the room running toward Nicolini. He fired three shots, but Nicolini had dropped behind the table and Mike's bullets missed their mark. Nicolini pulled a gun hidden under the table, and fired twice at Mike, hitting him once. Mike fell to the floor and rolled left behind a cabinet.

Nicolini, moved around the table trying to get a clear shot at Grady. At the same time, Franklin entered the room and fired twice. One bullet hit Nicolini in the arm and he dropped his gun. Jacob came in the room and fired three times hitting Nicolini all three times in the torso. Nicolini was still standing, the New York skyline showing through the large window behind his bulky body. His eyes opened wide as Grady, Jacob and Franklin emptied their clips into him.

The force of the bullets threw Nicolini backward into the window. The window broke with the force and Nicolini tumbled out. Jacob rushed to the window looked out and started laughing. He motioned the others to look, while he saw to Mike. Jacob helped Mike up.

"How you doing Mike?" Jacob asked.

"It's not bad. Grazed my arm," Mike said.

"Come on, you gotta see this," Jacob said as he helped Mike up and to the window.

Grady and Franklin were smiling when Mike looked out to see Nicolini hanging by his shirt that had been snared by a light for a sign. The sign was for a butcher shop and was in the shape of a pig. Mike smiled and pulled his head back in the room.

Franklin was still laughing when he heard a high-pitched scream as a women ran into the room and started hitting and scratching him. She raked her nails across his face leaving four bleeding scratches. The woman kept hitting Franklin, as Jacob, Grady and Mike stood laughing. Finally, Grady grabbed the women from behind, holding her arms at her side. She kicked out with her feet hitting Franklin in the groin.

"Put her in here," Jacob yelled as he opened the pantry door. Grady grabbed and tossed the woman into the room. Jacob closed the door behind her and propped a chair against it. She continued to scream and yell incomprehensible words while banging on the door.

"Let's get out of here," Franklin said still holding his aching privates.

All four men started toward the main doorway when they heard sirens. Jacob ran back to the window Nicolini fell out of and looked out. A police car had just pulled up. The officer got out of the car and looked up at Nicolini hanging from the sign. Another police car screeched to a halt. Both officers talked to each other and then ran to the front door of the apartment house.

"We gotta go," Jacob yelled. "Up to the roof."

Jacob led the way to the stairwell as the rest followed him. They ran up a flight of stairs and saw a door that opened to the roof. They ran onto the roof toward York Avenue where the car was parked. When they reach the last building, they tried to open the heavy metal door that led to the stairs. It was locked. Grady pounded on the door trying to force it open, but it was too strong for a person to knock down.

"Jacob, give me that hand grenade you have," Grady said. Jacob handed him the grenade.

Grady took the one he had out of his pocket and yelled, "Get behind the wall," Then he took the pins out of both grenades, let the safety loose, threw the grenades against to door and jumped behind the wall.

The explosion was deafening, and it did the job. The door was hanging off its hinges as all four men ran down the stairwell and into the hallway. As they approached the front entrance to the building, the doorman was standing in front of his desk motioning to them to stop. Franklin straight-armed him and the man flew over the desk and tumbled backward to the floor.

Franklin, Jacob, Grady and Mike pushed through the revolving doorway, and ran to their car. Jacob started the car and floored the accelerator. The big engine roared and the tires screeched leaving black skid marks on the asphalt as they sped off down York Avenue.

As soon as Jacob arrived in Philadelphia, he drove to Doctor Damiano's home to have him take care of Mike's gunshot wound. Don Amato had introduced Jacob to Damiano years before, and since then, Franklin and Jacob had used him numerous times. He was dependable, competent and, most of all, he kept his mouth shut, for a fee.

"Jesus Christ that hurts," Mike yelled.

"Sorry Mike," Doctor Damiano said. "If we were in my office I'd give you something for the pain."

"It's okay doc. Just saying." Mike grunted.

"Looks like a pretty deep graze. There's no bullet in you," Damiano said as he probed Mike's wound.

"Good," Mike grunted again.

"Mike, just lay back and try to sleep. I have to go to my office and get some sutures. I'll get something for the pain as well."

"What about infection doc?" Mike asked.

"I cleaned it well. You should be okay. I'll have you home for breakfast."

After Jacob dropped Mike off at Doctor Damiano's, he, Franklin and Grady drove home. All they could do now was to wait and see if Belotti and Rossetti would be able to smooth things over with the commission. If not, their biggest war was about to start.

# 57

**WHEN HE ARRIVED** home from New York, Jacob found Molly sitting alone in their dark living room. Her red-rimmed eyes and the crumpled tissues on the table told him she had been crying. Among the tissues were a number of old letters from Charlie.

"Did you hear from Charlie?" Jacob said urgently, expecting bad news.

"No. Nothing," Molly said and burst out crying.

Jacob took a second to quiet his pounding heart and said, "Oh God. I thought..."

"It's been two and a half months, Jacob. We haven't heard anything. What if he's a prisoner, or hurt somewhere. What if he's...," Molly put her head in her hands and cried.

"Don't say that. He's fine," Jacob said, trying to comfort Molly but only half believing it himself.

Jacob walked over to the table where he kept the whiskey and poured two doubles. He handed Molly one and said," Take this, it'll help you sleep."

"I can't drink this. It tastes awful," Molly said.

"Hold your nose then. It'll help. I promise," Jacob said.

Molly took a sip and said, "How can you drink this? It's disgusting."

"Drink it down in one gulp," Jacob said and clinked his glass against Molly's glass. "To Charlie and his safe homecoming."

"To Charlie," Molly said and drank the glass of whiskey. She made a contorted face and said hoarsely, "Oh my god that burns."

"One more and we'll go to bed," Jacob said as he poured another two shots in Molly's glass.

The whiskey worked and helped Molly fall asleep, but Jacob tossed and turned all night. Every time he dozed off, he was awakened by terrible nightmares where he saw Charlie being tortured by Japanese soldiers. Finally, at 6am, he just decided to get up and start his day early. It would be a busy one and maybe it would take his mind off unknown possibilities. Jimmy and Sally's wedding party started at 7pm and he had to check with Grady about security. With the New York Commission's actions for the Nicolini hit still in limbo, Jacob didn't want to take any chances.

When Jacob walked into the kitchen he found Rose and Mercy were already sitting at the table. Mercy got up, poured Jacob a cup of coffee and set it on the table.

"So why are you two up so early?" Jacob asked.

"Gerry had a fretful night. He woke me up at three and I just got him back to sleep," Mercy said.

"Is he sick?" Jacob asked.

"No. He's teething still," Mercy replied.

"How about you Mrs. Sunshine?" Jacob asked Rose, who was frowning.

"And what do you mean by that?" Rose quipped.

"Rose, you're sitting there looking like someone stuck a hot poker up...," Jacob paused, thought for a second and said, "on your back."

Rose gave Jacob a small smile and said, "I'm sorry. It's just there is so much to do for the party tonight. And..." Rose stopped talking for a minute, rubbed her eyes and said," It's Charlie. I'm so worried about him.

"I know Rose; we all feel the same, but we have to be positive. He's okay and he's just too busy to write," Jacob said.

"You're right Papa. I feel it in my bones. Charlie's okay," Mercy said.

Rose made the sign of the cross, Mercy and Jacob followed suit.

"Today's Jimmy and Sally's day and I'm going to do my part to make their party the best we have ever had," Rose said, regaining her composure.

Jacob raised his coffee cup and said, "To Jimmy and Sally."

Rose and Mercy clinked Jacob's cup and said simultaneously, "To Jimmy and Sally."

Three hours later, Jacob was in his office with Franklin, and Grady.

"Guards Grady?" Jacob asked.

"Yeah. I got them on six-hour shifts. Good men," Grady answered. Got the front and back covered and two more men in a car in front of the house"

"Good. Be sure the guys get some food during the party," Jacob said. Grady nodded.

"Anything from Tony yet," Grady asked Jacob.

"No I talked to him earlier and he hasn't heard anything. Doesn't expect too, until later today," Jacob said.

"How about Mike? He okay?" Franklin asked.

"Doc says he's good. He let Mike sleep at his house last night to keep an eye on him," Jacob said.

"Hope he makes it tonight," Grady said.

"Mike! Are you shitting me? He wouldn't miss a free meal and drinks if his arm fell off," Franklin said laughing.

"What do we do now?" Franklin asked.

"We wait," Jacob said.

Rose walked into Molly's room to wake her to help with the cooking. She found Molly staring into her mirror.

"As pretty as ever, Molly," Rose said.

"Do you really think so? I feel so old," Molly said.

"If you want to see old, look at me. You're still as pretty as you were when I first met you," Rose said.

"I see you've been kissing the Blarney Stone this morning Rose," Molly said and gave her a half smile.

"Come, on we need to get started cooking. Mercy's waiting for us. Jimmy and Sally said they would watch the baby while we cook," Rose said.

Molly finished brushing her hair and followed Rose to the kitchen. Mercy was sitting at the table peeling potatoes. Molly picked up a peeler and started to help.

"Morning Mama. I'd kiss you but I'm all potatoey," Mercy said.

"Good morning honey. How many pounds we peeling?" Molly said.

"Thirty pounds, around," Rose said. Mercy and Molly groaned.

"Do we really need that much potato salad?" Molly asked.

"I hope it's enough. You know how everyone loves my potato salad," Rose said.

Jimmy walked in the kitchen, with Bonnie following him, just as Rose proclaimed everyone loved her potato salad and said, "What's not to love? Mayo, bacon, celery, potatoes, hard boiled eggs, ummm ummm."

"Some chopped onions, a bit of vinegar, salt, sugar and my secret ingredient, mustard," Rose said.

While Rose was busy correcting Jimmy, Bonnie slowly got closer to the counter where Rose has just sliced the meat for the hot roast beef sandwiches she was serving for the party. Bonnie sniffed the air, then stood upright on her back paws and grabbed two slices of beef, with her mouth, from a platter. Just as Bonnie was about to eat the meat, Rose saw her and yelled, "You get away from that. No, no, no, bad dog."

Bonnie looked at Rose with her sad cocker spaniel eyes, as if to say, "I'm sorry." She tilted her head to the side with the roast beef still in her mouth.

"Oh, go ahead, eat it," Rose said. "Jimmy, can you please put Bonnie in the yard with the other dogs."

Jimmy walked over and took Bonnie's collar in one hand and then grabbed three slices of beef for himself and ran Bonnie out of the kitchen, and yelled, "It's better with the gravy."

Tony Amato had his consigliere Debello call Jacob to ask to have a meeting before the party started at 7pm. He requested that Mike, Frank and Grady be there as well. Amato was the last to arrive. He had deposited his wife Carmella and his daughters Sophia and Maria with Rose to help with the food, and then walked into Jacob's office.

He greeted each man with a kiss to the cheek, sat down and said, "First, I want to thank you for helping me squash the threat to my family. I can never repay you that debt. If any one of you needs something from me, all you have to do is ask. Anything."

"I'm hoping we'll be alive to be able to ask, Tony," Franklin said.

"I received a call from Don Rossetti this afternoon. He and Don Belotti have been able to smooth things over with the commission. They seem to be preoccupied with other things and besides, Don Bolotti offered them a small share of the New Jersey operation, which is now under his and Don Rossetti's control," Tony said and smiled.

Each man in the room relaxed in their chairs after hearing there would be no war over the Nicolini hit.

"It appears that Rossetti and Belotti will also take over Nicolini's turf. You know these Moustache Petes are very clever. They had planned this outcome all along. They used us to get rid of Nicolini and Delucia so they could take over. It was all about money and power. Still, it was a problem for us and I owe them for their support," Tony said. Then he placed a bottle of Jameson's Irish whiskey on Jacob's desk and said, "Time to celebrate."

Molly was standing by the kitchen sink fidgeting with the diamond-rimmed black opal crucifix on the pearl necklace, Jacob's father, Charles Byrne, gave to her the night he died. It belonged to Jacob's mother who succumbed to the Spanish flu in 1918. *Oh God, please bring Charlie home safe to me. If you must take someone to your bosom take me, not Charlie,* Molly prayed to herself.

"Are you okay Molly?" Carmella Amato asked.

"I'm sorry Carmella. I am not being a good host. I'm okay. Just thinking about Charlie," Molly said.

"I understand," Carmella said, remembering her own son Tony Junior who died in action. "You'll hear from Charlie soon."

I hope so. I pray so," Molly said.

"Mama, that's Grandmother's necklace. It's so beautiful," Mercy said pulling out a locket from her blouse and opening it, "I have the locket he gave me. That's her, Aunt Carmella," Mercy pointed to the picture in the locket. "And Grandfather," she said pointing to the other picture in the locket.

"She was so pretty," Carmella said. "I can see her in you Mercy."

Georgie ran into the kitchen and yelled, "Wait till you see Jake. He looks like a movie star."

Jake walked into the room after Georgie. He was dressed in a dark grey suit, a white shirt and wing tipped back shoes. His tie was lighter grey with blue stripes. Jake had his blond hair trimmed and combed back.

"Well, what do you think?" Jake said.

"Oh my God, you do look like a movie star," Mercy said.

Maria whistled a catcall, ran up to Jake and kissed him on the cheek. Jake's face reddened.

Jake put the dark gray fedora he held on, held his arms up and spun around.

All the women and Georgie hooted and hollered. When they stopped, Jake said, in a fake sophisticated voice, "Now, if you don't mind ladies, my women and I have a party to attend." He took Maria's arm in his and started to leave. As he did, he said to Maria, "You look simply ravishing my dear."

By 8pm, most of the guests had arrived and Jacob tapped a spoon on a glass to get everyone's attention. It didn't work, so he yelled, "Quiet. I have something to say," Everyone stopped talking.

"For the first time in a public setting I am pleased to introduce Mr. and Mrs. James Simms Byrne."

Jimmy and Sally walked into the room and everyone clapped and yelled their approval. Jacob held up his glass and said, "To Jimmy and Sally." Everyone repeated the toast.

Rose walked up to Sally and placed a wreath of wild flowers on her head. She whispered in Sally's ear, "This is to bring you good luck and many babies." She kissed Sally and then Jimmy. "I have a toast as well. Sally, Jimmy, may you be poor in misfortune, rich in blessings, slow to make enemies, quick to make friends, but rich or poor, quick or slow, may you know nothing but happiness from this day forward."

Everyone echoed their wishes for Jimmy and Sally's happiness.

"Excuse me everyone. I have something to say," Franklin yelled over the din of whoops and yells. I love Jimmy as if he was my own son and if he loves Sally, then I so do I. I wish them all the happiness in the world." He kissed Sally and shook Jimmy's hand.

"Wait. I'm not finished. Catherine, would you come here please," Franklin said. When Catherine stood by Franklin, he looked into her eyes and said," I can't think of a better time and place to tell you and everyone here that I love you," Franklin put one knee on the floor, took Catherine's hand and slipped a diamond ring on her finger. Will you be my wife?"

Everyone in the room was stunned to silence. Catherine looked to the ceiling, cocked her head as if thinking about the offer. She waited a full minute before saying, "Yes, of course, yes." Catherine pulled Franklin up and kissed him. The room erupted in bedlam as people yelled their approval.

Rose yelled over the crowd, "Time for a good old fashioned dance." Someone started the record player and the *Irish Washerwomen* started to play. Franklin took Catherine by the arm and started to dance the Irish jig. Jimmy and Sally followed. Rose took Jacob's arm and they started to dance. With one arm in a sling, Mike took Grady by the arm and danced. Nate and Sophia Amato danced along, not really knowing how. Alan Schechter and his wife did the same. Tonight, everyone was Irish.

Molly walked off into the hallway and dabbed her eyes to dry the tears. She was thinking about Charlie again. Georgie saw her, followed and hugged her. "Mom, it'll be all right."

Molly hugged him back, rubbed his hair and said, "Did you know my grandfather on my Mom's side had red hair like you? They say it's good luck to rub a red head's hair."

Georgie rubbed his head and looked at Jacob's office door as if he just realized something. He ran to the door and opened it. Rose had put the dogs in Jacob's office so they wouldn't be underfoot. Bunny, Bonnie, Zack and Simone ran on to the dance floor. Ginger tried to follow, but Georgie took her by the collar, guided her to Molly and said, "Ginger has red hair," and he started petting the dog.

Molly smiled and petted Ginger as well. Ginger's tail wagged in happiness as both Molly and Georgie rubbed her red fur. After a minute or so, she stopped wagging her tail and lifted her head. Ginger started barking and ran to the front door.

"What got into her?" Georgie said.

"She must hear the men your father has posted outside," Molly said and walked to the door. Ginger was jumping up at the door and scratching on it. "Stop it Ginger. You'll leave marks on the door," Molly chided.

The doorbell rang and Ginger became even more agitated. Molly bent down and hugged Ginger to quiet her. She opened the door, but at the same time, Ginger wiggled and tried to get out of Molly's grasp so she looked down at the dog as the door opened.

When Molly started to look back up, she first saw shiny shoes and then olive green trousers. Molly's heart skipped a beat and a stab of fear ran through her body. Ginger started to wiggle wildly and Molly lost her grip on the dog. Ginger ran forward, her tail wagging. As Molly moved her head upward again, she saw the green trouser leg bend down and two hands took Ginger and rubbed her head. Molly didn't want to look up, and kept her eyes on the man's knee. As he bent lower, the man's face came into Molly's view and her jaw dropped in stunned silence.

"Mom, it's me, Charlie."

# Author's Biography

*Harry Hallman*

Hallman was born in 1944 and raised in the Kensington section of North Philadelphia. That was a year before World War II ended. He was influenced by the stories told by returning servicemen and the proliferation of war movies that were shown on the then new invention of the television. With the influence of movie heroes such as John Wayne, and real heroes like Audie Murphy, he gained a healthy respect for his mother and father's generation and their sacrifices. His uncles on his mother's side both served in WWII, one in the Army and one in the Navy.

Hallman's father was Harry Hallman, Sr., a champion billiards player who also owned a poolroom called Circle Billiards, located at Allegheny Avenue and Lee Street. The younger Hallman spent many hours after school at his father's poolroom and watching his father play in other poolrooms in Philadelphia and New Jersey. The people he met, some belonging to the real K&A Gang, influenced his writing of the Mercy Row series.

He served four years in the U.S. Air Force, including two tours in South Vietnam, as a photographer. He is married to Duoc Hallman, whom he met in Vietnam, and has two children, Bill and Nancy, and one grandchild, Ava.

Hallman is a serial entrepreneur who has created several marketing services and digital media companies and continues to work as a marketing consultant.

Look for the continuation of the Mercy Row and Mercy Row Clann story with book three in 2015.

Keep informed at www.mercyrow.com or on Facebook at www.facebook.com/mercyrownovel.

Made in the USA
Middletown, DE
10 November 2021